Rachel Gibson's storytelling career began at the age of sixteen when she ran her Chevy Vega into the side of a hill, retrieved the bumper and broken glass from the ground, and drove to her High School parking lot. With the help of her friend, she strategically scattered the broken pieces and told her parents she'd been the victim of a hit and run. They believed her, and she's been telling stories ever since.

Rachel has three children and still lives in her native Boise, Idaho. When not writing, she can be found boating on Payette Lake with Mr Gibson, shopping for shoes, or forcing her love on an ungrateful cat.

By Rachel Gibson

ANY MAN OF MINE
NOTHING BUT TROUBLE
TRUE LOVE AND OTHER DISASTERS
NOT ANOTHER BAD DATE
TANGLED UP IN YOU
I'M IN NO MOOD FOR LOVE
SEX, LIES AND ONLINE DATING
THE TROUBLE WITH VALENTINE'S DAY
DAISY'S BACK IN TOWN
SEE JANE SCORE
LOLA CARLYLE REVEALS ALL
TRUE CONFESSIONS
IT MUST BE LOVE
TRULY MADLY YOURS
SIMPLY IRRESISTIBLE

ANY MAN OF MINE

Rachel Gibson

CORGI BOOKS

TRANSWORLD PUBLISHERS
61–63 Uxbridge Road, London W5 5SA
A Random House Group Company
www.rbooks.co.uk

**ANY MAN OF MINE
A CORGI BOOK: 9780552164498**

First published in the United States of America by Avon Books,
an imprint of HarperCollins Publishers

First publication in Great Britain
Corgi edition published 2011

Addresses for Random House Group Ltd companies outside the UK
can be found at: www.randomhouse.co.uk
The Random House Group Ltd Reg. No. 954009

The Random House Group Limited supports The Forest
Stewardship Council (FSC), the leading international forest
certification organisation. All our titles that are printed on
Greenpeace approved FSC certified paper carry the FSC logo.
Our paper procurement policy can be found at
www.rbooks.co.uk/environment

Typeset in Palatino.
Printed in the UK by
CPI Cox & Wyman, Reading, RG1 8EX.

2 4 6 8 10 9 7 5 3 1

Mixed Sources
Product group from well-managed
forests and other controlled sources
www.fsc.org   Cert no. TT-COC-2139
© 1996 Forest Stewardship Council
FSC

ANY MAN OF MINE

Chapter One

Any Man of Mine:
No Professional Athletes

S am LeClaire was a good-looking son of a bitch. Everyone thought so. Everyone from sports writers to soccer moms.

The girl wrapped up in his sheets thought so, too. Although she really wasn't a girl. She was a woman.

"I don't see why I can't go."

Sam glanced up from the knot in his blue-striped tie and looked in the mirror at the super-model in his bed. Her name was Veronica Del Toro, but she was known by just her first name. Like Tyra and Heidi and Gisele.

"Because I didn't know you were going to be in town," he explained for the tenth time. "Bringing a guest at this late date would be rude." Which wasn't the real reason.

"But I'm Veronica."

Now, there. There was the real reason. She was rude *and* narcissistic. Not that he held that against anyone. He could be rude and narcissistic himself; but, unlike the stories written about him, he really did know when to behave.

"I won't eat much."

Try not at all. That was one of the things that irritated him about Veronica. She never ate. She ordered food like she was starving, but she pushed it around her plate.

Sam slid up the knot and tilted his chin to one side as he buttoned down the collar. "I already called you a cab." In the mirror he watched Veronica rise from his bed and walk toward him. She moved across his carpet as if she was on the catwalk. All long legs and arms, big breasts yet hardly a jiggle.

"When are you going to be back?" she asked as she wrapped her arms around his waist. She rested her chin on his shoulder and looked at him through dark brown eyes.

"Late." He tilted his head to the other side and, as he buttoned the other collar point, he glanced at the big Stanley Cup champion ring on the dresser. The white- and yellow-gold ring had 160 diamonds, emeralds, and sapphires fashioned into the team logo on its face. On one side the Stanley Cup and the year had been engraved. On the other, his name and number. He'd had it out to show Veronica, but he didn't plan to put it on. Even if he had been a guy who wore jewelry, which he wasn't, the huge ring covered the finger on his right hand to his knuckle and was over-the-top. Even for a guy who liked over-the-top.

"How late?"

Looking in the mirror, he slid his gaze to the clock on his nightstand. It was already half past six, and the wedding started at seven. He really hadn't had the time to meet Veronica. But she wasn't in town that often, and she'd promised a quickie. He should have known better. She was Veronica and wasn't quick about anything. "Real late. When do you fly out?"

"In the morning." She sighed and slid her long hands up his dress shirt to his hard pecs. "I could wait."

He turned, and her palms slid to his waist. "I

3

don't know when I'll get back. This thing could run real late." Although with the regular season opener in just five days, he doubted it. He pushed her dark hair behind her shoulder. "Call me the next time you're in Seattle."

"That could be months, and by then you'll be on the road playing hockey." She dropped her hands and moved toward the bed.

He watched her skinny behind as she stepped into her tiny panties. There were a lot of things to like about Veronica. Her face. Her body. The fact that she was superficial, and there was nothing deep going on in her pretty head. There was nothing wrong with being superficial. Nothing wrong with living on the surface and avoiding lapses into deep thought. It made life easier. "We can always meet up on the road again."

"True." She reached for a red T-shirt and pulled it over her head before stepping into a pair of jeans. "But by then you'll have a black eye."

He grinned. "True." He grabbed his suit jacket and slid his arms inside. Last season, he'd hooked up with her in Pittsburgh. That night against the Penguins, he'd scored a goal, spent four minutes in the sin bin for a double minor, and got his first major shiner of the season. Maybe she'd bring him the same sort of luck this year. He reached for his wallet and shoved it into the back pocket of his khaki trousers.

"Last season your beautiful face was a mess," Veronica said as she slid her feet into a pair of pumps.

It hadn't been that bad. Just a few stitches and minor bruises. He'd certainly suffered worse during his sixteen years in the NHL.

"You should model."

"No. Thanks." A few years ago, he'd done an underwear ad for Diesel, and he'd found the whole process a colossal bore. He'd spent most of an entire day sitting around in white briefs while the crew set up for different shots. The end result had been huge billboards and magazine ads of him with his junk practically hanging out and looking particularly enormous. The guys on the team had razzed him endlessly, and his mother had been afraid to show her face in church for a month. After that experience, he decided to leave modeling to the guys who liked that sort of atten-tion. Guys like Beckham.

Together, he and Veronica walked from the bedroom of Sam's downtown loft. Within the open interior, gray shadow hugged the leather furnishings as fading sunlight cast dull patterns across the wood floor.

Sam held the front door open for Veronica, then locked it behind him. He moved down the hall, and his thoughts turned to the game in less than a week against San Jose. The Sharks had been knocked out of the first round of play-offs last season, but that didn't guarantee a win for the Chinooks in this season's opener. Not by a long shot. The Sharks would be hungry, and some of the Chinooks had partied a little too hard during the off-season. Sam had done his share of partying, but he hadn't gone to fat, and his liver was still in good shape. Johan and Logan were each carrying ten extra pounds around the middle, and Vlad was drinking like a sailor on leave. The organization had just given the captaincy to Walker Brooks. No shock there. Walker had been the alternate for the past few years.

"I love weddings," Veronica said through a sigh as they moved to the elevator.

Everyone assumed that Alexander Devereaux would put the A on his jersey, but nothing had been announced. They'd kind of floated the alternate captaincy in Sam's direction, but he hadn't taken the bait. Sam wasn't the most responsible guy, and that's how he liked it.

The elevator doors opened, and they stepped inside. "Don't you?"

"Don't I what?" He pushed the button to the lobby.

"Love weddings."

"Not particularly." Weddings were about as much fun as getting his cup rung.

They rode to the bottom floor in silence, and Sam placed his hand in the small of Veronica's back as they walked across the lobby. Two heavy glass-and-stainless-steel doors slid open, and a yellow cab waited by the curb.

He kissed her good-bye. "Call me the next time you're in town. I really want to see you again," he said as he shut her inside the taxi.

Misty clouds clung to the darkening Seattle skyline as Sam walked to the corner and headed two blocks toward Fourth Avenue and the Rainier Club. The sounds of the city bounced off the buildings around him, and he glanced at his image reflected in storefront windows. A slight breeze lifted his lapels and teased the lock of blond hair touching his forehead. He slid one hand to the front of his blazer and buttoned it against the damp, chilly air.

He turned his attention to the crowded sidewalk, and within a few short blocks, he caught sight of the exclusive old club with its aged brick façade and carefully trimmed lawn that reeked of money. As he moved down the street, he was aware of people turning to watch him. Several shouted out his name. He raised his hand in acknowledgment but kept on walking. That sort of constant recognition was new to him. Oh, he had his fans. Lots of them. Those who followed his career and wore his name and number on their jerseys. Since winning the Cup last July, his notoriety had increased a hundredfold, and he was fine with it. Fans just wanted an autograph or a handshake, and he could handle that.

In the middle of the block, he looked up the street and cut across. Life was good for Sam. Last season, the Seattle Chinooks had won the Stanley Cup, and his name would forever be inscribed on hockey's highest prize. The memory of holding the Cup over his head as he skated in front of the hometown crowd brought a smile to his lips.

His professional life was on a high. Through

blood, sweat, and hard work, he'd reached every goal he'd ever set for himself. He had more money then he'd ever thought he'd make in one lifetime, and he loved spending it on real estate, designer suits, fine wine, and finer women.

He walked beneath the Rainier Club's black awning, and a doorman greeted him. His personal life was pretty good, too. He didn't have one special lady in his life, which was how he liked it. Women loved him, and he loved them back. Probably a little too much sometimes.

The inside of the exclusive club was so stuffy, he had a sudden urge to take off his shoes just like when he'd been a kid, and his mom got a new carpet. A few of the guys were hanging out at the bottom of a wide staircase looking a little uneasy, but otherwise good in their expensive suits and summer tans. In another two months, several of them would be sporting black eyes and a few stitches.

"Nice of you to make it," forward Daniel Holstrom said as he approached.

Harp music drifted down the stairs as Sam peeled back the cuff of his dress shirt and looked at his TAG Heuer watch. "Ten minutes to spare," he said. "What are you all waiting for?"

"Vlad and Logan aren't here yet," goalie Marty Darche answered.

"Savage make it?" Sam asked, referring to the groom and Chinooks' former captain, Ty Savage.

"I saw him about ten minutes ago," Daniel answered. "First time I've ever seen him break a sweat off the ice. He's probably afraid the bride has come to her senses and is halfway to Vancouver."

Marty lowered his voice a fraction. "There are at least four Playmates upstairs."

Which wasn't surprising given that the bride was not only the owner of the Seattle Chinooks, but had been a *Playboy* Playmate of the Year. "Should be a good party," Sam said through a laugh, as a shiny auburn ponytail and smooth profile caught the corner of his eye. He turned, and his laughter got stuck in his throat. Everything inside him stilled as his gaze followed the woman with the ponytail moving across the lobby toward the front doors. She had on a headset and talked into the tiny microphone in front of her mouth. A black sweater hugged her body, and a little battery pack was clipped to her black pants. Sam's brows lowered, and acid settled in the pit of his stomach. If there was one woman on the planet who did *not* love him, and in fact hated his guts, it was the woman disappearing through the front doors.

Daniel put a hand on his shoulder. "Hey, Sam, isn't that your wife?"

"You have a wife?" Marty turned toward the front.

"*Ex*-wife." The burning acid in his stomach chewed its way upward.

"I didn't know you were ever married."

Daniel laughed like he thought something was real funny.

Sam sliced a gaze at Daniel out of the corners of his eyes. A silent warning that made the winger laugh even harder, but at least he didn't open his piehole and spill all the sordid details about Sam's drunken trip to a cheesy wedding chapel in Vegas.

He returned his attention to the front entrance for several more seconds before heading up the stairs. Her name was Autumn, and like the season, she was unpredictable. One day she might be pleasantly warm, the next, cold enough to freeze a guy's nuts off.

He reached the second floor and passed the lady playing a harp. Sam didn't like surprises.

11

He didn't like to be caught off guard. He liked to see which way the hits were coming so he could be ready for the blows.

He moved down a short hall sparsely littered with wedding guests. He hadn't counted on seeing Autumn that night, but he guessed he shouldn't be all that surprised. She was a wedding planner or, as she always insisted, "event organizer." Although, really, what was the difference? Wedding or event, it was the same damn circus. But it was typical of Autumn to make a big deal out of something little.

"Would you like to sign the guest book?" a woman seated at a small round table asked. Sam wasn't the kind of guy to sign anything without his lawyer present, but the woman with big brown eyes flashed him a smile, and he moved toward her. She wore something red and tight across her chest and had a sparkly headband in her dark hair.

Sam was a big fan of tight and sparkly and returned her smile. "Sure." She handed him a ridiculous pen with a big white feather. "Nice headband."

She raised a hand to the side of her head and kind of blushed like she wasn't used to getting compliments. "Are you making fun of my head-band?"

"No. It looks good in your hair."

"Thanks."

He bent forward and his tie brushed the white linen tablecloth. "Are you related to the bride or groom?"

"Neither. I'm employed by Haven Event Management."

His smile flattened. Which meant she worked for Autumn. Autumn Haven. While her first name fit, her last name was a total contradiction. Like jumbo shrimp or silent scream or cuddly cheetah.

"Don't have too much fun," Sam said, and handed the pen back to Autumn's employee. He walked the short distance toward a large room, where an usher showed Sam to a chair near the front. He moved down a red carpet strewn with white rose petals. Most of the seats were already taken up with assorted hockey players, wives, or girlfriends. He spotted the Ross twins, Bo and Chelsea, seated between former captain Mark Bressler and Faith's assistant, Jules Garcia. The twins worked in one capacity or another for the organization and were better known as Mini Pit and Short Boss.

He took one of the last remaining seats, beside sniper Frankie Kawczynski. In the front of the room, a man wearing a blue suit and holding a Bible stood before an enormous stone fireplace festooned with red roses and some kind of white flowers. The guy had to be the preacher, or he could be a justice of the peace for all Sam knew. One thing was for sure, though, he wasn't a fake Elvis.

"Hey, Sam. Are Daniel and Marty still hanging out downstairs?"

"Yeah." Sam glanced at his watch. The boys had better hurry if they were going to make it before the bride. This was one of those events where the guys needed to arrive on time, and completely blowing off the wedding of Faith Duffy, owner of the Seattle Chinooks, wasn't even an option. If it had been, Sam wouldn't be sitting there, suited up and looking at his watch, waiting for the show to begin. Dreading the pleasure of his former wife.

Some sort of wedding music poured through the room's sound system, and Sam glanced over his shoulder as a woman he recognized as the bride's mother entered the room. Her usual tight clothes and big jewelry had been toned down to

14

a simple red dress. Her only accessories were the small bouquet and the white yappy dog she carried. And like all yappy dogs, it had big ear bows. Red to match its nails.

Ty Savage and his father, Pavel, entered the room behind the bride's mother. Father and son were both hockey legends, and anyone with a passing interest in the game had heard the name Savage. Sam had grown up watching Pavel play old-school hockey, before helmets and fighting rules. Later, he'd played both against and with Ty, inarguably one of the best to ever lace up a pair of skates. Both men wore customary black tuxedos and, for one uncomfortable moment, Sam's brain flashed to his own wedding. Only instead of a tux, he'd worn a Cher BELIEVE T-shirt and jeans. He didn't know which was more humiliating, the wedding or the T-shirt.

Ty and Pavel took their places across from the bride's mother and in front of the fireplace. Ty looked calm. Not at all nervous or terrified that he was making a huge mistake. Sam figured he'd looked fairly calm at his own wedding. Of course, he'd been drunk out of his mind. That was the only explanation for what he'd done. The terror hadn't sunk in until the next morning. The memory of his drunken wedding was one he avoided like a whore avoided the vice squad. He pushed it away and locked it down tight, where he kept all unpleasant memories and unwanted emotions.

Soft harp music changed to the "Wedding March," and everyone stood as the bride entered the room. Faith Duffy was one of the most beautiful women on the planet. Tall, blond, gorgeous face, like a Barbie Doll. Perfect breasts. And he didn't think he was a pervert for acknowledging her rack, either. She'd been a Playmate of the Year, and most of the men in the room had seen her pictorial.

She wore a body-hugging white dress that covered her from throat to knees. Over the gauzy veil on Faith's head, he caught a glimpse of Autumn as she slipped into the back of the room. The last time he'd seen her, she'd called him immature and selfish. She'd told him he was an irresponsible horn dog, and she'd finished her rant by accusing him of having jock itch of the brain. Which wasn't true. He'd never had jock itch anywhere, not even in his jock, and he'd taken exception. He'd lost his cool with her and called her an uptight, ball-busting bitch. Which

16

in her case, *was* true, but that hadn't been the worst of it. No, the worst of it had been the look in Conner's blue eyes as his son had popped up from behind the couch. As if his parents had just plunged a knife in his three-year-old heart. That had been the worst of it. After that night, they'd mutually agreed that it was best not to be in the same place. This was the first time he'd been in the same building with, or even seen Autumn for what now . . . two years maybe?

Twenty months, two weeks and three days. That was how long it had been since Autumn had had the misfortune to be in the same room with the biggest horse's ass on the planet. If not the planet, at least the Pacific Coast. And that was a lot of horses' asses.

She stood at the back of the Cutter Room inside the Rainier Club, her eyes fixed on the bride as she handed her bouquet of white peonies, hydrangeas, and deep red roses to her mother. Faith took her place across from the groom, and he reached for her hand. In a completely unscripted move, he raised her hand to his lips and kissed the backs of her knuckles. Autumn had planned a lot of weddings in the past few years. So many that she could pretty much predict which couples were going to make it over the long haul. She knew by the way they spoke and touched each other and by the way they handled the stress of planning a wedding. She predicted that Ty and Faith would grow very old together.

As everyone sat, and the minister began, Autumn lowered her gaze to the bride's slightly rounded stomach. Just a few weeks ago, she'd received a call from the bride requesting the champagne at the bride and groom's table be replaced with sparkling cider. At three months, the pregnancy was hardly noticeable yet. The bride was one of those fortunate women who glowed with good heath.

Not Autumn. She'd been unable to button her jeans by month three, and her morning sickness had kicked in before she'd even known she was pregnant with Conner, turning her complexion very pale. And, unlike Faith Duffy, there hadn't been a man around to kiss her fingers and make her feel loved and secure. Instead, she'd been alone and sick and facing divorce.

Without looking directly at Sam, she was aware of where he sat. Aware of his big shoulders in his expensive suit and the light from the chandelier shining in his blond hair. When she'd slipped into the room, she hadn't even had to look around to know he sat in the fourth row, aisle seat. She just knew. Like the tension headache pressing against her temples. She didn't have to see it to know it was there. But unlike her headache, there was nothing she could take to make Sam LeClaire go away.

She tapped a finger against the event folder she held in one hand. She'd known Sam would be there, of course. She'd made sure the invitation had gone out on time and had overseen the RSVPs. She'd gone over the dinner seating with the bride and placed Sam with three other single hockey players and various big-busted Playmates at table seven.

She chewed on her bottom lip. He'd no doubt be pleased.

Autumn's earpiece beeped, and she turned down the volume as Ty and Faith spoke the traditional vows. The ceremony was short and sweet, and when the groom reached for his bride, Autumn waited. Even after all the weddings she'd organized over the past several years, even the ones she knew would fail, she waited. She wasn't the most romantic woman on the planet.

19

Still, she waited for that fraction of a second. That briefest magical moment just before a kiss sealed a man to his wife for the rest of their lives.

Ty's and Faith's lips touched and a little pinch squeezed a corner of Autumn's heart. She was a sucker. No matter the statistics, no matter the pain of her own divorce, no matter the cynical voice in her head, she was a sucker for the happily-ever-after.

Still.

For a fraction of a second, Autumn's gaze lit on the back of Sam's blond hair. Her temples squeezed a bit more, stabbing at her right eye, and she walked out of the room. For a lot of years, she'd hated Sam, hated him with a seething passion. But that kind of all-consuming hate took up too much emotional energy. After her last altercation with him, she'd decided, for the sake of their son, and her sanity, to let go of her anger. To let go of her hatred. Which also meant letting go of her favorite fantasy. The one that involved her foot, his balls, followed by an uppercut to his pretty jaw.

She'd never fantasized about Sam's death, nor even long-term maiming. Nothing that involved driving over Sam with a steamroller or Peterbilt semi. No, nothing as violent as that. Conner needed a father, no matter how crappy, and other than the foot-in-groin fantasy, she just wasn't a violent person.

Letting go of her hatred hadn't been easy. Especially when he made plans with Conner, then canceled. Or when it was his weekend, and he'd take off somewhere with his buddies and break Conner's heart. She'd had to work hard at letting go of her anger and was pretty successful at feeling nothing at all, but then again, she hadn't actually seen Sam in twenty months, two weeks, and three days. Hadn't been anywhere near him.

Applause broke out behind Autumn as she moved down the hall and into the Cascade Room. She walked between twenty round tables set with fine white linen and red napkins folded on Wedgwood china. The lights from the chandeliers and flickering tapered candles shone within crystal glasses and bounced off polished silver flatware.

The first day she'd met with Faith, the bride had expressed a desire for understated elegance. She'd wanted gorgeous flowers, beautiful table settings, and excellent food. Faith's lack of a clear theme hadn't been a problem, and she'd quickly become Autumn's favorite kind of bride.

A bride with good taste and no budget. The only real difficulties had arisen because of time constraints. Most weddings took eight months to plan. Faith had wanted everything done in three months. Looking around at the floral centerpieces of varying shades of roses and peonies interspersed with white honeysuckle, Autumn was proud of what she and her staff had pulled together.

The only thing that would have made the wedding perfect was if Faith had consented to let the local and national newspapers splash the wedding photo all over their pages. The marriage of elite player Ty Savage, who'd quit the sport to marry a former Playboy Playmate turned hockey team owner, was big news. Especially in the sports world. It would have been the kind of advertising that Autumn couldn't buy. The kind that could propel her business to the next level. The kind of break she'd been waiting for, but Faith hadn't wanted her wedding splashed anywhere. She'd wanted to keep it low-key. No photos released to anyone.

Autumn spoke into the tiny microphone in front of her mouth, and the catering staff, dressed in tuxedos, filed down the stairs from the kitchen above. Each carried trays filled with flutes of Moët et Chandon or hot and cold hors d'oeuvres. They moved into the wide hall and passed among the wedding guests.

Through the open door, Autumn watched the photographer, Fletcher Corbin, and his assistant, Chuck, scramble for candid photos. Fletcher was tall and thin, with a thinner ponytail. He was one of the best photographers in the business, and Autumn always booked him when he had the time, and the bride had the money. She liked working with him because she didn't have to tell him what to do or what shots the bride wanted. She loved that about Fletcher and most of the vendors on this particular job. They knew what they were doing. They adjusted and adapted and didn't cause drama.

The bride and groom stood in the middle of the wide hall, surrounded by a knot of guests. Autumn turned her wrist over and pushed up the long sleeve of the vintage black sweater she'd found at one of her favorite boutiques in downtown Seattle. It had tiny sequins around the collar, and she'd considered it a steal at forty bucks.

She looked at her watch and pushed her sleeve back down. Since her first job as a stager, she'd worn the face of her watch on the inside of her wrist to keep from scratching the crystal. For the past five years, she'd worn one with a large face and wide band for a totally different reason.

The wedding was five minutes behind schedule. Not bad, but she knew all too well that five minutes could easily turn to ten. Ten to twenty, and then she'd have a problem coordinating with the kitchen.

She pushed a button on the receiver hooked to her belt and walked to the far side of the room. She shoved her folio under one arm and reached for the bottle of sparkling pear cider sitting in a silver ice bucket at the bride's table.

"I'm here," her assistant, Shiloh Turner, said through the headset.

"Where's here?" She tore off the gold foil from the top and wrapped her hand around the neck of the bottle.

"In the Cutter Room."

"Any stragglers?"

"The maid of honor and best man are chatting it up by the fireplace. They don't look like they're in any hurry to vacate."

24

The day the bride's mother had insisted that her little yappy dog be a part of the ceremony, she'd suspected the woman might be trouble. Last night at the rehearsal dinner, the mother had shown up in pink spandex and stripper heels and confirmed Autumn's suspicions. "Give them a few more minutes, then do what you can to move them along," she said, and pushed at the cork until it came out with a soft pop.

Tiny carbonated bubbles filled the air with a soft fizz as she poured the cider into two crystal flutes. There was so much to do, and she mentally ran down her list. A lot went into planning a wedding, even a small one. Everything had to be timed perfectly, and even the smallest of mess-ups could turn a dream wedding into a wedding from hell.

Deep in her mental to-do list, Autumn shoved the bottle back inside the bucket and grabbed the glasses. She turned toward the room and almost plowed headfirst into a broad chest covered in white shirt, blue-striped tie, and navy blazer. Her leather portfolio slipped from beneath her arm as she lifted her gaze up the wide chest and passed the knot at the base of a wide neck. She looked beyond the square jaw and tan lips, along the slight curve of a crooked nose, and stopped at a pair of eyes the color of a hot summer sky.

Up close, Sam was even more handsome than from a distance. As handsome as the night she'd first seen him in a crowded bar in Las Vegas. A tall, blond-haired, blue-eyed god sent straight from heaven. The nose, the scar on his high cheekbone, and the evil intent in his smile should have been a huge tip-off that he was less than angelic.

Her stomach knotted, but she was happy to discover it was not a lump of burning anger. Nor did she feel a desire to kick him in the balls. While she disliked Sam, he'd given her the best thing in her life. She didn't know what her life would be like without Conner. She didn't even like to contemplate it, and for that reason, and that reason alone, she sucked it up and pasted a smile on her face. The same smile she used with brides who wanted white tigers or to be carried down the aisle on a pink throne. She was going to be pleasant even if it killed her.

And it just might.

Chapter Two

Any Man of Mine:
Has Human-Sized Ego

S am turned and looked behind him. It had been so long since he'd seen the corners of Autumn's pink lips turn upward into a pleasant little smile, he knew she couldn't be smiling at him.

No one else was in the room. He turned back and tilted his head to one side in an effort to gauge her temperament. "Hi, Autumn."

Her smile slipped a little. "Sam."

"It's been a while."

"About two years."

He looked into her dark green eyes for any sign

of trouble. "A little longer, I think." He didn't see a storm brewing in there and didn't feel the need to cover his crotch. Thank God. "I saw you earlier and thought I'd say hey, so you'd know I was here." He'd wanted to talk to her, gauge her reaction, and avoid any potential problems.

"I knew. You're on the guest list."

"Oh. Of course." He bent down and picked up the notebook. "Are you pouring yourself a drink," he joked as he straightened.

"It's pear cider, and it's not for me."

He wouldn't have mistaken any of the other guests for teetotalers. At least not the guests he knew. "What's Conner doing tonight?"

"Hanging out with Vince."

Vince. The male version of Autumn. Only bigger. Meaner and trained to kill. Sam hated Autumn's brother, Vince. "How have you been?"

"Good." She glanced at the big silver watch strapped to her wrist, the round face resting above her pulse, and he wondered if she still had his name inked there or if she'd had it removed. "I'd love to stay and chat with you all night, but I'm working," she said through that smile that didn't fool Sam for a second. She lifted her elbow away from her side, and he slid the leather folder beneath her arm. "Thanks. Have a good time tonight." She moved around him and walked from the room. Sam turned and watched her go. That went well. Too well, but he didn't trust her not to blindside him or spike his food with arsenic or MiraLAX. Maybe both to make his death really uncomfortable.

His gaze slid from her red ponytail and down her slim back to the nice curves of her waist. The flaps of two back pockets drew his attention to her rounded behind. Autumn was a pretty woman. No doubt, but she wasn't gorgeous. She had soft curves in all the right places. Slim hips and nice breasts, and he didn't believe that made him a perv to think it either. He'd seen her naked, but her body really wasn't anything special. Wasn't his type. He liked tall, thin women with large breasts. Always had been drawn to the overblown. So why, for those few days in Vegas, had he found an average woman so damn fascinating?

Sam walked out of the room and stood at the edge of the crowd drinking champagne and toasting the bride and groom. He could blame that odd fascination with Autumn on the city. Nothing ever seemed real in Vegas. He could blame it on the booze. There'd been plenty of that. He could blame the month of June. He always went a little insane in June, but he wasn't sure it was any of those things.

He grabbed a fresh glass of champagne from a passing tray and replaced the empty. The only thing that was real clear, that he was very sure about, was that he'd met a redheaded girl in a bar and married her a few days later, and the next morning he'd left her behind at Caesars like a used bath towel. He understood why Autumn hated him. He got it, and he didn't blame her. His behavior hadn't been his finest moment. Sadly, it hadn't even been his worst.

Through the crowd gathered around Ty and Faith, he caught a glimpse of a red ponytail. The guests parted for a brief second, and he watched her hand the bride and groom flutes of cider. There could only be one reason why Ty and Faith weren't drinking champagne at their own wedding. And it wasn't because they'd found religion.

Autumn moved to the edges, and Sam lost sight of her. He imagined that Ty and Faith were happy about having a child. They looked happy.

Sam took a drink from the crystal flute. Six

years ago, he hadn't exactly been happy to hear he was going to be a daddy, but once he'd held his son, all that changed.

"Hey, Sam."

He looked over his shoulder at the team's newest assistant coach, Mark Bressler. "Hammer." Up until about a year ago, Mark had been an elite hockey player and captain of the Chinooks. But last winter he'd been in a horrible car wreck that had ended his career and put Ty Savage in Mark's jersey. "It appears the captain knocked up the owner." He pointed his glass at the happy couple. "That has to be a hockey first."

"Jesus, LeClaire. Watch your language."

"What language?" Had he sworn and not known it?

"There are women present."

All he'd said was *knocked up*. Since when was *knocked up* "language" and "Jesus" wasn't? And since when did Bressler care? Sam lowered his gaze to the blond woman by Mark's side, Bressler's hand in the middle of her back. Ah. "Hi, Short Boss."

"Hi, Sam," Chelsea said, her attention riveted on the bride. "Faith's pregnant? Are you sure?"

He shrugged. "I can't think of another reason why she and Ty are drinking crappy cider instead of the good stuff?"

"Oh my God!" Her blue eyes lit up, and she pushed her hair behind her ears. "I know something before my sister does."

The ring on her left finger about blinded him. "That's some ring?"

She held up her hand and smiled. "You noticed it?"

"Hard not to." He was pretty sure the moody man at her side had given it to her. "Honey, don't break my heart and tell me you're off-limits now."

She grinned. "Sorry."

He took her hand in his and looked at the huge diamond. "Is it real, or did some joker get you a cubic zirconia?"

"Of course it's real, numb-nuts."

"Language," he reminded Mark, and dropped Chelsea's hand. "There are women present." He looked around for Chelsea's twin. "Is your sister still here? She's not as nice as you, but . . ."

"She's kind of taken now, too."

"Damn." He smiled and stuck out his hand to his former teammate and friend. "Congratulations. You're a lucky man."

Any Man of Mine

Mark shook Sam's hand as he slid his arm around his fiancée and pulled her against his side. "Yeah, lucky me." Chelsea looked up at Mark, the two smiling at each other as if they shared an inside joke. The kind that people in love shared.

Sam raised his glass. The kind he'd never shared with anyone and found sappy and annoying. Never in his life would he have ever figured the Hammer for one of those sappy annoying guys. "See you two," he said, and moved away before they started making out or something.

He cut through the crowd and approached the bride and groom. "Congratulations, Ty," he said, and shook the groom's hand. He didn't know if the bun in the oven was common knowledge yet, so he decided not to mention it.

"Thanks for coming."

"Sam." The bride reached out and gave him a big hug. She was beautiful and soft and smelled great. She'd make Ty a good wife. Hell, any man a good wife. Any man but Sam. Sam wasn't the marrying kind of guy. Obviously.

"You're a beautiful bride," he said, and pulled back to look into her face.

"Thank you." She smiled. "And don't think

I've forgotten about that conversation we had in St. Paul."

They'd had a conversation? She was smiling, so he must have kept it clean.

"I couldn't get you all invited to a party at the mansion, but I did invite a few Playmates here tonight."

Oh, that conversation. She'd promised him and the guys an invitation to the Playboy mansion if they won the Stanley Cup. "I noticed."

"I'm not surprised." She laughed. "I had the wedding planner make sure she sat you at their dinner table."

Under normal circumstances, that would have been welcome news. He pushed up the corners of his mouth. "Fabulous. Thanks."

"I hope that makes up for my broken promise."

"We're square." He took a step back, and general manager, Darby Hogue, and his wife stepped forward to offer the bride and groom their congratulations.

Sam took a drink, and over the top of his glass, he spotted the Playmates. They weren't hard to pick out in a crowd. They were the four girls with big hair and bigger breasts, surrounded by Blake, Andre, and Vlad. Four on three was an uneven play. He figured it was his duty to even things out. He lowered his glass but didn't move.

Autumn. He just couldn't work up the proper enthusiasm required to chat it up with women in short skirts and low-cut blouses. Not while his baby-mama circled, looking for a reason to hate him even more than she already did. If that was even possible.

Instead, he struck up a conversation with Walker and Smithie and their wives. He smiled and nodded as the women talked about their own weddings and the births of all their children. Thank God Walker interrupted his wife just as she was warming up to a poop story.

"Did you hear the front office is looking to trade Richardson?" Walker asked.

Yeah, he'd heard. He liked Richardson. He was a good, solid wingman, but with Ty retiring, they needed a more versatile guy. One who could kill penalties as well as play the wings. "Do you know who they're looking at?"

"Bergen, for one."

"The Islander? Huh." The last he'd heard, Bergen was still in a slump.

"And then," Walker's wife said through a laugh, "he called out, 'I poo in the potty, Mommy.'"

Screw it. "See you around," Sam said, and headed for the playmates. He didn't care what Autumn thought. She was an uptight ball-buster, and there was nothing wrong with a little conversation with four beautiful women.

Autumn knelt between the bride's and groom's chairs and went through the rest of the schedule. Autumn was a list maker, both in business and in life. When it came to weddings, she knew the list by heart. Just in case, though, she had every detail written in her folio.

It was after eight, and the dinner and toasts were just about over. Faith looked exhausted, but she only had to get through the cake cutting and first dance before the groom could take her home.

Autumn herself might get home at midnight. If she was lucky.

"Thank you," Faith said. "You've kept everything running smooth."

"And on time," Ty added, who'd never made an effort to hide his desire for a very small wedding. But like most grooms, he'd caved to the desires of the bride.

"You're welcome." She looked at her watch. "In

about five minutes, Shiloh will invite everyone to meet you in the Rainier Room."

"Could you do it now?" Ty asked, but it was more of a demand than a question.

"Not everyone is through eating," Faith protested.

"I don't care. You're tired."

"You can't expect everyone to just get up and leave."

"Mention the open bar," Ty suggested to Autumn. "They'll trample over each other to get to the free liquor."

Autumn laughed as she rose. She buzzed her assistant and told her to mention the open bar when she invited the guests to join Faith and Ty in the other room. As she moved from behind the bride and groom's table, her gaze landed on Sam, where he sat charming the pants, or more appropriately, the thongs, off the Playmates. They laughed and touched his shoulder and looked at him like he was a god.

There had been a time when the sight of Sam with a beautiful woman or two would have carved out her heart. When she would have wanted to curl into a ball, but those days were long past. He could do what he wanted. As long as he didn't do it in front of her son. Which she suspected he did because he was an irresponsible horn dog with jock itch on the brain.

She moved from the room as Shiloh picked up the microphone and made the announcement. She checked and rechecked her list. The cake was ready to be cut, the band ready to play, and the two bartenders ready to sling drinks. She had a few moments and ducked into the ladies' room. As she washed her hands, she looked at her face in the soft lighting. Growing up, she'd hated her red hair and green eyes. All that color against her pale skin had been too much, but she liked it now. She'd grown into her looks, and she liked the woman she'd become. She was thirty years old, had an event-planning business that allowed her to pay her bills and raise her son. The child support she got from Sam more than covered the expense of raising a child. It allowed her to pay cash for her home and vehicles and take vacations. But at the same time, she knew that if she had to, she was financially able to take care of Conner on her own.

She dried her hands and opened the door. The economy always affected her business, which was why she'd expanded it to encompass a variety of events instead of just limiting herself to weddings. She was currently planning a Willy Wonka birthday party for twenty ten-year-olds for next month. Getting all the props and vendors for the party had been a challenge, but fun. Not as much fun as weddings. Planning weddings was what she loved best, ironic given her past.

She moved down the hall through clumps of wedding guests making their way to the Rainier Room. There were a lot of beautiful and wealthy people at that night's event. There was nothing wrong with that. Autumn made her living catering to beautiful, wealthy people, as well as those on tight budgets. She enjoyed both, and as she knew all too well, wealthier didn't always mean easier. Or that the bill was paid on time.

As she passed Sam, he separated himself from a group of his teammates and a few of the Playmates.

"Autumn. Do you have a minute?"

She stopped a few feet in front of him. "No. I've got thirty seconds." They had a son, but she couldn't imagine what they had to talk about. "What do you need?"

He opened his mouth to answer, but the cell

phone clipped to her belt rang, and she held up one finger. There was only one person in her phone with that "Anchors Aweigh" ring tone, her brother, Vince. And Vince wouldn't call unless there was a problem.

"Hey, Carly just phoned," he said. "She's sick and can't watch Conner. I have to be at work in half an hour."

It was still too early for Autumn to leave. She moved to a quieter spot in the hall and said, "I'll call Tara."

"I did. She didn't answer."

Autumn ran through a metal list of options. "I'll call his day care and see if they'll take him . . . Crap, they closed a few hours ago."

"What about Dina?"

"Dina moved."

"I guess I can call in sick."

"No." Vince had only had this latest job a week. "I'll think of something." She closed her eyes and shook her head. Sitter problems were difficult for every single mother. The odd hours of an event planner turned those hours into a nightmare. "I don't know. I guess you're going to have to bring Conner here, and I'll have one of my workers entertain him for a few hours."

"I'll get him."

Autumn looked up over her shoulder. She'd forgotten about Sam. "Hang on." She lowered the phone. "What?"

"I'll get Conner."

"You've been drinking."

He frowned. "Obviously, I'll have Natalie pick him up."

Natalie. The "personal assistant." Autumn didn't have anything against Sam's latest "assistant" other than she thought it was ridiculous that he called his girlfriends "assistants." She shook her head. "I don't know."

"Is this really something to fight about?"

Conner could either go to his dad's with the "assistant," a place he knew, or he could come to the Rainier Club and hang out until she could take him home. On the surface, the decision appeared to be a no-brainer, but she liked Conner with her at night. She slept better knowing he slept safe and sound in the room across from hers.

"Forget it." He shook his head and turned away.

But being a good parent wasn't always about her. She reached out and grabbed his arm.

41

"Wait." His blue eyes met hers, and, through the wool blazer, his body heat warmed her palm. His biceps turned hard beneath her touch, and she dropped her hand. There had been a time when the heat would have leaped to her chest and burned her up. These days, she was immune and returned the phone to her mouth. "Sam's going to take him."

"What's that idiot doing there?"

She bit the side of her lip to keep from smiling. "He's at the wedding."

"Tell Vince hi," Sam said as he reached into his pocket and pulled out his cell. He pushed a few numbers, then spoke into the receiver. "Hey, Nat. I know it's your night off, but can you go pick up Conner for me?" He smiled and gave Autumn a thumbs-up. "Yeah, just take him to my place. I should be there in a couple of hours."

Autumn hung up her phone and looked down as she hooked it to her belt. "Thanks, Sam."

"What?"

She looked up at the smile on Sam's face. "You heard me."

He laughed. "Yeah, I did. It's just been a while since you've had a nice word for me."

With Sam, it had never been so much what he

said as they way he said it. All oozing with nice-guy charm. Good thing she was immune to him, or she might actually mistake him for a nice guy. "I'll have Vince pick Conner up in the morning."

His laugher stopped, and his smile disappeared. "Vince is an idiot."

Which was a lot like the pot calling the kettle black.

"I'll have Nat drop him off home." A few of Sam's hockey buddies walked down the hall. Handsome, rich, beautiful women on their arms. This was Sam's life. Beautiful women and designer clothes. Invitations to weddings at the Rainier Club. Adoration and fan worship.

"Thanks again," she said, and moved around him. She'd been his wife and had given him a son, but she'd never really known him. Never would have fit into his big, over-the-top, life. She didn't shop at Neiman Marcus or Nordstrom or Saks. She haunted vintage shops, or, when she bought new, she shopped at Old Navy or the Gap or Target.

She walked into the Rainier Room and toward the four-tier red velvet cake. She had her own life, and except for Conner, her life had nothing to do with Sam LeClaire.

Chapter Three

Any Man of Mine:
Likes Children

Autumn pulled her Subaru Outback into her garage a little after midnight. She'd stayed at the Rainier Club until the last vendor had packed up, and she'd written a final check to the band.

She grabbed her tote bag off the passenger seat and made her way into the lower level of the house. She'd purchased the split-level in Kirkland a year ago because it was on a quiet cul-de-sac and had a huge, fenced backyard that bordered dense forest. For the past three years, she'd saved a portion of Conner's child support and paid cash for the home. She needed that kind of security.

That kind of stability. She needed to know that no matter what happened with her job or with Sam, she would always have a home for Conner.

The house certainly wasn't lavish by any means. It had been built in the late seventies and, while it did have new paint and appliances, it needed some work. The previous owner had been mad for wallpaper with flower borders, wood paneling, and faux bricks. It all had to be taken down, but unfortunately Autumn didn't have a lot of time to take care of it, and remodeling the house got pushed farther down the to-do list. Vince said he'd help her, but he didn't have a lot of time either.

In the family room, the overhead light burned, and the television blasted the Discovery Channel. Her tote pulled one shoulder lower than the other as she stepped over a Nerf Recon Blaster and a green plastic golf bag filled with two plastic clubs. She shut off the TV and checked the wooden dowel in the sliding glass door before hitting the light switch.

The blaster was the latest toy Vince had bought for Conner. It was Vince's opinion that Conner spent too much time with girls and needed a manly influence and manly toys. Autumn thought Vince was ridiculous—but whatever. Conner loved Vince and loved to spend time with him. God knew he spent little enough time with his own father.

In the quiet of the house, the stairs creaked beneath her feet. Normally, she liked peace and quiet. She liked those few hours of calm after she put Conner to bed. She liked having that time to herself. When she didn't have to work or make dinner or keep one step ahead of her five-year-old. She liked reading a magazine while soaking in the tub, but she didn't like Conner not being there at all. Even after these past several years when he'd had overnight visitations with his dad, she still got a bit anxious knowing her baby wasn't in his bed.

She moved across the dark living room and into the lighted kitchen. She set her tote on the table, then opened the refrigerator and grabbed some string cheese. On the outside of the refrigerator door, Conner had spelled out "hi mommy" in alphabet magnets, and he'd tacked up a new picture he'd obviously drawn while she'd been at work. In crayon, he'd drawn a figure with a red ponytail and green eyes, one arm longer than the other and holding the hand of a smaller figure with yellow hair and a big smile. He'd drawn a bright tangerine sun and green grass. Off to one side he'd drawn another figure with long legs and yellow hair.

Sam.

Autumn opened the cheese and threw away the wrapper. She pulled a long string and took a bite. For the past few months, Conner had started to randomly include Sam in his family pictures, but always off to one side. Which, Autumn supposed, was a true representation of his relationship with his dad. Random. Off to one side.

She grabbed a glass from the cupboard and poured filtered water into it. Seeing Sam that night, it was hard to remember what she'd found so fascinating about him. Oh, he was still gorgeous and rich and as magnetic as ever. He was big and muscular and larger than life, but she wasn't the fool at thirty that she'd been at twenty-five.

She raised the glass to her lips and took a drink. It was embarrassing to admit, even to herself, that she'd ever been that big a fool, but she had been. She'd married Sam after knowing him a total of five days because she'd fallen madly, desperately, in love with him. It had been foolish but had felt so real.

48

Any Man of Mine

She stared at her reflection in the window above the sink and lowered the glass. When she looked back on that time in her life, it was difficult to believe she'd actually felt those things. That she'd married a man she'd known for so short a time. Difficult to believe her heart had turned so soft and squishy at the sight of him. Difficult to believe she'd fallen so fast and hard. Difficult to believe she'd been a woman who would do something so impulsive.

Perhaps it had happened because she'd been at a real low point in her life. Her mother had died of colon cancer a few short months before that fateful trip. Vince had been in the Navy—off doing his scary SEAL stuff. And for the first time in two years, she hadn't had anyone to take care of but herself. She hadn't had to run anyone to doctor appointments or to chemo or radiation therapies.

After the funeral, after she'd packed up her mother's life in boxes for storage, there'd been nothing left for her to do, and for the first time in her life, she'd felt alone. For the first time, she'd *been* alone—alone with only two things to check off her long to-do list. Sell the house and go to Vegas for an overdue break.

49

She would like to think she married Sam because she'd been lonely. That she'd had too much to drink and been stupid. Which was true. She *had* been alone and drunk and stupid, but she'd married Sam because she'd fallen head over heels, madly in love with him. It was embarrassing to admit, even now, how quick and hard she'd fallen.

But he hadn't loved her. He'd married her like it was joke. He'd left her like she meant nothing. Less than nothing. He'd left her without looking back.

She set the glass in the sink, the sound of the glass against porcelain echoed in the empty house. He'd left her devastated and confused and with a lot of other emotions. She'd arrived in Vegas alone. She'd left married and alone. She'd been alone and scared when she'd taken her first pregnancy test. Alone and scared when she'd felt the first gossamer flutter of her baby in her womb, and the first time she'd heard Conner's heartbeat. She'd been alone and scared when she'd discovered she was having a boy, and she'd been alone and scared when she'd delivered Conner with no one in the room but a doctor and two nurses.

A week after Conner's birth, she'd called Sam's

lawyer and informed him that Sam had a son. A few days later, Conner had been given a paternity test, and a week later, Sam had seen his baby for the first time.

She turned off the kitchen light and moved down the hall. Autumn no longer felt alone and scared, but it had taken her a few years to stitch together a life from the shattered pieces. To make a secure place for Conner to live and forge a protective shield around her heart.

There was a part of her that wished she'd kept Conner a secret from Sam. A part of her that wanted to keep Conner to herself. A part of her that didn't think Sam was worthy of her beautiful boy, but she knew that it was best for Conner to know his father. Autumn had hardly known her father, and she knew from experience it was best that Conner grew up having Sam in his life. Even if Autumn didn't approve of him or his lifestyle, Sam was Conner's father, and that was that.

She paused by Conner's bedroom door and looked at the empty bed. His Barney pillow lay on the Barney quilt she'd made him, and her heart squeezed a little. Conner should be in his bed, hugging his Barney pillow. Sam didn't deserve Conner. She'd seen him leave the Rainier

Club with a group of his hockey buddies and the playmates. A child didn't fit in with Sam's lifestyle. He was an athlete, a playboy, and he was no doubt spending the night somewhere with one of those Playmates. Heck, he was probably spending the night with more than one while Autumn went to bed alone.

All by herself. Every night.

Not that she minded being alone all that much. She was too busy to be lonely, but . . . but sometimes, after she'd planned a wedding like Faith and Ty's, she got a little wistful. She wanted that. She wanted a man to look at her the way Ty looked at Faith. She wanted a man to love her like that. She wanted to be the pinch in a man's heart. The catch in his breath. The reason his stomach tumbled, and he lost sleep.

She'd married Sam, but he'd never felt those things for her. And if she married again, and she wasn't ruling that out completely, she would not be fooled by a pretty face and charming smile. She wanted a man to look at her like he wanted to look at her for the rest of his life.

The problem was that between her job and her son, she didn't have a lot of time and even less energy. She'd tried dating a few times, but men wanted girlfriends who had time for them. When Autumn did have a few hours, she longed for a massage or a pedicure more than she longed for a man. She could give herself an orgasm, but she couldn't give herself a deep-tissue massage or paint daisies on her own toes.

She turned away from Conner's room and moved down the hall. Dating was way down on her list of priorities. Maybe someday when Conner was older and her business wasn't so demanding, she'd be ready to move dating up on her to-do list.

Light poured through the open door, stretched across the beige carpet and onto the dark blue and red Transformers quilt. Sam loosened his tie as he walked across the floor. He unbuttoned the neck of his shirt and stood within the spill of light at the side of his son's bed. Conner lay on his side, his eyes closed and his breathing slow and steady. Like Sam, Conner was a heavy sleeper and threw off heat like a furnace. His blond hair stuck up in the back, and his hands were stretched out on the bed as if he were reaching for something.

The first time he'd seen his son, his heart had

shifted in his chest, and his world had shifted beneath his feet. The first time he'd seen Conner, he'd been afraid to touch him. He'd been so sure he'd bruise him or drop him or break him somehow. Conner had been about six pounds and wearing some sort of footed blue thing. The enormous responsibility had hit Sam like a club to his spinning heart. He hadn't planned to be someone's dad. Knew he probably wasn't going to be good at it, and the irony of it all had not escaped him. For a guy who avoided anyone's depending on him whenever possible, he'd been handed the biggest responsibility of his life. All because he'd been irresponsible.

He moved from the room, pausing at the door for one last look at his little boy. He loved his son. The kind of love he'd never known existed before he'd seen his tiny face for the first time, but he didn't always know what to do with Conner.

He unbuttoned his collar and pulled the tie from his neck. By the time he'd seen Conner that first time, the paternity test had been a fait accompli, but he hadn't needed a test to know the child belonged to him. Conner looked like him. Fair-haired and blue-eyed. Conner was tall for his age, and Sam had dreamed of teaching his son to skate. But as much as Conner looked like a LeClaire, the kid didn't like to skate, which was just inconceivable given that the boy *was* a LeClaire, and half-Canadian.

The few times Sam had tried to teach him, Conner had cried every time he fell. There was no crying in hockey, and after about the fifth time of trying, Sam had given up. Hell, Conner hadn't even been there in the stands last season when Sam had won the Stanley Cup. He'd stayed home with a *cold.* True, Conner was only five, but Sam had been skating for two years by the age of five, and there was absolutely no way he would have let a little thing like a cold keep him from attending the final game of the playoffs. He blamed Autumn. She'd never hidden the fact that she thought hockey was too violent.

He shrugged out of his blazer and moved down the hall. Because of all the Stanley Cup events the past summer, he hadn't spent much time with his son. Now, with school and the hockey season, he was going to see him even less. He wasn't thrilled, but there wasn't anything he could do about it.

The door to the spare bedroom was ajar, and he shut it. The latest assistant, Natalie, slept inside. She was young and beautiful and seemed to be good at her job. Most important, Conner liked her.

The shades in the master bedroom were open, and the Seattle skyline poured its light across the floor and onto the king-sized bed. He hit the light switch and saw a note on top of the white-and-blue quilt on his bed. It was from Natalie, letting him know that she had to leave at 6:00 A.M. Since she'd come to work for him at the last minute, he wasn't going to get all twisted about her leaving early. He folded the note and glanced at the clock on his nightstand. It was a little after midnight. If he wanted Nat to take Conner home, he'd have to get up with Conner at five thirty. He reached for a pen inside the nightstand. *I'll take Conner home*, he wrote, and slipped it under Natalie's door. As he moved back to his room, he realized that he didn't know where Conner lived these days. He knew they'd moved to Kirkland last year, and he had a vague idea, but he hadn't been to the house.

He walked into the closet and tossed his tie on the center island. Contrary to what Autumn thought of his assistants—heck, what a lot of people thought—he didn't sleep with them. Most of them were part-time students who needed extra money, and he paid them well to be at his beck and call. Their job description ranged from general gofer to nanny, and they were too important, and he depended on them too much to mess it all up with sex.

His pants hit the floor as he stepped out of his shoes. And he knew why everyone thought it, too. Because the assistants were all pretty. If any of the assistants had been homely girls with hairy warts, no one would think a thing about it. But he didn't worry about what other people thought. He was only concerned with himself and, as far as he was concerned, why have an unattractive woman in the house if he could hire someone nice to look at? It just made perfect sense.

He stripped to his boxer-briefs and, because Nat was down the hall, stepped into a pair of pajama pants. He didn't like anything restrictive and tended to overheat. He preferred to sleep bare-assed.

Sam scratched his bare chest and turned off all the lights. He'd have to call Autumn in the morning and let her know, but he didn't think she'd have a problem with him dropping Conner off home. And if she did, tough shit. Yeah, they'd agreed not be in the same room together, but tonight they'd been in the same room and hadn't killed each other. Hadn't even thought about it. Of course, he could only speak for himself.

A remote control lay on his dresser, and he picked it up and pointed it at the windows. The shades slowly lowered as he crawled into bed. Daniel and Blake and some of the guys had gone out after the wedding. This was the last weekend before the start of the season, and they'd probably party all night. One last blowout. Of course, they wouldn't let a little thing like work stop them completely, but they would have to slow down.

He adjusted the pillow beneath his head and thought of Autumn. He hadn't laid eyes on her for two years, but he still felt the same knot of confusion and guilt that he'd felt the day he'd walked out of the hotel in Vegas, leaving her behind. Sam didn't like feeling those things and avoided them as much as humanly possible.

He pushed all that guilt aside and thought of everything he had to do the next day and the season opener against San Jose Thursday. He thought of the Sharks' strengths and weaknesses. How best to exploit their lack of mental toughness. Within minutes, he drifted into a heavy dreamless sleep, and when he woke the next morning, he woke with a feeling of being watched.

"You're up now," Conner said, as soon as Sam opened his eyes. Wearing Incredible Hulk pajamas, Conner stood by the bed, his light blond hair sticking up on one side of his head. He looked at Sam as if he'd been trying to stare him awake. The morning sun lit up the blinds but left the room in dusky shadow.

Beneath lowered lids, Sam looked at the clock. It was just past eight. He cleared his throat. "How long have you been standing there?"

"A long time."

Which could mean an hour or a minute. "You wanna climb in here with me?"

"No. I want Toaster Sticks."

"Are you sure you don't want to sleep in?" Sundays were his only days to sleep in. The rest of the week he was practicing or playing, often both in the same day. "I could turn on the TV." He pointed to the big screen across the room.

"Nope. I'm hungry." That's one thing he knew about Conner. The kid liked to eat the second his feet hit the floor.

Sam groaned and swung his legs over the side of the bed. "Get the toaster out while I take a leak."

Conner smiled and took off out of the room, his little feet thumping across the carpet and hardwood floors. The bottoms of his pajamas fit snug around his calves instead of his ankles. Conner had always been tall, but it seemed as if he'd grown a few inches over the summer when Sam hadn't been looking. He stood and, after using the bathroom, joined his son in the kitchen.

He'd bought the loft a year ago and had the kitchen remodeled with brushed nickel, glass, and Italian marble. Instead of a conventional wall, a waterfall separated the kitchen and the dining room. From the ceiling, continuous water slid down a thin piece of glass giving the appearance of a sheet of water. The interior designer called it a "water feature," and it was Conner's favorite place to play.

Everything in the loft was modern and masculine and suited him. Sam opened the Sub-Zero freezer and crouched to look inside. Freezing air hit his bare chest as his gaze roamed over the contents: frozen juice, ice packs and numerous bags of peas. "I'm out of Toaster Sticks."

"Mom makes me heart pancakes."

Which explained a lot. "I don't have anything

to make pancakes." Not that he'd make them into little hearts even if he did.

"I like Egg McMuffins," Conner piped up.

"Your mom feeds you that crap?"

"When we're in a hurry."

"Well, don't eat that stuff. It's not good for you." He opened the pantry. "In the morning, a guy needs 80 percent carbs and 20 percent protein to start his day right."

Conner sighed. He'd heard it before. "I hate oatmeal."

Sam knew that and grabbed a box of Cheerios. "Oatmeal will fill you up, give you energy, and put hair on your chest."

"I'm in the kindergarten."

Sam laughed and turned to look at his son, sitting at the bar on a tall stool, his blue eyes bright and alert. "You don't want to be the only kid in your elementary school with a hairy chest?"

His eyes got even wider. "No!"

He took the milk out of the refrigerator and grabbed a cereal bowl. "Well, maybe next year."

"Maybe in sixth grade." Conner lowered his gaze to intently study the dark blond hair growing across Sam's chest. Then he pulled out the neck of his pajama's and peered inside. "Does it itch?"

"When it first grows in." He set the bowl in front of Conner and poured the cereal.

"My nuts itch sometimes." He rested his cheek on his fist. "But they aren't hairy. Mom says I can't scratch my nuts in public."

Sam smiled. That was such a boy thing to say. Sam sometimes worried that Autumn raised his son like a girl. Made him wimpy. Good to know he thought like a boy.

"Did you wash your hands?"

He looked up from the bowl. "What?"

"You gotta wash your hands when you cook."

Sam rolled his eyes and moved to the sink. So much for sounding like a boy. "You obviously live with a woman." He turned on the faucet and pumped some antibacterial soap into his palm.

"Mom yells at Uncle Vince about it all the time."

Good. Someone needed to yell at the idiot. Sam grabbed a paper towel and dried his hands.

"Does that hurt?"

"What?

He pointed to Sam's bare arm. "That?"

"This?" Sam ran a finger over the heavily

inked *veni vidi vici* tattooing his skin from the inside of his elbow to his wrist. "Nah. It did a little when I had it done."

"What does it say?"

At one time it had said his mama's name. Something he rarely recalled any more. "It's Latin and means: I came, I saw, now someone's gonna get his butt kicked." He wondered if Autumn had covered over his name on the inside of her wrist.

Conner laughed, showing his little white teeth. *"Butt.* That's a bad word."

"Butt?" He purposely cleaned his language up for Conner. Always did. He shook his head and threw the paper towel away. "What do you say instead of *butt?"*

"Bum-bum."

"Bum-bum?" He was right. Yet more proof that Conner spent too much time with a woman. *"Butt* isn't a bad word."

"Mom thinks so."

"Just because your mom's a girl, doesn't mean she's always right. *Bum-bum* is a sissy word and will get you beat up. Say *butt* instead."

He thought it over and nodded. "I got a picture." He jumped off his chair and ran from

63

the kitchen. When he returned, he set a piece of white notebook paper on the bar.

"You drew it?" Sam poured cereal and milk into the bowl.

"Yeah. I'm a good drawer." He crawled back up on the stool and pointed to two lopsided figures with yellow hair and blue eyes. One was smaller, and it looked like they were standing on an egg. "This is you, and this is me. We're fishin'."

"Fishing?" He grabbed a banana and sliced it up.

"Yeah."

The only time Sam fished was in Cabo. And that was more about drinking with the guys than actually fishing. He dumped half the banana in Conner's cereal, the other half in a blender. He grabbed a spoon and slid the bowl to his son. While Conner ate, he tossed some frozen strawberries, milk, protein powder, lecithin, and a splash of flaxseed oil into the blender. He pushed *smoothie*, then poured his breakfast into a big glass.

"I saw you on the boat."

"What boat?" He was pretty sure no one had taken photos on those trips. It was kind of an unwritten rule. He turned and raised his glass to his lips.

"In the paper." A Cheerio stuck to the corner of Conner's mouth, and he pushed it in with the back of his hand.

Ah. *That* picture. The one taken of him on a yacht last June pouring beer from the Stanley Cup on a few big-busted bikini models.

"I didn't like those girls."

"That's 'cause you're five." Sam lowered the glass and licked his top lip. "You will someday."

Conner shook his head, and one disapproving brow rose up his forehead. Good God, he looked just his mama. "Take me on your boat. Not those girls."

"That wasn't my boat."

"Oh." Conner took a big bite and chewed. "Josh F's dad takes him to the kindergarten," he said around a mouthful of Cheerios. "Dads should take their kids to the kindergarten sometimes."

How had they jumped from boats and fishing to kindergarten? "Doesn't your mom take you?"

Conner nodded and swallowed hard. "You can take me, too."

"Maybe when I'm in town sometime." He took a drink. "How do you like 'the' kindergarten?"

"It's okay. I like my teacher, Mrs. Rich. She reads to us. And I like Josh F."

65

"Is he your friend?"

He nodded. "Yep. Not Josh R. though. He's dumb. I don't like him." He scratched his cheek. "He punched me."

"Why?"

Conner shrugged a skinny shoulder. " 'Cause I touched his Barney backpack."

"The purple dinosaur?"

"Yep."

Sam licked his top lip. "Did you punch him back?"

"Oh no." He shook his head. "I don't like to punch people. It's not nice."

If the kid didn't look just like him, Sam might wonder. He'd spent so much time in the penalty box for fighting last season, he'd been tempted to hang a picture and maybe set up a lava lamp, it had felt so much like home. "I thought Barney was for babies."

Conner thought a minute, then nodded. "I liked Barney last year."

"Barney sucks."

Conner laughed, again showing his little white teeth. "Yeah. Barney sucks."

Chapter Four

Any Man of Mine:
Is Responsible

By noon, Autumn was dressed in jeans and plain white T-shirt. She flat-ironed her hair until it was smooth and shiny and brushed on a little mascara and tinted lip gloss. And yeah, she'd made the effort to look presentable because Sam had called and said he was dropping Conner off himself at noon. No, she didn't care about impressing him, not that she could, anyway, but neither did she want to open the door looking tired and scary. Which was how she usually looked on Sundays.

By half past twelve, she stood in the living room,

looking out the big window. By one, she paced with her cell phone in hand dialing Sam's number. He didn't answer, and all sort of horrible scenarios ran through her brain. Everything from a car accident to kidnapping. Every time she heard an engine in the distance, she pressed her forehead to the glass and looked down the street. Every time it wasn't Sam, her anxiety shot up a notch.

When Sam finally pulled his big red truck into her driveway at one thirty, she was out the door before he put the vehicle in park.

"Where have you been?" she asked as she tore down the steps, her gaze scanning the inside of the truck and stopping on Conner strapped inside. At the sight of her son, all her worry and anxiety turned to anger.

Sam slid his long legs out of the truck. His running shoes hit the pavement, and he stood there in jeans and a dark blue pullover fleece as if he were in no hurry. As if he weren't an hour and a half late.

"Hey there, Autumn." A pair of old-school Ray-Bans sat on the bridge of his slightly crooked nose, and the afternoon sun shone in his hair like he was some golden warrior.

Her cheeks felt all hot, and she had to take a

deep breath to keep from screaming. "Do you know what time it is?" There, that sounded calm.

Sam pulled back the sleeve of his North Face fleece and looked at the big platinum watch on his wrist. "Sure, it's about one thirty," he answered as if she'd merely inquired. He reached inside the truck and pulled out Conner's little SpongeBob backpack.

"Hi, Mom," Conner said as he followed his backpack out the driver side.

"Where have you been?" she asked again.

Conner jumped to the ground beside his father. "Shorty's."

Was that some sort of bar? Strip club? God knew Sam loved the strippers. "Whose?"

"It's an arcade downtown," Sam elaborated. "Just a few blocks from my condo."

"We had hot dogs." Conner's blue eyes got wide with excitement. "I played pinball. I got lots of points."

The two high- and low-fived each other, and Autumn felt the familiar tic behind her right eye whenever she had to deal with Sam. She didn't know if it was an aneurysm or blood clot. Neither was good. "Great. Wonderful." She forced a smile for Conner's sake. "Tell your dad good-bye."

Sam squatted down, and Conner stepped between his widespread knees. "Bye, Dad." He wrapped his arms around Sam's neck and held tight. "Maybe we can go to Shorty's again."

"Sure." He hugged him, then pulled back to look in his face. "Or we'll go to a movie or you can come to a game like we talked about."

Autumn didn't need to see Conner's face to know he was looking at his dad like he was the best thing since double hot fudge cake. All the guy had to do was feed him the crumbs of his attention, and Conner totally ate it up.

Conner nodded. "And fish."

Sam laughed as he rose. "Maybe next summer."

Conner grabbed his backpack from the ground. "Okay."

"Run inside and put your stuff away." She laid her hand on her son's cool, fine hair. "I'll be in in a minute."

Conner looked up at her, then back to Sam.

"See ya, buddy."

"See ya, Dad." He gave his dad's leg a quick hug, then headed up the steps to the front door.

Autumn folded her arms beneath her breasts and waited until he was inside. Then she turned to face Sam. She didn't want to yell or scream or sock him in the head. She didn't want to be that crazy person. Like before. She was in control of herself now. "You said you'd have him here at noon."

"I said ish."

"What?"

"I said noon-*ish*."

The tick in her eye moved to the center of her forehead. "What is that? Some sort of special Sam time? While the rest of the world lives and operates in time zones, you're special and operate in *ish*?"

He smiled like he thought she was funny. "I wanted to spend a little more time with him, Autumn. There's nothing wrong with wanting to spend a little time with my son."

He made it sound so reasonable. "You're an hour and a half late. I thought something might have happened."

"Sorry you were worried."

That wasn't good enough. Besides, she didn't believe him. He threw the word around, but he didn't mean it. Sam was never sorry about anything. "When you didn't show up, I called."

He nodded. "I forgot my phone at home. When we got back, I saw that you'd phoned."

71

"What? You didn't think to return my call? To let me know Conner was okay?"

He folded his big arms over his equally big chest. "It occurred to me, but by the way you blew up the phone with all your calls, I knew you'd chew my ass. Just like you're dying to do right now. And to tell you the truth, I'm never going to purposely call anyone who's dying to chew my ass."

She took a deep breath and glanced up at the big window and Conner's little face glued to the glass. Holding on to her control by a thread, she calmly said, "You're immature and irresponsible."

"Well, sweetheart, I've never said I wasn't irresponsible. But you're too controlling."

"He's my son."

"He's my son, too."

"He's your son when it's convenient for you."

"Well, it was convenient today. Get over it."

Get over it? Get OVER it? The tic in her forehead stabbed her brain, and her control snapped. "What about next time? What about when you blow him off next week or the week after? What about when he's looking forward to seeing you, and you blow him off for a party with your buddies?"

"I have events that I am required to attend."

"Were you required to attend that harbor cruise with half-naked women? Or how about all your trips to Vegas for craps and lap dances?" Although how, given their history, he could ever set foot in Vegas again was beyond her.

He rocked back on his heels. "Is this about jealousy?"

She rolled her eyes. Pain squeezed the bridge of her nose, and she was instantly sorry. "Get over yourself, Sam. You might think the sun rises and sets on your sorry ass, but I'm here to tell you that it doesn't." She glanced up at Conner, staring down at her. "And the one person who thinks it does, you totally blow off."

"I'd be with him more if I could. You know my schedule makes it difficult."

"If he were a priority in your life, you'd make time." She pushed her hair behind her ears. "You had this past summer off, but you only spent three weekends with Conner. You canceled on him at least eight different times, and every time you did, I had to try and make it up to him. Every time you've ever let him down, I'm the one who has to tell him that you love him and would be with him if you could. I'm the one who has to lie to him."

73

His jaw tightened. "I do love him."

"And we all know how much your love is worth." She shook her head. "While you're off playing hero to thousands of other little boys, your own son cries himself to sleep like his heart is breaking."

His arms fell to his sides, and he rocked back on his heels as if she'd hit him. "I'm no one's hero."

"I know that." She pointed toward the window without looking up at her son. "But he doesn't. Not yet. He doesn't know you're just a selfish prick unworthy of him, but he'll figure it out someday." She gasped and covered her pounding forehead with one hand. "Oh my God. I wasn't going to do that. I don't want to do this. I don't want to lose control. I don't want to be angry and call names. No matter how true."

He said just loud enough for her to hear, "He cries himself to sleep?"

"What?" She glanced up at the window. At her son looking down at his parents. He didn't look upset. He hadn't heard her call Sam a bad name. "Yes."

"I didn't know that."

"Why would you?" She brushed her hair back

and sighed. Suddenly tired. "You never stick around to pick up after yourself. I'm sure you never even give it a thought."

"Are you talking about Conner?"

"Who else?"

Over the top of his sunglasses, one brow rose up his forehead.

"Other than how your actions affect my son's life, I don't care about you, Sam. I haven't for a long time. My only concern is Conner."

"That makes two of us."

Hardly, she thought. "I see that he has everything he needs."

"He needs a man's influence."

Had he been talking to her brother? "He has Vince."

"*Vince* is an asshole."

"So are you, but at least Vince keeps his promises. Conner knows he can count on Vince."

He took a deep breath through his nose and let it out as if *she* exhausted *him*. "I told Conner he could come to my games, and I'll make sure he gets a good seat."

"He can't stay up that late, or he'll fall asleep at school."

"Not on Saturdays he won't." He climbed

inside his truck and shut the door. "I'll have Natalie call you."

Conner didn't like hockey. He was a pacifist, but if he wanted to go, she didn't have a problem with Natalie taking him. Besides, Sam would lose interest, and it wouldn't be an issue anyway.

Sam didn't wait for her response. Just shoved the truck in reverse and backed out of the driveway. From the window above, Conner waved, but typical of Sam, he didn't look up and notice. Autumn frowned and shook her head as she moved up the steps to the front door. Off in the distance, the rumble of bad-dog pipes rattled the air.

Great. Vince. Like she didn't have enough drama.

She paused on the top step and raised a hand to shield her eyes from the afternoon sun. The hatred Vince and Sam shared was no secret, and she hoped the two didn't stop and duke it out on Morning Glory Drive. She held her breath as the two passed, and although she couldn't see that far, she wouldn't put it past either to flip each other the bird.

She stood on the porch and waited. She loved her big brother. Loved him for a lot of good reasons, but mostly because he had her back. No matter what. He was loving and fiercely loyal. He fought for her. Always had, but sometimes he took his job as big brother and uncle a little too seriously. But that was Vince. He was a former Navy SEAL who didn't believe in half measures. He had dark demons that he never talked about and lived by the motto: "Sometimes it is entirely appropriate to kill a fly with a sledgehammer."

He pulled the Harley to a stop in the driveway where Sam's truck had just been parked and killed the engine. He swung one long leg over the bike, stood, and ran his fingers through his short dark hair.

"I thought the idiot was supposed to stay away from you," he said as he walked up the steps. His boots thudded on the concrete.

"He just dropped Conner off. No big deal." No need to mention that he'd been an hour and a half late and had worried her. No need to poke the bear with a sharp stick. "So, why are you here?" Although she figured she already knew.

"Maybe I just wanted to see you today."

"You saw me yesterday." She made a motion with her hand. "Come on. Get it out before we go inside."

He smiled, his bottom teeth slightly crooked

but very white. "After last night, I just wanted to make sure you're okay."

"You could have called."

"You would have lied." He dipped down and looked into her eyes. "Do I need to kill him?"

She might have laughed if she knew with a hundred-percent certainty that he was joking. She wasn't certain, but she didn't hold it against him. There were probably a lot of people who wanted to kill Sam. She'd seen him play hockey, and a few minutes ago, she'd wanted to kill him herself. "No. I didn't really even see him last night." Which wasn't technically true. She'd seen his blond head every time she'd entered a room. "We didn't talk much." Which was true.

"So, you're okay?" She suspected that Sam and Vince hated each other so intensely because they were alike in some ways. They were both handsome and arrogant and total horn dogs. The difference between them was that Vince put his family above all else.

There'd been a time when Conner had been younger when she'd relied a lot on her brother, but she was stronger now. As much as she loved and still needed Vince, there were times when she wished he'd find a nice girl, get married, and have his own family. He'd make a great dad, but of course, that whole horn dog thing always got in the way of a serious relationship. "You didn't need to tear over here."

"I wanted to come anyway."

Right. Autumn opened the door, and Vince followed her inside. "I'm a big girl now. I can handle Sam." They moved upstairs to Conner's room. He stood by his bed, pulling his dirty pajamas out of his backpack.

"Hey, Nugget," Vince said, using Conner's nickname as he crouched by his side and ruffled his hair.

"Hey, Uncle Vince." Conner pulled out his little undies. "I played pinball with my dad."

"Oh, yeah? That sounds like fun."

He nodded. "I ate a hot dog." He turned to his mom. "Can I have a new quilt?"

"What's wrong with your Barney quilt?"

"Barney sucks."

She gasped, and her mouth fell open. "But—but—You love Barney. He's your purple friend."

He shook his head and sniffed. "Barney is for babies."

"Since when?"

He shrugged. "Since I'm in the kindergarten now. I'm big."

He'd just torn a chunk of her heart. They'd picked out the material and made the quilt together. The pillow, too. "You don't want your Barney pillow?" He loved his Barney pillow.

"Nope."

Autumn gasped and grabbed the T-shirt above her heart. This was Sam's doing. She couldn't prove it without quizzing Conner, but she was sure Sam was responsible for Conner's sudden Barney defection.

Vince rose and turned to face her. "The kid's got a point," he said, totally going to the dark side with Conner. "Barney sucks hairy dinosaur balls."

"Language!"

Conner laughed, but Autumn was not amused.

While you're off playing hero to thousands of other little boys, your own son cries himself to sleep like his heart is breaking.

Sam stood on the balcony and looked out at Seattle and Elliott Bay beyond. The 2:05 ferry slid through the water, loaded with cars and passengers and headed for Bainbridge Island. Below him, the sound of traffic drifted upward to the tenth floor, and a brisk breeze brushed his face, carrying the scent of car fumes and the Puget Sound.

While you're off playing hero . . .

Sam moved away from the rail and sat in a padded patio chair. He reached for the Beck's sitting on the table next to him. He'd always assuaged his guilt by telling himself that when Conner was older, he'd make it up to him. He'd spend more time with him. Doing father-and-son stuff. Not that he knew anything about father-and-son *stuff.*

He raised the beer to his lips and tipped his head back. He was an even worse dad than his own. He would never have thought that was even possible, but he'd outshittied Samuel LeClaire Sr. in the father department. Because he knew better. He knew he never wanted to be the guy who treated strangers better than his own family. He never wanted to be the guy whom everyone else in town thought was great. One hell of a guy. A hero, but a hero who had nothing left for his family by the time he got home and took off his uniform.

Sam knew all too well how that felt. Sam was thirty-five. His old man had been dead for twenty years, but he could still remember waiting for his dad to come home and falling asleep before he arrived. He remembered throwing himself into hockey. Excelling. Standing out. Being a star, thinking that maybe, just maybe if he was good enough, his dad would come and see him play.

He doesn't know you're just a selfish prick unworthy of him, but he'll figure it out someday. He remembered the night he'd stopped waiting up, stopped caring if his dad came to one of his games. He'd been about ten when he'd realized his dad was never going to do the things he saw other dads do with their sons. His dad was never going to shoot the puck with him or come to one of his games. He was never going to look up and see his dad in the stands, sitting next to his mother and sister.

He ran his thumb up the cool bottle, collecting dewy droplets that slid to the crease and dripped over his knuckle. It was true that his work schedule was tough. During the season, he spent half his time on the road, but it was equally true that he'd left the responsibility of raising his son to Autumn. Breezing into town, spending some quality time with Conner before breezing back out. Autumn was more responsible than he was. So much so that it was sometimes hard to square her with the girl he'd met in Vegas.

A cool damp breeze brushed his face and the side of his hot neck. He'd always told himself that quality was more important than quantity. Wasn't that true? He was pretty sure he'd heard some child psychologist say that on a news program once, and this past summer, he'd had more obligations than usual. Because of the Cup win, he'd been expected at more fan and press events.

He raised the beer to his mouth and took a long drink. The weekends in Vegas and the blowout parties with his buddies hadn't been obligations. And yeah, a few times he'd canceled on Conner to party with his friends. And maybe it was more than a few times, but he'd never thought Conner was affected by his absence. Never dreamed his son cried himself to sleep.

He lowered the bottle and balanced it on the arm of the chair. Out of all the men on the planet, he should have known better. Out of all the men on the planet, he did know better. He also knew that sometimes shit happened, and, when it did, it was too late.

He remembered the night two Mounties knocked on the front door and told his mother that her husband had been killed during a raid on a farm in Moose Jaw. Constable LeClaire had been the first through the door and the first out of four others to die. He remembered looking at his dad's casket, one in the line of three others. He remembered seeing him in the red uniform he loved and had chosen over his family. He remembered hearing the cries of all the other kids who'd lost their fathers. He remembered holding his sister, Ella's hand while she cried and listening to his mother's quiet sobs. He remembered feeling ashamed. Ashamed because he felt very little for the man everyone else loved and thought was a hero.

He'd been fourteen when he'd had to step into his father's shoes. Just a month shy of his fifteenth birthday when he'd assumed the responsibility of man of the house. When it came to his ten-year-old sister, he'd taken the job seriously. He'd always looked out for her, and she'd followed him like a shadow. A shadow with a bouncy blond ponytail. In Ella's big blue eyes, he'd replaced their father. He was a damn hero.

Sam grabbed the neck of the bottle and turned it slowly on the wooden arm of the chair. He'd never wanted to be anyone's hero. God knew what a piss-poor job he'd done for Ella, but he did want his kid to sleep at night knowing his daddy loved him.

Which brought his thoughts around to Conner's mama. So, maybe he should have called Autumn and told her they were going to be late. Honestly, he hadn't given it a thought, and it hadn't occurred to him until he'd seen how many times she'd called his cell. By then he figured the damage was done. He hadn't needed to see her flying down those steps toward him to know he was in trouble. Hell, he'd known it before he'd turned onto her street. What he hadn't counted on was her looking so wild and hot. All that red-and-gold hair flying about her head and her green eyes on fire. If she hadn't opened her mouth and started bitching, he might have found himself in the uncomfortable situation of remembering the last time she'd looked like that. All crazy and wanting to do damage. Only that time she hadn't been angry. She'd torn at his clothes until he was naked, and her mouth was all over him, doing her worst, leaving him gasping, spent, and wanting more.

The first time he'd seen her, she'd been dancing by herself, one hand over her head, the other on her stomach, and moving her hips slow and seductive. He'd been on his feet walking toward her before he'd had a coherent thought in his head. He'd moved up behind her and put his hands on her waist. The second he'd touched her, he'd felt something. A spark of some little something hit him in the belly.

She'd thrown a sharp little elbow into his stomach, right about where he'd felt that little spark of something, then she turned to face him. Her eyes had rounded with fear, and she looked like she was thinking about running. He hadn't blamed her, but he hadn't been about to let that happen either.

Autumn hadn't fallen into bed with him that first night, but once he got her there, they hadn't left. Seeing her fly at him today, brought back memories of her naked against him. Of her white skin and firm white breasts in his hands and mouth. Autumn might not have his perfect body type, but her body was perfect. And for those few days in Vegas, when nothing had been real, she'd seemed perfect, too.

Sam raised the bottle and took a long drink. Then he'd woken up, hungover and wrung out and wondering what the fuck he'd done. He'd married a girl he had just met and didn't know. Hell, he hadn't even known where she lived.

The month before that disaster in Vegas, he'd signed a five-million-dollar, three-year, contract with the Chinooks. With one reckless act, he'd put it at all risk. With one reckless act, he'd changed his life forever. Autumn's, too.

He had never been sure what had pissed Autumn off more—him leaving her alone in Caesars without so much as a good-bye, the way he'd handled the divorce, or his insistence on a paternity test. Out of those three things, the only one he would change if he could was the way he'd left. He'd man up and say good-bye. It would have been the hard thing, but it would have been the right thing to do.

Sam placed the heels of his palms on the arms of the chair and rose. He wasn't as bad a dad as Autumn portrayed him, but he wasn't as good as he needed to be either. All that had to change. He had to do the right thing. He had to go as hard at seeing his son as he did at playing hockey. He looked at his watch and took one last pull from his beer. Some of the guys were getting together at Daniel's for poker night. Sam was down three thousand and would love the opportunity to win it back.

Getting more serious about his personal life didn't mean he had to give up everything else. Didn't mean he had to give up poker night.

Chapter Five

Any Man of Mine:
Likes a Good Buffet

I want a renaissance faire wedding. With a castle and moat and magicians."

Autumn looked down at the tip of her ballpoint pen and forced herself to write renaissance faire in the theme heading. It was a little after six on a Saturday night, and she was in her office planning the Henson/Franklin wedding. Renaissance, apparently. In the office next door, she could hear Shiloh clicking on the computer and talking on the phone. "You have to keep in mind that the venue you've chosen is fairly small." She rose from behind her desk and straightened the red-

and-black floral dress she'd bought at a vintage store in downtown Santa Cruz the last time she and Conner had gone on vacation to California. The soles of her red leather flats barely made a sound as she closed the door. Shiloh was a great assistant, but she tended to dial up the volume when she was excited. "I don't know if we have room for a moat." This was her first face-to-face meeting with the couple, but she'd had several phone conversations with the bride.

"Oh. Well how about snake charmers and jesters?"

She retook her seat and looked up at the young woman across from her. Carmen the bride appeared so normal with her clear blue eyes and straight black hair. She wore a sweater set and little brooch, but the ear tapers sticking out of her lobes like black spikes were a tip-off that some kind of freakiness lay beneath that demure sweater set. "I'm not sure we can get the permits for exotic animals at your venue."

"Bummer." Carmen snapped her fingers. "Juggling dwarfs. We saw that at a faire in Portland."

Autumn hoped the bride was talking about little people who juggled as opposed to little people who *were* juggled. It was probably the former, but she'd heard of stranger things. "We might have better luck getting jugglers if we didn't put height restrictions on them," she suggested.

Carmen turned to her groom, Jerry. "What about pirates?"

"Pirates can be fun but totally unpredictable," the groom answered as if they were talking about real pirates. "Grandma Dotti and Aunt Wanda are uptight and might have a problem with the pirates."

Thank God for an uptight aunt and grandma. Autumn wanted all brides and grooms to have the weddings of their dreams. She wanted them to have everything *they* wanted, but she knew from experience that simple was always better. "If you have too much going on, it takes the focus off the bride and the groom. It's your day, and the two of you need to be the center of attention."

Carmen smiled. "That's true. I've dreamed of my wedding day all of my life." Traditional or alternative, all little girls had that in common.

"We want the servers in fools hats and masks," Jerry added.

"And wearing our wedding colors."

91

Which were blue and gold. She tilted her head as if she were giving the suggestion serious thought. While she wanted to give the bride and groom what they wanted, it was her job to keep it within their budget, too. "Well, those sorts of costume would have to be especially made for the reception. As opposed to rented, and your budget is . . ." She flipped a page like she'd forgotten and needed a reminder. "Twenty thousand. Twenty thousand is barely going to cover your catering, flowers, photography, and venue." Twenty thousand was a lot of money unless you were talking about planning a wedding. "If you want the servers to have specially made costumes, we can always cut back on the food. Perhaps serve chicken as opposed to a roasted pig."

The bride sat back in her chair and bit her lip. "Jerry and I met at a renaissance faire in Gig Harbor. We've always envisioned our wedding with a renaissance theme and a roasted pig."

Autumn gave the couple her most reassuring smile. "And you can and will have a great wedding with a renaissance theme. I'll talk to some of my vendors and see what kind of deals they can give you. In this economy, they are a lot more open to giving price breaks. And I'll contact the local Society for Creative Anachronism and see what they can do, too. I think we can come up with something fabulous and still stay within your budget. I'm looking forward to helping you with this wedding. It's going to be fun." At least it wasn't a pink princess theme, which was Autumn's least favorite. "Have you picked out a dress," she asked Carmen, and by the time the bride and groom left her office, they'd signed a contract, put down a deposit, and were upbeat and optimistic about their June wedding.

Autumn tossed her pen and pressed the heels of her palms against her brows. She wasn't going to get rich planning weddings with budgets of twenty grand. Every little bit helped, and she was grateful for each job. But the commission off Carmen and Jerry's wedding would barely pay the lease on her office for two months, which was why a lot of planners worked out of their homes, but not Autumn. She'd always believed that the image of success attracted success. Her office wasn't anything big and splashy, just a seven-hundred-square-foot space she rented in a strip mall not far from her house; but it did give her the appearance of professionalism that a planner just couldn't get from meeting clients in her home.

Autumn depended on the big events and big weddings, like the Savages', to survive the leaner times and keep her business going. To put food on the table and pay the utilities. Although she hated to admit it, the money she got each month from Sam went above and beyond helping to pay her personal bills. She and Conner lived modestly, and she'd like to be able to say she didn't use any of the child-support money Sam provided. She'd like to throw it all back in his face, but she wasn't a martyr, and raising a child was expensive. She'd like to say she was socking the money away for Conner's education, but Sam had that covered, too.

The amount Sam paid for one child was ridiculously high, but she was the only one who seemed to think so. Neither her lawyer nor Sam's or even Sam himself seemed to think he should pay less. Which, she supposed, showed how much money the man made a year. She didn't need half that much, and she'd put a lot of it aside so that when it had come time to buy a house, she'd paid cash. The house was thirty-five years old, but it was her and Conner's, and they'd never be homeless. Never have to move around to avoid landlords and eviction notices like when she'd been growing up. Never moving from town to town, one step ahead of the repo man.

If Autumn did have a weakness, it was traveling. Every year, she took Conner on an awesome vacation. Usually in January because Januaries were notoriously slow months in the planning business. But with Conner in school now, they would have to take minivacations and wait until spring break to head off to St. Barts or Atlantis.

"Hey, Autumn." Shiloh, Autumn's twenty-five-year-old assistant stuck her dark head into the office. "I talked to Tasty Cakes, and they'll do the cake for the Kramer anniversary for a thousand if we use them for the Peterson birthday party."

"Fabulous." The Kramer's fiftieth wedding anniversary was planned for the second week in November and included three hundred family members and a five-tier wedding cake. "We can use the savings on better wine." She flipped her wrist over and looked at her watch. Seven thirty. Free weekend nights were rare. "Don't you have a date or something?"

Shiloh raised one dark brow over her brown eyes. "Don't you?"

Autumn laughed. "Yeah right. I have a five-year-old."

Shiloh rested a shoulder against the door-frame. "Not tonight you don't."

True, Conner was at the hockey game watching his dad skate around and punch people in the head. Sam had actually come through this time. Of course, it wouldn't last. "No one asked me out tonight."

"That's because of the repellent."

"What are you talking about?"

"Your man repellent."

She blinked. "My what?"

Shiloh's mouth fell open. "I thought you knew. I thought you did it on purpose."

"Did what on purpose?"

"Put on the man repellent. You know, sprayed yourself with 'stay away' vibe. If my friends and I are out, and we don't want to be bothered, we put out the vibe."

"I have a vibe?" She put a hand on her chest.

Shiloh shook her head, and the light caught in the sparkly headband she favored. "No! Geez, sorry." She walked farther into the room. "Forget it. Forget I said anything."

"That's like saying my face looks like a dog's butt, then telling me to forget you said it."

"Your face doesn't look like a dog's butt. You

have a really pretty face and a smoking body—and I mean that in a totally nonlesbian way." She took a deep breath and let it out slowly. "Which is why I thought you put on the repellent. To purposely scare men away. We all do it sometimes."

She scared men away? Seriously? When had that happened? She'd thought she wasn't dating by choice. Not because men found her repellent, but come to think of it, she hadn't been asked out in a really long time.

"I'm soooooo sorry, Autumn. Are you mad?"

"No." She wasn't mad. Just a little shocked and a *whole lot* confused. She couldn't even recall the last time a man had even flirted with her.

Shiloh gave a weak smile, then asked in an obvious attempt to change the subject and fill the awkward silence, "So, what's your brother doing tonight?"

She reached for an empty binder and pulled the rings apart. "Out somewhere." She'd have to ask Vince if she had a bad vibe. He'd tell her the truth, maybe. "Why?"

"I thought I might call him."

"You know he's a dog?" She reached inside a desk drawer and pulled out a planning packet. She looked up, and added, "Right?"

"Sure." Shiloh shrugged. "I don't want to marry him. Just maybe have dinner."

Uh-huh. Vince didn't do dinner. "Shi—" She should warn her assistant. She liked Shiloh, and Vince wasn't relationship material. He had issues.

"Yeah?"

Shiloh was a nice woman, and Autumn didn't want to lose her as an assistant, even if she did think she sprayed man repellent on herself, but who was she to give anyone advice? "Nothing. Have a good night."

"See ya Monday," Shiloh said over her shoulder as she walked away.

"Lock the door on the way out." She placed a business card in the binder sleeve, a packet inside, and snapped the rings shut. She hadn't had a date in a really long time. She'd thought it was because she was just too busy. That she wasn't ready. That it was *her* choice. Was there more to it? Did she really give off some sort of vibe?

No. Yes. Maybe. She reached inside another desk drawer and pulled out a remote. *God, I don't know.* She turned on the television across the room and clicked around until she found the Chinooks' game. She watched for a few moments, hoping to see Conner's face in the crowd. She was a single mother. A small-business owner. A very busy woman. Way too busy for a relationship just then, but that didn't mean she wanted to repel men.

"The puck is shot up ice by LeClaire, who tries to pass to Holstrom," the hockey commentator announced just before the whistle blew. *"Five and a quarter left in the second period, and icing is called."* The camera zoomed in on Sam's jersey. On the Chinook swatting a puck with its tail, then the lens panned up to his face beneath the white helmet resting above his brows. His blue gaze looked up at the scoreboard. The Dallas Stars were up by a goal. *"That man right there is a huge part of the Chinooks' cup-winning defense,"* the commentator continued. *"He's always one of the biggest, most intimidating guys on the ice."*

A second commentator laughed. *"If you see LeClaire coming, it's best to get out of the way. With his team down by one, he'll be looking to put the big hurt on someone."*

Sam skated into a face-off circle to the left of his own goal. He put his stick on the ice and waited, his steely blues focused on the opponent across from him. The puck dropped, and he fought for domination, battling it out. He shot the puck up ice, but it was stopped by a Dallas player who had the audacity to skate along the boards toward the Chinooks' goal. The "big hurt" Sam put on him lifted his skates a foot off the ice and rattled the Plexiglas. A Star slammed into Sam, who turned and threw a punch. Several players from both teams piled on, and Autumn couldn't tell if they were hitting each other or holding each other back. Gloves and sticks hit the ice, and two referees finally blew their whistles and skated into the middle of the scrum. Sam pointed to the left and argued with the ref, but in the end, he straightened his white jersey, picked up his gloves and stick from the ice, and skated to the penalty box. His eyes narrowed, but a smile twisted one corner of his lips. He wasn't at all sorry.

Of course, Sam was rarely sorry about anything.

She remembered the first time she'd looked up into those blue eyes. She'd been so incredibly naïve, and he'd been so impossibly handsome. She'd been alone in Vegas. All alone in Sin City. She'd been a small-town girl, and Vegas had been foreign and like nothing she had ever experienced. Maybe if she hadn't been alone, she wouldn't have been so vulnerable to Sam's evil ways.

Maybe if she hadn't paid nonrefundable money for the seven-day, five-night vacation package to Caesars Palace, she would have taken one look at the debauchery in those beautiful eyes and run home. Maybe if her mother hadn't warned her about the decadence in Vegas, she wouldn't have been so intrigued to see it for herself.

She'd spent the previous two years caring for her mom and taking care of her affairs after her death and she'd needed a break. A vacation from her life. She had a list of everything she wanted to do in Vegas, and she was determined to wring every last dime out of that vacation.

That first day by herself she'd spent walking up and down the Strip, staring at all the people and collecting stripper/hooker cards. She'd window-shopped at Fendi, Versace, and Louis Vuitton. She'd found a pink bead bracelet at a sidewalk vendor and played a few slots in Harrah's because she'd read somewhere that Toby Keith stayed at Harrah's. But she'd only fed the slots until she lost twenty bucks. Even then, she'd been very tight with her money.

She'd lounged by the pool, and that night she put on a white sundress she'd bought at a Wal-Mart in Helena and hit Pure. She'd heard about the nightclub inside Caesars. Read in *People* and *Star* magazines that celebrities hosted parties in the bar.

At first, things inside Pure were slow. She sat within the stark white interior and rolling pastel lights, nursing a few drinks and wondering, "Is this it?" Is this what everyone raves about? But by eleven, the bar picked up, and by midnight she was dancing and having a good time. By 1:00 A.M., the dance floor was a crowded mash of warm bodies, and she was in the middle of it, moving her butt to Jack Johnson, letting go, being young, and having more fun than she'd had in years.

Within the mix of hot bodies and warm tequila glow, she'd become instantly aware of a pair of big hands on her waist. For a second or two she hadn't thought much of it. The floor was crowded, and people were bumping into each other. She took the touch for an accident, but when it became obvious to her booze-soaked brain that the touch wasn't accidental, she threw an elbow into a solid wall of muscle and looked over her shoulder. Way up into baby blue eyes and a face that dropped her jaw. Yellow light slid through his hair and lit him up like a golden god.

He didn't smile or say anything. Not even "hello." He just looked at her, his hands lightly resting in the curve of her waist, not a bit sorry that he was touching her. Blue and green lights flashed across his face as sex rolled off him in hot waves. His gaze held hers, and she knew trouble when it stared down at her. She knew it by the tumble in her stomach and the catch in her breath. She knew she should run.

But she didn't. Instead, she stood there, feeling the pulsing beat of the music through her feet up to her heart. She stood there, staring into those mesmerizing blue eyes like she'd fallen into some bizarre, dizzying trance. Either that, or she'd downed more tequila than she thought.

He lowered his face and asked next to her ear, "Are you afraid?" His deep, rough voice touched the side of her throat and raised the tiny hairs on the back of her neck.

Was she?

No, but she definitely should be. Maybe it was the alcohol or Vegas or him. Probably all three. She shook her head and he pulled back and looked into her face as an easy, confident smile pushed up the corners of his lips.

"Good." He raised one of her hands to his

shoulder and once again rested both palms in the curve of her waist. "That's real good."

For such a big guy, he could move. He was fluid and at perfect ease with his body. He pulled her closer until the front of her sundress almost touched his blue T-shirt. Almost. She could feel the heat of his chest and smell the scent of soap and skin and beer. He moved his hips with hers, his knee finding a spot between her thighs. Her hands slid across his hard shoulders to the base of his wide neck. This wasn't happening. This sort of thing didn't happen to her. Not the pounding in her heart or the hot pulse down low in her belly. It wasn't real. He wasn't real. He certainly wasn't on her to-do list.

His lids lowered a fraction as he looked down at her, her body in perfect time with his, his hips flirting with hers but never actually touching. "I saw you," he said next to her ear. "And I like the way you move."

She liked the way he moved, too. Any man who could move like he was making love on the dance floor had to know how to make love in the bedroom. Autumn wasn't exactly a virgin. She'd had a few boyfriends. Some of them had even been pretty good in bed, but she had a feeling that this guy *knew* things. The kinds of things that came with lots of experience and dedicated practice. Things that turned up the heat in her abdomen.

"Are you a dancer?"

She was almost insulted, but this *was* Vegas. "Like a stripper?"

"Yeah."

"No. Are you?"

He laughed. A low rumbling next to her throat. "No, but if I were, I'd give you a free lap dance."

"Bummer. I've never had a lap dance." She had a feeling he couldn't say the same.

"I've never given one, but for you I'd be willing to give it a try."

As she pulled back to look up into his face, his lips slipped across her cheek and brushed the corner of her mouth. She sucked in a hard breath, and her chest got tight.

"But not here," he said. "Come with me."

She didn't know him. Didn't even know his name, but she wanted to. She wanted to know all of him. She wanted to go anywhere he wanted to take her.

She should run.

This time she listened. She took a step back,

and his hands fell to his sides. He raised one brow, and before she lost her mind completely, she turned. He reached for her. She felt his hand on her arm, but she kept on going. One foot in front of the other, all the way up to the sixth floor. She shut herself inside her room and locked the door. Him out or her in, she wasn't sure.

This sort of thing did not happen to her. She didn't dance like that with guys she didn't know. She didn't stare at their lips and wonder what it would be like to kiss them.

Her mother had been right. Las Vegas was a decadent, morally dangerous place, and she should have heeded the warning. Nothing was real there. Not the canal at the Venetian, the volcano at the Mirage, or the people at Pure. Handsome men did not look at Autumn Haven as if she were the only woman in a bar filled with beautiful women. And she, Autumn Haven, did not contemplate sex with complete strangers. Not even strangers who looked like the guy in the bar.

She packed her bags, but when she woke the next morning, her head cleared, and she decided she'd overreacted. She'd had too much to drink and blown everything out of proportion. Her memory of the night before was a bit hazy, and she was fairly sure she hadn't really contemplated hooking up with some random guy. The touch of his hands on her waist hadn't been as hot, and he wasn't as impossibly good-looking as she recalled through her tequila goggles. But even if it was all true, the chances of its happening again were as about as likely as running into that same guy in a town crammed with hundreds of thousands of guys.

She spent most of the morning in her room getting over the slight headache she had earned the night before. After lunch, she put on a black bikini with gold hearts she'd splurged on at the Fashion Show Mall the day before. She slathered herself with sun screen, dumped it along with several magazines in her beach bag, and headed down to the pool.

From the hotel's brochure, she knew that the pool was called Garden of the Gods Pool Oasis. Which pretty much described the elaborate pools, massive columns and urns, rows of palm trees and winged lions. In the brochure, she thought Caesars should have added *decadent* to the description. The Garden of the Gods Pool and Decadent Oasis

By the time she made it to the pools, it was a little

before one in the afternoon and inching toward a hundred degrees. The sun toasted the top of her head, and she took a big floppy hat out of her bag and found a white lounge chair in one corner beneath a cluster of palms. Being a natural redhead didn't mix with the hot sun. She either burned or freckled. Neither was an attractive option.

A cabana boy took her drink order, and she relaxed with a tall glass of tea. Not the Long Island kind. At least not right then. With her hat dipping over her left eye, she sat back with a *Cosmo* magazine and settled into an article about the most intense erogenous zones on a man. According to the article, it was just beneath the head of the penis called the frenulum. Autumn had never heard of it and brought the magazine closer for a better look at the diagram.

"There you are, Cinderella."

She slapped her *Cosmo* closed and raised the brim of her straw hat. She looked way up into a pair of black Oakley's covering eyes she knew were a beautiful blue. He was even bigger and better-looking in the sunlight. He wore a pair of gray Quicksilver board shorts and a white tank with large armholes around his massive shoulders.

"What are you reading?"

"Makeup tips." She tried to act cool as she shoved the *Cosmo* into her bag. Like she wasn't reading about penises and like outrageously good-looking men talked to her every day. "Have you been following me?"

He chuckled and sat on the chaise next to her. "Keeping my eyes open for you."

"Why?"

He dug in his back pocket, then handed her the pink bead bracelet she'd worn the night before. "You lost this."

This was Vegas. Nothing was real in Vegas. Certainly not good-looking men tracking her down to return a cheap bracelet. She opened her palm, and he dropped it in her hand, the beads still warm from his body. "Thank you."

"I was fairly drunk last night." His brows lowered, and he looked around. "So is there anything I need to apologize for?"

"No."

"Damn. I was kinda hoping we got into trouble." He returned his gaze to hers. "Why are you hiding way back here in the corner?"

"I'm not hiding. I'm just avoiding the sun."

"Hungover?"

She shook her head. "I burn."

He gave her that slow easy smile she'd seen the night before. The one she'd thought her tequila buzz had made up. "I could put sunscreen on your back."

She lowered her hand from the brim of her hat and tilted her head to look at him. There was only one sensible option. Run away again before she got herself into trouble.

He held up his hands as if he were completely harmless. She wasn't fooled. "I won't touch you anyplace you don't want to be touched."

But she didn't want to run. She was on vacation. Nothing counted on vacation. And certainly nothing counted in Vegas. Wasn't that their motto? What happened in Vegas stayed in Vegas? "Sorry. I already put some on."

"That makes one of us." He looked up at the broiling sun and cringed. "I can practically hear my skin sizzle."

She pointed up at the palm trees. "In the shade?"

"I'm sensitive."

"Uh-huh." She reached into her beach bag and pulled out a tube of sunscreen. "It's SPF 40 and—" He whipped off his shirt, and she about fell out of her chair. Holy crap! He had big pecs and shoulders and a six-pack of killer abs. She'd never seen anything like him. Not in person, anyway. Not close enough to lick. Would probably never see anything like him again. Where had he come from? What did he do for a living? Lift small buildings? "What's your name?"

"Sam."

He looked like a Sam. "Autumn," she said, and swung her legs over the side of her chaise. "Autumn Haven."

He chuckled. "And that's your real name? You're not just shitting me?"

"Not shitting you." She'd always hated her name. "I know. It sounds like a retirement home. Like Meadow Lakes or Summer Village." She kept her eyes on his face in a desperate bid not to rudely stare at his chest and drool. Although really, staring at his face was no hardship. "Here you go." She shoved the sunscreen toward him.

Instead of taking it, he lay back in his chair. "Your name doesn't sound like a retirement home. More like one of those paradise destinations."

A thin golden happy trail ran down the middle of his six-pack, circled his navel, and disappearing beneath the waist of his shorts, pointing the way to *his* paradise destination. God help her. She wanted to say something clever. Something smart and sexy, but she couldn't think of anything. Not when the blood was draining from her head.

"The all-inclusive kind," he added. "The kind that promises endless pleasure and an all-you-can-eat buffet."

Autumn had a choice. Run like hell. Again. Run and save herself from endless pleasure and the all-she-could-eat buffet laid out in front of her like a smorgasbord of sin.

She rose from the lounge chair, looked down at all that yummy temptation, and popped the top of her Coppertone.

Chapter Six

Any Man of Mine:
Fits into My Life

S am left his truck running and groaned a little as he hoisted Conner to his shoulder. Beneath the neoprene ice pack wrapped around his waist, the muscles in the small of his back tightened, still in protest over the hit Modano had put on him in the third frame. He leaned a bit to his left and carried his son up the concrete, the soles of his leather loafers a thump on the concrete. He was getting old. His body couldn't take the same punishment at thirty-five that it had at twenty-five.

The weak porch light shone down on his head as he rang the doorbell. The cool night air seeped through the tight weave of his thin gray sweater and white T-shirt beneath. He'd had Natalie call Autumn to tell her that Conner was staying after the game to meet some of the guys. He wondered if she'd mentioned that Sam would bring him home.

The door swung open, and Autumn stood within the soft glow of the entry. She wore a yellow T-shirt with a white wiener dog on it, yellow-and-white flannel pants, and white wiener-dog slippers. Her deep auburn hair shone like fire beneath a brass chandelier, but she didn't look all fired up to see him. Not like last time.

"He passed out about ten minutes ago."

Autumn opened the door wider and let him in. He followed her up a set of stairs and down a hall lined with framed photos. The house smelled of homey things. Like cooked meals, wood polish, and old carpet. It wasn't the kind of house he expected her to live in with his son. It wasn't a bad house. Not all that much different from what he'd lived in as a kid, but she could afford newer.

They moved into a bedroom painted with cartoon characters, and his muscles protested as he laid his son on a bed covered with a Barney quilt. Conner hated Barney. Didn't he?

114

Sam straightened, and Autumn took over. She unzipped Conner's jacket, and his eyes fluttered open. "I got a foam finger," he said.

Her hands moved over him, and she helped him sit up as she pulled at his jacket. "Did you have a good time, little nugget?"

He nodded and yawned. "Yes."

Sam moved to the doorway and watched Autumn carefully pull Conner's arms through his Chinooks' T-shirt. It had been a couple of years since he'd seen mother and son together. He didn't think he'd ever seen Autumn so . . . soft.

"Dad told me a joke."

Her head whipped around. Her eyes huge.

Sam put up his hands. "A knock-knock joke."

"It was funny." Conner laughed, sleepy and silly. "Knock knock."

Autumn returned her attention to undressing Conner. "Who's there?"

Conner waited until the shirt was pulled over his head before he answered, "Goat."

"Goat who?"

"Goat is at . . . Goat ask . . ." He lay down, and Autumn moved to the end of the bed and untied his shoe. "I forgot."

"Goat to the door and find out," Sam provided.

Autumn turned her face and looked at him as she untied his laces. A smile worked one corner of her lips, and she rolled her green eyes as if she went through this sort of thing a hundred times a day. "You're right. That is funny." She took his shoes and socks off his feet and dropped them on the floor. "Peee–yew!" She waved a hand in front of her face. "Those are the stinkiest feet in the whole world."

"You always say that, Mom."

Conner and Autumn had a whole ritual, a whole life that he knew nothing about and that had nothing to do with him. He'd always known it, of course, but actually seeing it made him a little uncomfortable, and he really couldn't say why.

He took a step backward into the hall. "I'll go get the foam finger."

"And my puck, Dad."

Sam looked into Conner's sleepy eyes and nodded. "Okay." He moved back down the hall, past the walls lined with photos of Conner and Autumn and Conner with Vince the idiot. The small of his back hurt like hell as he moved down the steps and out into the chilly night air. When he got home, he'd shove a bag of peas against his back. He preferred peas over anything else. They fitted better to his back or knee or shoulder, and when they were hard, they kind of massaged his muscles like cold beads.

The Ford F–250 was still running, and he thought about turning it off, but he figured he wouldn't be much longer and left it on. A guy didn't buy an F–250 because he worried about gas consumption. He drove it because of the payload and because it hauled serious ass. Although he never hauled anything heavier than his sports bag, it was good to know it had the power if he ever decided to tow twenty four thousand pounds.

He moved to the passenger side and found Conner's foam finger and the puck Johan had given him while he and Nat had sat in the lounge waiting for Sam to finish with reporters and getting his back iced in the locker room. You'd have thought the puck was made of gold, the way Conner had acted about it. Shit, if he'd known his kid would get so excited about a puck, he would have given him one years ago.

He shut the truck door and headed toward the house. *You should know. You're his father,* his

117

guilty conscience reminded him. His conscience seemed to be more active lately, a fact that bothered him as much as his guilt. He didn't like to feel guilty about anything. Seeing Autumn again had triggered something inside him, and seeing that his son lived in an old split-level in Kirkland while he lived in a five-million-dollar loft in the middle of Seattle didn't sit very well with him either.

The front door to the older house squeaked as he opened it. She could afford better. He paid her enough in child support to make sure his child lived well. He paid enough that he shouldn't feel guilty about anything anymore.

He moved up the stairs and looked around the living room. At the oak furniture and sofa and love seat that were made out of durable microfiber. The house was crammed with little homemade knickknacks and art projects. Pictures of Conner at every age and stage of his life were all over the place. He had photos of Conner, too, but nothing like this.

The cell phone in the front pocket of his black wool pants rang, and he pulled it out. Veronica's number flashed across the screen, and he sent it to voice mail. He was tired and not in the mood to talk about Milan or Paris or wherever the hell she was staying. If by chance she was in Seattle, he wasn't in the mood for that either. Sometimes he just wanted to crash by himself. Tonight was one of those times.

He set the big blue finger and puck on a coffee table and moved to the fireplace mantel. He reached past a photo of Vince with Conner on his shoulders and grabbed a photograph of Autumn sitting on a swing in a park somewhere. Conner sat on her lap, grinning. Conner was young, perhaps a year. His mother looked young, too. Maybe it was the smile. He hadn't seen her smile like that in a long time. Five years or more. He put the photo back and looked up at a grouping of photos that hung above the mantel. Each individual photo was framed with black-and-white matting, and the theme seemed to be Halloween.

Conner at the age of three dressed as a mouse standing next to Autumn dressed up like a cat. Not a sexy kitty, either. Just a black cat. In another photo, Conner in a little cow costume and Autumn was a milkmaid. Again, not a sexy milkmaid. When Conner had been a baby, Autumn had dressed him as a monkey, and she wore a banana suit. At every Halloween party Sam had ever gone to, the women put the goods out on display. Sexy Snow White. Sexy cop. Sexy devil. Sexy harem girls and sexy nuns. That was what Halloween was about.

"He's out like a light again," Autumn announced as she walked into the living room.

He looked over his shoulder, then back at the photos. "What is Conner going to be for Halloween this year?"

"He hasn't made up his mind yet. The latest is a vampire, but I'm sure he'll change his mind several more times before the thirty-first."

"I think I'm going to be in town this year." Which wasn't always the case and one of the reasons he never made a fuss about not seeing Conner on Halloween. He was fairly certain he'd be in Toronto on the thirtieth, but back in town the thirty-first. He remembered because Logan had said something about hitting a bar downtown known for their wild costume contests. A few years ago, he'd been a guest judge and recalled a certain Alice in Wonderland who'd forgotten her underpants. For some reason that he never understood, but certainly appreciated, Halloween seemed to give normally reserved women permission to dress slutty and make out with each other.

God love 'em.

"I put Conner's finger and puck over there," he said, and pointed to the table. "I think he had a good time tonight."

"I think he did." She raised her arms and pushed her hair back, gathering it in her hands and twisting it into some sort of loose knot that immediately fell apart. "He'll probably sleep until noon."

There wasn't anything overtly sexy about Autumn. Not what she wore nor how she stood. Not even the way her shirt pulled across her breasts and distorted the wiener dog on front, kind of lifting his back end higher up her chest while his head was stuck under her right breast. In her dog shirt and slippers, she looked like a mom, and Sam had never been attracted to moms. Moms had baggage, and he didn't mean kids. He already knew this mom's baggage. Knew that when she got together with friends and talked about "that son of a bitch," she was talking about him. Yet he couldn't stop himself from wondering if she still liked to be kissed in the crook of her neck. Right where the collar of her shirt touched her warm neck. "I'm a little surprised to see you living in a house like this," he said to change the direction of his thoughts. Fast before his mind wondered down that dangerous path. A path leading down her chest to her cleavage.

Autumn folded her arms beneath her breasts. "What's wrong with my house?"

A lot. Starting with the carpet that looked a good ten years past warranty. Not to mention the hideous wallpaper border. He could see her eyes getting all squinty like she was about to get worked up. He didn't want to fight, so he said, "Nothing. It just seems like it might need a little work, and I never figured you for a fixer-upper."

"That's probably because you don't really know me."

He could point out that he knew she had a little birthmark shaped like Oklahoma on her ass, but he was pretty sure that wasn't the "you don't really know me" she was talking about. "Are you handy with a hammer and nails?"

She relaxed a bit, and her hands dropped to her sides. "No." She shook her head, and her red hair brushed her shoulders. "I can manage a hot glue gun, and I rock at table arrangements." She cast her eyes about the room and let out a breath. "When I bought the house, I thought I'd have it completely renovated by now, but I just haven't had the time."

He asked what he thought was an obvious question. "Why not buy a house you don't have to renovate?"

She shrugged. "Several reasons. One of which is that I wanted a nice, safe place for Conner to play." She started toward the kitchen and motioned for him to follow. "I'll show you what attracted me to this property."

He moved past an oak dining-room table with fresh roses in a pink vase in the center. The kitchen was surprisingly updated and shockingly without those knitted cozies that some women favored.

She flipped on the outside lights and lit up a huge backyard with one of those play sets that had a fort, slide, four swings, and a climbing wall. "Conner loves it back there," she said.

"Does he climb the wall?"

"Oh yeah, but I think he prefers to climb up the slide."

Were they really standing this close to each other and not yelling? So close that her shoulder almost touched his arm? The last time they'd stood this close without yelling, they'd been naked.

He looked at her profile. At the smooth white skin of her forehead, straight nose, and full red mouth. They might be standing close, so close he could smell her hair, but there was a big distance between them.

"You can't really see it, but behind the fence is a nice wooded area." She raised her left hand and pointed outside. "Sometimes we have lunch in the woods on a little table Vin made for us." She laughed and said something else. Something about slugs, but his attention was on the pair of angel wings tattooed on her wrist. The wings were blue, outlined in black, and totally covered what had been there before.

"–and ran screaming into the backyard as fast as his little legs would carry him. I told him—"

She'd tattooed over his name. Good. That was good. He'd tattooed over her name years ago. He should be relieved. He was relieved. Yeah.

She chuckled about something. A breathy little sound that made him antsy, and he backed away from her for no apparent reason. "I gotta go. I left the truck running."

"Oh." Autumn turned and looked up at Sam. He had a red mark on his cheek, probably from the fight she'd seen earlier, and his hair was slightly damp as if he'd recently showered. She'd been telling him about Conner's funny little slug phobia. Trying to be *nice* to him. Trying to prove to herself that she could be civil to the jerk. "I'll show you out." Typical of Sam not to care about stories concerning his own child.

The cell in his pants pocket rang, and he shoved his hand inside and turned it off without looking. "I'll be in town until Wednesday. After that, I have a grueling six-game grind," he said, as she followed him through the living room. "My next home game isn't until Friday, the twenty-third. I'll have Natalie look over my schedule and call you."

She wanted to tell him that Conner's life did not revolve around his schedule, but during the long hockey season, it did. As a result, so did hers. "That's fine."

He opened the door, then turned to look at her. She stood on the step above him as the cool night air leaked inside. She folded her arms around herself and waited for him to leave. He didn't. Instead, he tilted his head to the side and looked at her. His gaze moved across her face as if he was looking for something.

"Huh," he said, just above a whisper.

She untucked one hand and held it palm up. "What?"

He shook his head. "Nothing." He turned on the heels of his Prada loafers and shut the door behind him.

Autumn took a step down and flipped the dead bolt. Okay, so she didn't know for sure that his shoes were Prada, but she figured it for a fairly safe bet. Sam liked the best, in everything from his shoes to his women.

Which was why she didn't fit into his life any more than he fit into hers. Never had. And was probably the reason he didn't like her house. It wasn't new and flashy. The latest model.

She chuckled as she moved downstairs to her office at the back of the ground floor. According to what she'd read online, Veronica Del Toro was Sam's latest model. Tall. Big lips. Bigger boobs. Typical Sam.

And yes, she occasionally read articles about Sam and his latest escapades. She was Conner's mother. It was part of her job. A tiny part, but still part of her job was to know what sort of women Conner was exposed to although she never heard her son mention anyone but the "assistants."

Autumn walked to a big leather chair, spun it around, and sat. An event binder, several bride magazines, and a red laptop sat on her desk. When she googled Sam, she found articles that usually started off with: "When Sam LeClaire winds up for a slap shot, defenders duck, forwards flee, and goalies pray to God the puck hits them in a well-padded place." Or links that led to stuff like "Greatest Hockey Fights" or "Hockey Brawlers" or "Sam LeClaire vs. Domi or Brown or Parros or whoever." It was ridiculous, and she tried her best to teach Conner that violence was never the answer. That it was much better to be nice to people.

She flipped open the event binder she'd put together for the Willy Wonka party and reached for a pencil. She adjusted the catering cost and looked for some place to cut.

The last thing Autumn wanted was for Conner to grow up and be like his dad. It was up to her to make sure Conner treated people better than

Sam did. Treated *women* better. No superficial su-permodels. No revolving door in his bedroom. No getting married to girls he didn't know in Vegas. Best just to stay out of Vegas–maybe the whole state of Nevada—altogether.

Once she'd popped the top on her Coppertone sunscreen that day by the pool at Caesars, her life changed forever. Once she'd run her hands all over those washboard abs and hard chest mus-cles, she'd fallen head over heels in lust. He was a gorgeous man who'd thought she was an exotic destination. Looking back, she'd like to say she'd put up some resistance to the deep desire pulling her under, but she hadn't.

Instead of grabbing her beach bag and back-ing away from that smorgasbord of sin laid out in front of her, she had knelt beside his chaise and squirted sunscreen into her palms. "Are you here alone?" she asked, and dropped the tube on the ground. Beneath the brim of her hat, she glanced at his ring finger. It was bare, but that didn't mean he wasn't married or had a girlfriend.

He shook his head and turned his face to the sun. "I'm here with a couple of buddies."

That didn't mean anything either, but this was the second time she'd seen him alone. She rubbed the lotion in her hands, then touched his abdomen. The heat from his skin warmed her palms and tingled the pulse at the base of her wrists.

"Are you here with friends?" he asked, his voice all calm and cool as if her hands on him had no effect. Like she was the only one getting all tingly.

"No. Just me. I asked a friend, but she didn't want to come."

He looked at her, the intense Nevada sun cut through the leafy palms overhead and bleached the corner of his mouth and a patch of his left cheek. "Why?"

Autumn shrugged, and her thumbs brushed the trail of hair on his hard stomach as she slid her hands to his heavily defined chest. She wondered if he was in town for some muscleman competition. "She said she doesn't like Vegas." Which was the excuse that her friend had given, but Autumn suspected that the truth was she'd grown in a different direction than the friends she'd had before her mother's illness.

"But you came anyway," he said matter-of-factly. Still sounding unaffected, but the muscles beneath her fingers bunched and turned hard.

"Of course." She'd had a rough few years. "I made a to-do list."

"Really?" One corner of his mouth lifted. "What's on it?"

"Different things." Good Lord was she really rubbing lotion on a gorgeous stranger. "Some of them I've already done." Apparently she was.

"Like?"

And having a good time doing it, too. "Like I watched the Bellagio fountains and bought a flamingo from the Flamingo." She rubbed lotion onto his solid pecs. Beneath the brim of her hat, she stared at defined muscles and tan skin and swallowed the drool in the back of her throat. "And I went to Pure last night."

"I remember." Her thumbs brushed across his flat brown nipples, and he sucked in a breath. "What's left?"

She smiled. "I really want to see Cher's Farewell Tour here at Caesars, but I can't get tickets."

"Cher? You have seriously got to be kidding me."

She shook her head and slid her hands down to his belly just above his board shorts. "Don't you like Cher?"

"Hell no." He let out his breath as her palms slid along the waistband. "Only gay guys like Cher."

"That's not true." She tilted her head back and

glanced up into his face. Her hat dipped over her left eye. His blue gaze stared back at her, kind of hot and smoldering. Heat shimmered across her skin. The kind of heat that had nothing to do with the Nevada sun.

"I can pretty much guaran-goddamn-tee it."

She returned her attention to his corrugated belly and fought a sudden urge to fall face-first onto his warm abdomen and kiss him there. To let her hands and mouth go on an exotic vacation and suck him up like an *all-you-can-eat buffet*. "Not all guys at a Cher concert are gay."

"Maybe there are a few straight bastards that let themselves get dragged to a Cher concert." He cleared his throat. "But I can also guaran-goddamn-tee that they're only sitting there, listening to Half Breed and watching a shitty light show because they're desperate to get laid."

She sat back on her heels and laughed. "How do you feel about Celine Dion?"

"I've never been that desperate to get laid." He sat up and grabbed her wrists. As he rose from the chaise, he pulled her up with him. In the little shaded spot in a corner of Garden of the Gods, he ran his hands up her arms to her shoulders. "Am I on that list?"

Even if she'd thought to put: rub-lotion-on-random-hot-guy on her list, she could not have envisioned Sam. "No, but I could pencil you in." She touched his sides and pecs, anywhere her hands could reach. "Right after: meet an Elvis impersonator."

He touched her, too. Her arms and shoulders and the bare curves of her waist. His thumbs fanned her bare belly, back and forth and pressed into her navel. She tore her gaze from the etched muscles of his chest and looked up into his eyes, the same hot, smoldering blue as the Nevada sky above his head. The fine hairs on her arms tingled and sent a shiver down her spine. Her nipples and belly got all tight, and he slid his palms to the small of her back. Slowly, he pulled her against him until the tips of her breasts brushed his chest. He raised one hand and took her hat from her head. He tossed it on the chaise and stared into her eyes. "That hat has been driving me crazy. Teasing me with little glimpses of your pretty face." His gaze slid down her cheeks and stopped at her mouth. "There's something about you that makes me want to catch you in my hands and touch you all over."

She knew the feeling and rose onto the balls of her feet.

"It's hot out here," he whispered against her lips.

Yeah. Even in the shade, it was unbelievably hot and sweaty.

One of his palms slid down her arm to her hand. "Let's go."

"Where?" She liked Sam. She liked talking to him, and she really liked touching him. She wanted to spend more time with him, she wasn't so sure she wanted to spend that time in bed. Okay, she did want to, but she knew she shouldn't.

"Someplace cooler." He raised his face, and she dropped to her heels.

Cooler?

He turned and pulled her across the hot concrete, past towering lions and columns, to the edge of the pool. He dropped her hand and eased himself into the waist-deep water. She sat on the side of the pool and dangled her legs over the side.

"Are you afraid to come in?" Sunlight turned strands of his hair gold while the water lapped his navel.

"No. I'm just not a very strong swimmer." And she didn't want to get her hair wet.

He slid his hands up the outsides of her thighs and stepped between her knees. "I won't let you drown." His fingers toyed with the gold-cord bows tying her bikini bottoms together at her hips. "I like you too much to let you drown."

Which begged the question. "Why?" Why her out of all the women in Vegas?

"Why do I like you?" He raised his gaze from the ties at her waist, up her stomach and breasts to her face. "You're pretty, and I like the way you dance. I like your hair."

"It's red."

"Naturally?"

"Yes."

"I've never been with a natural redhead." He flashed her a smile and slid two fingers beneath the golden cord. She half expected him to make some lame comment about her having a fiery crotch. Like some of the guys she'd dated, but he didn't. Instead he said, "I want to know more about you, Autumn Haven. A lot more."

She sucked in a little breath that got all tangled up in her chest. "Like if I'm married, have kids, or committed a felony?" That wasn't what he wanted to know more about, and they both knew it. Did she want more, too? She knew she shouldn't.

"For starters."

"No to all three." She slid her hands up his arms to the hard balls of his shoulders. There were a lot of things in life she shouldn't do. A lot of things she'd missed out on over the past two years. "How about you?"

"Not married. No kids." He grasped her thighs and eased her off the side of the pool. Her legs automatically wrapped around his waist, and he said, just above a whisper, "No felony, but by the time this weekend is over, I just might do several things that could land me in jail."

The crotch of her bikini pressed into the front of his swim shorts. Pressed into the long hard length of his erection. Beneath the surface of the water, she squeezed her legs against him and against the hot, tight pressure building between her thighs. A lot of things like sex. "Like what?"

"I don't know. I've only lived in the U.S. for about two years now, and I don't know what's illegal here." He lifted one wet hand and pushed her hair behind her shoulder. His cool fingers brushed down her spine to her bottom. "Sexually speaking."

The cool water swirled about her legs and behind and the hot, liquid press of her body into his. The sensation of hot and cool heightened her sexual awareness, and she glanced around at the other people lounging about or standing in the large pool. She and Sam were far from alone. People could see them. This wasn't her. She didn't do this sort of thing. Not with a man she'd just met. Not in public. "Where are you from?"

"Originally Saskatchewan." He moved backward until the water lapped at the bottom swells of her breasts. "Canada."

Growing up, she'd lived close to the Canadian border in three different states. She summoned up her best Canadian accent and wrapped her arms around his neck, pressing her hard, aching nipples into his chest. "I think everything is legal in Vegas, eh?" she said next to his ear.

His chuckle was low and deep in his throat and ended in a groan as he grabbed her behind in both hands and lifted her slightly. "Everything?" Slowly, she slid back down his body. Down his hard chest and harder erection. He kissed the side of her neck, right where it met her shoulder. He sucked her skin into his hot, wet mouth, and any reservations she might have had about spending time in bed with Sam burned to a crisp beneath the hot Nevada sun.

Her head fell back and her breasts lifted. "Everything."

Chapter Seven

Any Man of Mine:
Good in Bed

G ood didn't begin to describe sex with Sam. It was more than good. More than satisfying. More than anything she'd experienced. It was hot and greedy. Wet and soul-shattering. He was methodical and spontaneous, raunchy and gentle. Autumn was twenty-five and not a virgin, but Sam knew things. He knew more than just where to touch. He knew *how*.

He took her to his bedroom inside a thirteen-hundred-square-foot suite. She had a quick impression of oversized leather furniture, black marble, stocked bars, and towering windows before he tossed her on a big king-sized bed covered in dark blue velvet. He'd said he shared the suite with buddies, but Autumn hadn't seen them. She never heard them either.

Being with Sam wasn't making love, but it was more than just sex. More than just a few hours of fun in the sack. Her whole body felt alive. Like she was speeding a hundred miles an hour, on fire, racing toward orgasm that arched her back and curled her toes. They had sex twice. The second time much slower and more methodical than the first time, which had began earlier in the pool and ended with them falling off the bed and finishing on the floor.

When she left the suite three hours after entering it, her elbow hurt and her knees were a little tender. She didn't remember hitting her elbow, but she did remember hitting her knees.

A smile twisted one corner of her lips as she stepped into the bathtub in her own room. Sam told her he'd call after he showered. She wanted to believe him. She wanted to believe that she was more than just an afternoon hookup; but if not, that was okay. He hadn't used her any more than she'd used him. She had no expectations and no regrets.

She reached for a white washcloth and unwrapped a small bar of soap. A drop of water fell from the spigot into the bath, and the scent of the finely milled soap filled the room as she washed her face and the spot where Sam had kissed her throat. She ran the soapy cloth over her breasts and belly and slid down in the water until the back of her head rested against the edge of the tub. She brought her feet close to her behind under the water and closed her eyes. She'd never hooked up with a random guy before. One she didn't really know. The one-nighters she'd had in the past had been with men she'd known. At least somewhat. She wasn't all that sure those counted as one-nighters. Most of those times, though, she'd done the clothes scramble, afterwards followed by the walk of shame.

This time, she didn't feel ashamed. Although she probably should. She'd been raised on shame. Been raised to believe that the price of sin was not a good time but a good guilty conscience. After Autumn's father had left, her mother embraced religion with both arms. Holding it tight against her chest like a shield. Autumn had been seven, Vince ten, when everything they knew changed. They went from a two-parent home to living with a mother incapable of adapting to the changes in her life. For the first few years, her mother sat around waiting for her husband to come back. When he remarried and began a new family, and it finally became apparent that he wasn't going to return, Joyce Haven turned to God. She replaced her husband with Him.

As a general rule, Autumn didn't have a problem with religion or people who lived their faith. If religion made a person better, more grounded, then she was all for it. But she did have a problem with people who couldn't make a decision without consulting God about everything from buying a car to radiation treatments. She believed God gave her a brain and the wisdom to make decisions on her own. The bad decisions she made were just part of life's learning curve.

For almost two years, she'd put her life on hold to take care of her mother. She'd fought hard, most times harder than Joyce, but in the end, nothing had worked. She didn't resent taking care of her mother. She loved her mom and missed her every day. There was a permanent hole in her heart and life and family. If given the choice, she'd do it again. She wouldn't even have to think twice about it.

But now. Now her life felt empty. Vince was gone, she was alone, and she had to figure out what she was going to do with the rest of her life. She could go back to school and get her business degree. Before her mother's illness, she'd been enrolled part-time at the University of Idaho and working two jobs. She'd worked days for a florist and nights as a server for a local caterer. She'd enjoyed both jobs and wouldn't mind getting those jobs back when she returned to school.

Autumn felt her fingers get pruney, and she unplugged the tub. She grabbed a towel and looked at her watch, sitting next to the sink. It was half past five. An hour and ten minutes since she'd left Sam's suite. The phone hadn't rung.

It didn't ring as she rubbed coconut-scented lotion into her skin or when she pulled on a fluffy hotel robe. Nor when she brushed her teeth and dried her hair. She assumed she wouldn't see Sam again. That was okay. She wouldn't have minded seeing him again, but she had her to-do list, and riding the roller coaster at New York New York at night was next on it.

As she moved from the bathroom, she jumped as someone pounded on the door. She placed a hand over her thudding heart and looked through the peephole at Sam, standing there in jeans and a black polo shirt. She bit the inside of her cheek to keep a smile from spreading across her lips. "You lost?" she asked as she opened the door.

He tilted his head to one side. "You're not dressed?"

"I just got out of the bathtub." She let him in and leaned her back against the door.

An unrepentant grin flashed across his lips. "I was hoping to catch you naked." He lowered his mouth to hers and slid his hand inside her robe. He cupped her breast, and they stayed inside her room until the next morning. They ordered room service and a movie and stayed in bed. Between bites of mint-crusted lamb, she learned that Sam lived in Seattle and played hockey for the Chinooks. Autumn didn't know a lot about hockey, but his being a professional athlete made perfect sense given his muscles and incredible stamina. It also somehow made the time she spent with him more final. Not that she thought their friendship, or whatever it was, would last beyond tomorrow, let alone Vegas. But just knowing who he was, what he was, put an end to any thought of a lasting relationship before one started. She'd dated a football player in college, but he'd dumped her for a cheerleader. Jocks always ended up dating cheerleaders or sorority girls or starlets.

While in Vegas, she just wanted to enjoy her time with Sam for as long as it lasted. She liked him. He was easy to be with, and he was amazing in bed. Or in the tub, on the floor, or up against a wall. He did things with his mouth that made her scream, and someday, when she was old and barely able to scoot her walker down the hall of some nursing home, she would remember her wild week in Vegas with a gorgeous hockey player. She'd smile, and the other old ladies pushing their walkers would just think she was senile. They'd never know about Sam. No one would know about Sam. Ever. Sam would always be her naughty little secret.

That afternoon, they left Caesars and ate lobster bisque, mushroom-covered tenderloin, and asparagus tips at Delmonico in the Venetian. They washed it all down with a bottle of red wine. He asked about her life, and she told him about her dad leaving when she'd been young and about taking care of her mother.

"I have one brother, but he's in Afghanistan somewhere doing whatever it is that he does." She took a bite of tender asparagus and looked across the table at Sam. She told herself that the little pang she felt in her stomach was from hunger and not from Sam's blue eyes looking back at her. "How about you? Any brothers or sisters?"

He took a big drink of his wine and glanced across the crowded restaurant. "I had a sister."

When he didn't offer any more information, she lifted a palm and prompted, "And . . . ?"

"And she died."

"When?"

"A few years ago."

She put her hand over his. "I'm sorry."

He looked back at her, anger setting his square jaw and leaking out of him like a dark shadow spilling across the table. "What's on your to-do list?" Subject closed.

She kept her hand on his, and her thumb brushed across his knuckles. Mixed within all that anger was dark pain. She could see it. Feel it, sharp and tangible. The kind of pain she knew all too well. The kind that could steal your breath if you let it. "Tonight, I want to ride the roller coaster at New York New York. I think it'll be cool to look down on the Strip all lit up."

He took another drink of his wine, and she felt

the tension ease, sucked back inside wherever he kept it. "I have to meet the guys at the Voodoo Lounge tonight. Why don't you come with me instead of riding a roller coaster."

She slid her hand toward her and tucked it into her lap. There was only one part of her body that she wanted to ache for Sam, and it wasn't her heart. Anything beyond lust was too risky. She shook her head. "Why don't I meet you there?"

His brows drew together, and the corners of his mouth lifted in a bemused smile. "Are you playing hard to get?"

She needed some distance. Needed a little space to breathe and clear her head before she did the unthinkable and started to have feelings for him. "Maybe."

"Honey, it's a little late. Don't you think?"

Maybe, but she had to try. If not, she was afraid she might start to think of him as more than just a wild Vegas hookup. And that couldn't happen. That was impossible.

He reached into his wallet and pulled out a VIP pass. "This will get you in the door," he said as he handed it across the table toward her. "We have a table on the balcony. Try not to be too late."

How late was too late? Autumn was an on-time girl and had never understood the concept of fashionably late. But that night she arrived at the Voodoo Lounge after eleven. It just about killed her to wait that long. She spent her time shopping for a strapless dress and a black thong. She took a long bath and put her hair up in big curlers. She put on more makeup than usual, and beneath the black tube dress, she only wore her tiny panties. She caught one last glimpse herself before leaving the room. She looked like herself, only different. She looked . . . sexy. Which was a new look for her. Especially after the last few years.

It was Sam. Sam made her feel good about herself. It was the way he looked at her. The touch of his hands. The way he whispered her name in her ear. He made her feel desired and sexy.

The Voodoo Lounge was on the fiftieth and fifty-first floors of the Rio, and Autumn walked to the front of the line and flashed her VIP pass. She'd never had a VIP pass to anything and was immediately taken up in a glass elevator and shown down a black-lighted foyer. Like most bars, the Voodoo was dark and smelled like booze and too much perfume. It had neon pink and blue lights, and a hip-hop band played in one corner of the small space. She rose onto the toes of her black pumps and looked through the crowd. She didn't spot Sam right away, so she made her way through the bar to the large outdoor balcony. A breeze caught her hair, and she pushed it behind her ears. In one corner, a DJ spun records from the sixties and seventies, and on the perimeter of the balcony, were groups of cozy tables and chairs and Sam. He stood within a cluster of people, mostly women, laughing and chatting and having a good time. He wore a blue dress shirt with the sleeves rolled up. Compared to the women, Autumn looked conservative. A platinum blond, wearing a tiger-print haltered minidress, put her hand on his arm, and he didn't seem to mind. Autumn turned toward the bar and looked over the menu. A gentleman parked at the bar suggested a Witch Doctor, but she didn't want anything big and bulky that she would have hold with two hands. She ordered a mojito and watched as the bartender threw the glass into the air and caught it behind his back. She cast a glance over her shoulder at Sam, who was still occupied. This time, one of the women touched his chest. She turned back and dug a twenty out of the little black purse hanging from a silver chain on her shoulder. The guy next to her tried to buy her drink, but she declined. He seemed okay, and if it weren't for Sam, she might have struck up a conversation with him. He had short dark hair and a thick neck and kind of reminded her of Vince.

She pointed to the smoke rising from the guy's big fishbowl of a drink. "What's in your Witch Doctor?"

"Rum, coconut rum, banana rum, more rum. Wanna sip?" He turned the straw toward her.

She shook her head and laughed. "No thanks. Four shots of rum is about three too many for me." She handed the bartender a twenty and felt Sam behind her a fraction of a second before he slid his hand around her waist and pulled her hair to one side.

"Who's the asshole?" he asked next to her ear.

She supposed she could get all jealous and indignant because he let women touch him, but she didn't have any right, and jealousy was such an ugly emotion. "Hi, Sam."

"What are you doing?"

"Getting a drink."

"I see that." His voice was a dark, seductive

rumble across her skin. "What took you so long to get here?"

She smiled at the bartender, who put her change and mojito on the bar. "I was buying underwear."

"Mmm. What kind?"

She shoved her change into her little purse, then turned her face into Sam's. "Black thong. " He smelled a little boozy. Like he'd been at it a while. One thing she did notice about Sam, besides his six-pack and massive good looks, was that he drank a lot. At least to her, and she'd spent three years at the University of Idaho. A notorious party school, but this was Vegas. Most people drank a lot in Vegas.

"Sexy."

For the first time in a very long time, she felt sexy. "I'll show you later." Another thing she noticed about Sam, besides his smooth voice and smoother hands, was that he never really seemed drunk. He didn't slur or get sloppy. He was never obnoxious, and all that booze did nothing to impede him in the bedroom. He never forgot a condom or the job at hand.

He kissed her neck, then took her hand, and they weaved their way past the dance floor to a table near the edge. They passed a big staircase leading to the upper deck, where a big American flag waved in the breeze.

He introduced her to a guy named Daniel and another named Vlad. One was Swedish, the other Russian. They were both huge and both had women hanging off their arms. Over "Sweet Home Alabama" playing in the background, the two introduced the women in the party. Vlad's accent was so thick, Autumn thought she caught the names Jazzzzzz and Teeeeeena, but she wouldn't bet on it.

Daniel's quizzical gaze seemed to pick her apart and put her back together. "You're the reason Sam can't make it to Scores."

"Or Cheeetaz," Vlad added.

The boys obviously loved the strip clubs, and Autumn wondered if the women with them grabbed poles for a living. "The first night we met, Sam thought I was a dancer." She took a drink, then set the glass on the table. "I think he was disappointed."

"I wasn't disappointed." He slid his arm around her and pulled her against his side.

Daniel's brows lowered. "You okay, Sam?"

"Yeah." He turned his attention to the glittering city below. The brilliant, flashing skyline of the

Strip and the surrounding area lighting up the desert like stars. "You wanna get out of here?"

She looked up into his profile, at the blue neon light and night shadows against his cheek and jaw. "Is something wrong?"

His grip on her waist tightened. "It's the thirteenth."

"Are you superstitious?"

The last strains of "Sweet Home Alabama" trailed off into the breeze, only to be drowned out by the city below. "Yeah." He looked down at her. "Is 'have sex in a limo' on your list?"

She felt his grasp ease to a soft caress. "No."

"Wanna add it?"

He had to be joking. "Got a limo?"

"Yep." He flashed her a grin as he reached inside his pant's pocket and pulled out his cell phone. "Good night, everyone," he said, as his hand moved to the small of her back, and they headed toward the bar. In the elevator on the way down, his palm slid to her behind and stayed there until they stepped outside the Rio.

A stretch Hummer waited by the curb, and she guessed he wasn't joking. He helped Autumn into the enormous vehicle and paused a moment to speak with the driver before crawling in after her.

"Does he know what you have planned?" she asked, as the door shut and closed them in the dark interior. Running lights lit up the floor like a 747, and a small bulb shone on the control panel. Even if he wasn't joking about sex in a limo, could she really go through with it?

"Probably." Sam fiddled with buttons, and the privacy window slid up.

"I've never had sex with someone watching." And she wasn't so sure she could do it now.

"He can't see."

"Are you sure?"

"Reasonably." He found a radio station and turned up the volume of Green Day's "Boulevard of Broken Dreams."

Through the dark interior, his mouth found hers, and there was a sort of desperation in his kiss that she'd never felt before. A sort of need and greed. Like he wanted to eat her up. Consume her, right there in the back of a stretch Hummer.

She was leaving in a few short days, and so was he. She'd never see him again, and having sex while speeding through Vegas was a lot better than thinking about going home, alone. The car sped away from the curb, and Billy Joe's voice filled the limo. As he sang of loneliness and shallow hearts, Autumn straddled Sam's lap and placed her hands on the sides of his face. She kissed him long and hard as his hands crept up her thighs because this was Vegas, and apparently she didn't have a problem with sex in a limo. Not even with only a reasonable assurance that the driver couldn't see. Nothing was real there. Not the façades, nor the fake canals and volcanos. Not the promise of easy money or the feelings threatening to overtake her good intentions. Certainly not the affair that had nothing to do with love.

Sam's big hands slipped over her hips and up her sides. He tugged at the top of her dress until it was around her waist, and her bare breasts rested in his palms. His thumbs brushed across her hard nipples, and he said things.

"I need you," he groaned. "I need you to fill me up." He said other things. Dirty things. Things about what he wanted to do to her and how. Things about what he wanted her to do to him. Things that only a man like Sam could get away with saying.

He reached between her thighs and pushed her thong aside. He touched her and did those things he said he was going to do. Later, in her hotel room, she did things to him that made him groan and beg her not to stop. Things that brought a smile to his lips.

It was good to see him smile.

The next morning, she woke alone. She didn't know whether to be sad or glad. She turned over and went back to sleep. At noon, Sam called her room to tell her to meet him in the lobby at six and to wear something comfortable but not flip-flops. She wondered what he had planned, and when the time came, she wore a jeans skirt, white tank top, and leather sandals. He wore jeans and Clint Eastwood T-shirt, and they ate Chinese and drank Tsingtao.

"What's left on your to-do list?" Sam asked, and took a long pull from the green bottle.

"A lot. I haven't done half the things on it."

"Yeah." He smiled and lowered the beer. "Sorry about that."

"You don't look sorry."

He shrugged. "You should thank me. Your list sucks."

She gasped. "No, it doesn't."

"I've never seen a suckier list. It's like you got

out Frommer's and circled things you wanted to see."

She folded her arms across her chest. "Fodor's online."

"Same thing. I wasn't on your list. Sex in a limo wasn't on your list. Hell, you're in Vegas, and you don't have one damn strip club on your list. Not even a male review. If I didn't know better, I'd think you were a nun."

Her nose wrinkled. "I really have no desire to see men dancing around with their wieners out."

He blinked. "I can't believe you just said 'wiener.'"

She ignored him and glanced about the Chinese restaurant to make sure no one was listening in on the conversation. "I don't want some guy's balls flying around my head, and if one of them actually put his . . . penis . . . on my shoulder, I'd freak out."

He tilted his head back and laughed. Long and loud and attracting attention. She didn't care. He had a great laugh, and she wished he'd laugh more.

"I cannot believe you're the same girl who jumped on me in the limo last night."

She couldn't either.

"And you didn't seem to mind my balls flying around your head last night."

She bit the corner of her lip to keep from smiling.

He lifted one hip and pulled out two tickets from his back pocket. He handed them to her.

Her mouth dropped open. "Cher?" She looked up into his face. "How did you get tickets?"

"I got my ways."

"Are you going to Cher with me?"

"That's why there are two tickets."

He hated Cher. "But you're not gay or desperate to get laid."

"That's true."

"You don't like Cher."

He grinned. "I like you."

Oh no. She was in trouble. Big bad horrible trouble with blond hair and smiling blue eyes. Her throat got tight, and the air left her lungs. Her heart felt like it was expanding in her chest, and if it didn't stop, it would burst. Right there in Beijing Noodle No. 9. Her eyes watered. This was horrible. From that very first night, she'd known he was the kind of trouble she should avoid. She just hadn't realized he would overwhelm her and make her fall for him.

"Don't cry. It's just Cher, and they are nose-bleed seats. No big deal."

It was a big deal. Huge. She swallowed hard, past the big lump in her chest. She didn't care about Cher. She'd only wanted to go because she was in Vegas, and it was a farewell tour. She wiped the tears beneath her eyes. "I don't know what to say." And she didn't. Despite knowing better, she was developing dangerous feelings for him. It was stupid and rash and real. It felt real, but she didn't know if he felt the same way.

During the concert, she wrapped her arm around his and watched the bright stage show and Cher's parade of costumes. She liked it more than she thought she would, but when Sam started to snore, she woke him, and they left early. They moved to the casino and played blackjack and craps and roulette. Mostly he played and she watched. They drank free booze until about 1:00 A.M. Autumn felt light and hazy, and as a joke, she bought Sam a Cher T-shirt. They'd both laughed like it was the height of hi-larity when he put it on. And when Sam decided that they needed to find an Elvis impersonator, she thought it sounded like a great plan. "Elvis impersonator" was on her list, but unfortunately, the only one still awake was at the Viva Las Vegas Wedding Chapel.

Even years later, she was never quite sure how they'd arrived at the chapel or whose idea it had been to go inside and watch Elvis marry people, but what was clear, what had always remained clear, was standing outside the chapel, looking up at the marquee and the bright flashing names of the most recently wed. In big orange letters: Just Married, Donna and Doug.

"We should get married."

She looked at him, the orange light bathing his face and glowing in his blond hair. "Are you kidding?"

He shook his head. "No. It just feels right."

Her heart pounded boom boom boom in her chest, and her stomach got all light and queasy. "Sam . . ." She swallowed hard. "I don't think—"

"Don't think." He pulled her against him, and his mouth swooped down to take hers in a full, wet kiss that sucked out her breath and over-whelmed what little wits she had left. She loved him. Somehow, she'd fallen in love with Sam, and she wanted to be with him. Maybe it was fate. Meant to be. Love at first sight. Right?

He pulled back. His lips wet from the kiss, he looked at her from beneath lowered lids. "Say yes."

"Yes."

He smiled, and within an hour, they were Mr. and Mrs. Samuel LeClaire. He'd paid for the Hound Dog Special, which in hindsight was apropos given Sam's hound-dog ways. But hindsight was always twenty-twenty, and that night the Hound Dog Special meant goodies that included four candid wedding photos, roses, and a plush Hound Dog keepsake. Once outside, they'd watched their names flash in bright neon, and instead of rings, they got their names tattooed on the other's body. By the time they made it back to the hotel room, the sun was just rising over the desert. They ordered room service and made love without a condom. At least she thought it was love. She'd felt it in every part of her body, including her heart.

She woke just after noon, alone except for her stuffed Hound Dog. Sam was gone, but she wasn't worried. He'd come back. He always did, and they were married now. Their future was together. He'd never come right out and said he loved her, but he had to. He'd pursued her since that first night at Pure, and last night they'd promised to "love each other tender." She smiled and stretched. The wedding had been impulsive and rash, to be sure, but she didn't regret it.

By three, she got a little concerned, and by four she was worried that something had happened to him. She didn't have his cell number and called the front desk. She asked to be connected to his room and was informed that he and the rest of his party had checked out.

Checked out? She slid her feet into a pair of flip-flops, grabbed her room key, and headed to his suite. Except for the maids changing beds and vacuuming, the place was empty. No suitcases. No Sam. He must have checked out to move into her room. So where was he?

She'd spent the rest of the day and night waiting for him to come pounding on her door. Every time someone passed her room, her heart stopped, but it was never Sam. She couldn't believe he'd left her without a word. She was confused. Where was he? As she stared at the photos of them, standing before the Elvis impersonator, she told herself that he'd come back. He would. He had to because they were married.

She told herself he'd be back as she waited and worried and watched the news for any report of an accident. She even stayed an extra day, waiting, but he never even called. By the next afternoon it became clear that he wasn't coming back, and she boarded a small plane to Helena.

She arrived home a few hours later, numb and hurt and confused. Had anything that had happened been real? It had sure felt real, and her heart ached like it had been real.

The wedding certificate was real. Sam had turned her head, broken her heart, and knocked the wind out of her, and what was she to do? He'd married her and left her in a hotel room. She didn't know if she should fly to Seattle and talk to him. He probably wouldn't be that hard to find. She didn't know what to do and felt like she was living in a fog. When she did finally hear from him at the end of the next week, it was through his lawyer, demanding a divorce. He'd left her stunned and her heart crushed. Too bad that hadn't been enough for him.

A month later, when she'd informed his attorney of her pregnancy, she'd been so scared and alone, and she'd hoped—hoped even though she knew better—that he'd tell her it was okay. That he'd be there for her and the child. That he'd help her out so that she wasn't totally alone. Instead, he'd demanded a paternity test.

The next time she laid eyes on him again was the day she'd put Conner in his arms. He'd had tape across his nose and one of his eyes was black-and-blue. Her heart had squeezed, and her throat had hurt from holding back emotion. He'd looked at her as if he really didn't remember her, and any love she'd felt for him turned into a deep, burning hatred. Right there in his lawyer's office, and she'd wished she'd been the one to punch him. If he hadn't been holding her son, she might have.

Autumn shut the notebook on her desk and rose from her office chair. Now she felt nothing. Peace settled across her heart as she walked from her office and moved upstairs. Life was good. Her son was in the bedroom asleep across the hall from hers. Her business was great, and she didn't hate Sam. She was sure that he would always do things to make her mad. He was selfish and couldn't help himself, but she didn't hate him. Her heart didn't ache; nor did her head feel like it was going to explode when he walked into a room. When she'd opened the door that evening and seen him with Conner in his arms, she'd just felt relieved that her son was home. Safe.

She was free from the hot and cold emotions. Free from the push and pull of love and hate. Free to feel nothing for Sam.

Nothing at all.

Chapter Eight

Any Man of Mine:
Isn't Ninety Percent Testosterone

S am stood in the tunnel of the Joe Louis Arena and waited to hit the ice. He hated playing in Detroit. Hated the stinking octopus.

He stood behind Logan Dumont and in front of Blake Conte. Captain Walker Brooks hit the ice first amidst a wall of booing Red Wing fans. Sam had always found jeering crowds amusing. He fed off all that passion, and no one was more passionate about a sport than hockey fans. When it was his turn to step onto the ice, he stuck his glove under one arm and skated across the ice, waving like he was a conquering hero. He looked up at the filled seats and laughed. He might hate playing at the Joe Louis, but he loved playing hockey. He'd been on the road for over a week and was exhausted and jet lagged, but the second the puck dropped, that all went away. Adrenaline pounded through his veins and rushed across his skin. He dominated behind the blue line, using his body to agitate and intimidate. He closed firing lanes and spent four minutes in the sin bin for cross-checking and hooking. The latter was complete bullshit. It wasn't his fault that Zetterberg got tangled up in Sam's stick. He should go back to Sweden and learn how to skate like a big boy.

Pansy ass.

The coaches sometime bitched about stupid penalties, but they all knew that was just the way Sam worked. It was the cost of doing business, and when the Chinooks won, like they did that night against the Red Wings, no one bitched. He drew his paycheck—and these days it was a big one, with lots of zeros—for hitting hard, shutting down goal-scoring opportunities, and making plays for the wingmen. He had one of the hardest slap shots in the league and one of the hardest right hooks. He liked to think he used both judiciously. Of course, that wasn't always true. Most of the time he started shit to intimidate and make his presence known. To make an opponent hesitate. To make a mistake, but sometimes he just started shit for the sake of starting shit. Sometimes he went toe-to-toe because he liked it.

It wasn't as if he fought as much as Andre; but, as Mark Bressler repeatedly pointed out, Andre was the team enforcer, and fighting was his main job.

After the Detroit game, Sam and the rest of the Chinooks boarded the team jet and flew home. He spent a week in Seattle before heading out for Phoenix, Nashville, and Pittsburgh. While he'd been in town, he split his time between work, Conner, and a couple of female friends. But when he boarded the jet and headed toward Phoenix, it wasn't the friends he thought about. By the time he touched down in Pittsburgh a week later, it wasn't female companionship he missed. He missed his son even though he'd talked to him several times on the phone. In the past, he'd always called Conner when he was on the road. Always missed him and made the effort, but this time he felt a bigger tug. Spending more time with him made him miss Conner's silly knock-

knock jokes and his drawings. He missed his questions about anything and everything, and he missed his little hugs.

That night, the game against the Penguins started out badly and went straight to hell. Everything just felt off, starting with the drop of the first hinky puck. Pittsburgh dominated down the middle, and number eighty-seven, Sidney Crosby, was on fire. The kid from Nova Scotia scored a goal and an assist off bouncing pucks from Sam's stick. He'd been so pissed off, he'd retaliated and sat out a double minor in the penalty box. During his stint in the sin bin, the Penguins scored on a five on four and won four to three.

That night, Sam boarded the jet, turned his iPod to shuffle, and stuck in his earphones. He just wanted to forget about that night's game. He didn't want to think about bouncing pucks and bad penalties. He really didn't want to think about anything. His life was easier that way.

But he'd been thinking about his sister, Ella, the past week or so. More than usual. Maybe because he was making an effort to spend more time with Conner. Taking on more of the responsibility for his son. The weight of that responsibility scared the hell out of him. It wasn't a new weight. Just one he hadn't carried in a long time.

After the death of his father, he'd become the man of the family. Responsible for his mother and sister, Ella. Not financially, not back then, but responsible. He'd taken his job seriously, or at least as seriously as a kid could. His mother had been a strong, competent woman. Still was, but Ella . . . Ella had been lost without her dad. Lost and empty, and Sam had filled the void for her. He'd looked out for her and made sure nothing bad ever happened. When he could, he'd take her to fun places. During the summer, her shiny blond ponytail was never out of his peripheral vision. And during the school year, he'd made sure she did her homework and hung out with the right kinds of kids.

At nineteen, he'd been picked up in the first round of drafts and moved nearly five hundred miles away to Edmonton. He'd visited home as much as he could, and he talked to her almost every day. When she'd turned sixteen, he'd bought her a car, and when she graduated from high school, he took her to Cancún to celebrate. That same summer, he was traded to the Maple

171

Leafs, and Ella moved with him to Toronto. She attended York University and graduated with a bachelor's degree in education. He'd been so proud of her. She was beautiful and smart and funny, and her future was wide open.

Then she met Ivan, and she changed. Not long after the two began dating, she became withdrawn and sullen and secretive. The first time he saw a bruise on her face, he caught up with Ivan at his construction job. He knocked the little shit on his ass, planted his size-fourteen shoe on the guy's chest, and told him he'd kill him if he ever saw another bruise on Ella. As a result of his interference, he saw less and less of his sister. But after a year and a half of the roller-coaster ride that was Ella and Ivan's relationship, she finally left him. Sam moved her back home to Regina, and she lived in a small apartment not far from their mother. Sam was relieved and ecstatic. Ella got reacquainted with old friends and gradually came back to herself. The last time he'd seen her, the old, happy, full-of-life Ella shone from her big blue eyes.

He'd been at home in Toronto when he got the call that changed his life forever. It was June 13, and he'd just finished a round of golf with some of the guys and was sitting at his dining-room table, eating a peameal sandwich and chips that he'd picked up on the way home. He'd been half-way through his lunch when his mother had called with the news that Ella had been killed. That Ivan had traveled across Canada to find her, and when she wouldn't get back together with him, he'd shot her, then himself. Beautiful, smart Ella was dead with a bullet in her head. And one of the tragedies of it all, but certainly not the biggest, was that Ivan was dead, too, because Sam would have dearly loved to kill him.

His sister was dead, and he hadn't been able to help her. He hadn't been there when she'd needed him most. He'd been the man of the family, but he'd failed to keep his sister safe.

The first few years after Ella's death were a nightmare. A blur of excessive partying and self-destruction. During that low point, the only time his life came into focus, the only time it made any sort of sense, was on the ice. Fighting it out. Working his guilt out on whoever dared to skate across his personal piece of real estate. Off the ice, he'd backed away from anything that re-sembled taking on the responsibility for anyone but himself. He could only take care of Sam, and sometimes, he royally fucked that up.

He'd hooked up with Autumn on the anniversary of Ella's death. A real low point. A point where he'd felt the huge hole his sister had left behind. Nothing had filled that hole, but for those few days in Vegas, he'd given it one hell of a try. He'd binged on booze and sex. He didn't recall a whole lot about that time, but he did know that for a few short days, he hadn't felt so goddamn empty. He'd filled up with a redheaded girl with dark green eyes. There'd been something about her, something that had made him pursue her like she could save him from himself. Then he'd woken up married, hungover, and sober for the first time since arriving in Nevada.

These days, he no longer felt the need to fill the void with booze and random women. The void was still there. Nothing could ever replace a sister. She would always be the missing part of his family, but he was no longer so self-destructive. The women in his life weren't random. No more rink bunnies and hockey groupies, but neither were they long-term. He always kept that part of his life separate from his life with his son. At least he thought he had until Conner mentioned that photograph of him pouring beer on bikini models. Conner was old enough to be affected by

Sam's life. Old enough to know his dad had time for other people but not for him.

He'd always felt Conner was safer with Autumn. That she would do a lot better job of taking care of him than Sam would. That was probably still true, but Conner needed him, too. Not some guy he saw in sports clips and on occasional weekends. His son needed him to step up.

The jet engines slowed as it prepared to descend into Seattle. It was about 3:00 A.M. Saturday morning, and Sam looked out at the lights below. He planned to sleep for about the next ten hours, then some of the guys were going to meet downtown to judge a Halloween contest. When he'd talked to Conner earlier, he'd learned that his son had decided to dress up as a hockey player. A Chinook hockey player like his dad. He wouldn't mind seeing Conner wearing a sweater with Sam's number on it, but Halloween wasn't his holiday, and Autumn was a real stickler about holiday visitation. Normally, he might just risk showing up and incurring the wrath of Autumn, but after the night he'd dropped Conner off home after the game, they'd been getting along. Although *getting along* might be a bit of an overstatement. The few times he'd dropped

Conner off instead of relying on Nat to do it for him, they were civil, and he hadn't felt the urge to cover his nuts. He figured that as long as he didn't bring Conner home late without calling, or try and muscle her out of her holiday, he was probably safe from her foot in his crotch.

He'd see Conner the day after Halloween. Maybe take him to that arcade he liked so much. Spending more time with his son was important to him, but getting more serious about his son's life didn't mean he had to give up other things on his free nights. Things like hanging out in a bar filled with slutty Snow Whites and naughty nurses.

"Vince?"

"Yeah?"

Through the dark Halloween night, Autumn watched Conner run between the flickering lights of jack-o'-lanterns and knock on the door of a neighbor a few blocks from their house. A candy bag in one hand, a Chinooks' jersey over his coat. "Do you think I'm man-repellent?"

"What?" Vince looked down at her. "What's that?"

176

"A few weeks ago, Shiloh said I act like I've sprayed myself with man repellant?"

Conner ran toward them, the black eye she'd drawn on him a little smeared, but his red scar still stuck to his cheek. "I got some Nerds."

Goody. Straight sugar. They moved to the next house, and Vince said, "Don't pay attention to Shiloh. She's one of those girls who isn't really serious about anything. She's not like you."

"What does that mean?" Conner ran up toward another door decorated with a spider.

"It means you're a mother and a business-woman. You have a lot going on and a lot going for you."

"Yes, but I'd like to think men find me attractive. That I'm more than a mother and a business-woman."

He hooked his arm round her neck. "You're a beautiful woman, and if you wanted a man in your life, you'd have one."

She and Vince had always been close, even when he'd been away, but he was also her brother and would lie to spare her feelings. "You really think so?"

"Yeah, but don't hang out in bars to meet men.

That didn't work out so well the last time you tried it."

Autumn laughed. "True." They rounded a corner and, from half a block away, she saw a red trunk parked next to Vince's Harley in her driveway

"Dad came." Conner switched his candy bag from one hand to the other.

"Yeah." Vince dropped his arm to his side.

It wasn't Sam's day. Why was he there? "Don't run," she called out, as Conner took off down the sidewalk. He ran beneath a pool of light from the streetlamp, then cut across the yard filled with happy scarecrows and smiling jack-o'-lanterns.

Beside her, Vince muttered something she couldn't quite hear. Which was probably for the best, then he asked, "What does that idiot want?"

"I don't know. I thought he was out of town." Within the shadows of her house, Sam rose from the bottom step of her porch, and Conner disappeared into his dark wool coat. So typical of him just to assume he could show up without calling.

"Has he suddenly decided to be father of the year?"

"Something like that, but it won't last." She shook her head, and her ponytail brushed the shoulders of her navy peacoat. The sound of Vince's bootheels was heavy and ominous as the two of them closed the distance to Sam. "Promise me you won't start anything."

A stitch on his leather bomber's jacket popped as if he was flexing his muscles like the Incredible Hulk. Vince was a kind, loving brother and a good uncle. He was protective, but he had a few anger issues. He could also hold a grudge longer than anyone she knew. Even her. While Autumn had moved on from her bitter feelings for Sam, Vince had not and probably never would. Even though their mother had been very religious, "Forgive and forget" was a foreign concept for the Haven kids. Especially for Vince, and while Autumn had moved on, she couldn't say she'd forgiven Sam. Not that Sam had ever asked for her forgiveness. Never said he was sorry, and she'd never forget. That was impossible. Too much to ask. It was more like she'd just let go of it all and didn't care.

As she and Vince walked up the driveway, the tension between Sam and her brother pinched the back of her bare neck, and her ponytail felt too tight. "Behave," she said under her breath. She stopped in front of Sam and looked up into his face, light from the house spilled across his forehead, the slight crook in his nose and across half his lips. "I didn't know you were in town."

"I am."

Obviously. "I didn't know you were coming over."

"I didn't either until about half an hour ago." His chin jerked up a little. "Vince."

"Sam."

"I need to talk to you a minute," Sam said as he stared down Vince.

"Me?"

"No. Your brother."

She was afraid of that. She grabbed Vince's arm. "Don't hit him."

Vince pried her fingers from his jacket. "I won't hit him first."

Sam chuckled. "You wouldn't get the chance to hit me second, frogman." He walked past them to the end of the driveway and stopped beneath the deep inky shadow of an old oak.

Vince laughed, too, but it wasn't funny. Vince had been trained to kill, but Autumn had seen Sam knock people out. People bigger than Vince. "Promise?"

He headed across the driveway, his "No," trailed after him.

"What's a frogman?"

She glanced down at Conner's shiny blond head. She should probably take him into the house, but she didn't think either man would throw a punch in front of Conner. While they hated each other, they loved Conner more. At least she hoped so. "I think it's a Navy SEAL."

"Oh. Is Dad going to hit Uncle Vince?"

"Of course not." At least she hoped not. "They were just joking around."

"What are they talking about?"

She strained to hear what they were saying, even leaning forward a little, but only a low murmuring timbre reached her ears. "Man stuff."

"What's 'man stuff'?"

Like she knew? "Cars."

"Uncle Vince doesn't have a car. He has a motorcycle and a truck. But his truck isn't as big as Dad's."

From the little she could see, it looked like Sam's hands were on his hips, and Vince still had his arms crossed.

Again she heard Sam chuckle, then he walked

from the inky darkness and across the drive-way toward her. "You got a Reese's in that candy bag?" he asked Conner.

"Maybe ten or twenty!"

"Good. You can give your old dad one."

"I got lots of candy. Come in and see."

Sam looked over at Autumn. "Do you mind?"

Like it mattered. She shook her head and watched Vince move from the shadow toward her. "Give your uncle a hug good-bye," she told Conner.

"Okay." Already hopped up on Halloween candy, Conner ran to Vince and wrapped his arms around his waist. "Bye, Uncle Vince."

"See ya, Nugget. Give me knuckles."

Conner held up his clinched fist, then quickly pulled it back. "Too slow, Joe." He ran back to Sam, took his hand, and pulled him up the steps. Autumn waited until they disappeared inside before she asked, "What was that all about?"

"We came to an understanding."

"What understanding? What did he say?"

Vince swung a leg over the Harley and righted the bike. "Never mind."

"Vince! What understanding?"

He sighed. "He told me he was going to be

around more, so I better get used to seeing him."

"And?"

"Nothing." The motorcycle rumbled to life, filling the night with dual exhaust and putting an end to the conversation. He backed out of the drive and took off, leaving Autumn to stare after him. There was more to it than "nothing." She knew Vince too well to believe him.

She let out a breath and headed up the steps to the front door, decorated with a friendly ghost. She was tired from trick-or-treating for the past three hours and hoped that Sam didn't plan on staying long. She was meeting two prospective brides in the morning and needed to be sharp. She opened the door and headed up the steps as Conner told his latest knock-knock joke. Sam laughed like it was the height of hilarity.

It wasn't.

Conner sat next to Sam on the mint green couch, his coat thrown on the table. Father and son's blond heads were close together as they hovered over the bag of candy sitting between them. The big number sixteen on Conner's youth jersey was not only Sam's number; apparently it had also belonged to someone named Bobby Clarke. "Bobby had a hard shot," Conner had informed her a few weeks ago. "But Dad's is harder. He won three times for the hardest shot."

"Nice shiner," Sam complimented Conner's black eye.

"It's like yours. Last season."

"I don't have a scar on my cheek."

"I know. You probably will, though."

Autumn shrugged out of her coat and moved into the dining room. "Don't make yourself sick on all that candy."

Conner pretended not to hear her. "You can have a Kit-Kat, Dad."

"I like Dots. I used to stick all the different colors on my teeth and chase Ella around."

"Who's Ella?"

"My sister. I told you about her."

"Oh yeah. She died."

Autumn hung her coat on a chair and moved back into the living room. She was used to having a man in the house. Vince was over all the time, but Sam brought a different energy with him. It wasn't as aggressive or defensive as in the past, but it wasn't altogether comfortable either. It was too much. Too much rugged testosterone radiating from her sofa and filling the room.

"You better let me have those Dots so your

teeth don't rot," he said, poking around in the bag. "Maybe some of those M&M's, too. There might be some green ones in there, and I know how much you hate anything that reminds you of veggies."

The last thing Sam LeClaire needed was green M&Ms.

"You can have them all."

Sam glanced at Autumn, then returned his eyes to the bag. "Thanks, but I—" His head whipped up, and he stared at her as if she'd suddenly turned into an alien. His brows shot up his forehead, and the corners of his blue eyes pinched. An evil alien.

She looked behind her, saw nothing, then returned her gaze to his. "What?"

He pointed at her white Jersey. "What the hell are you wearing?"

"A hockey jersey." She looked down and pointed at the penguin on the front. "Hockey is our Halloween theme this year."

His voice was quiet. Deadly. "It's Pittsburgh."

"I like it. The penguin has little skates on his feet." She looked back up. "It's cute."

"It's gay."

"Sam. Language."

185

"Jerseys aren't supposed to be cute." He frowned and pointed an accusing finger at her. "You're wearing Crosby's number."

She looked at the 87 on her sleeve. "Who?"

"Jesus. The bastard just scored on me with a hinky puck. He should have been embarrassed instead of skating around like a prom queen."

Whatever that meant. She pointed at Conner, who was hanging on Sam's every word. "Language, please."

Conner shook his head. "I told her, Dad."

Autumn gasped. "Told me what?"

"To wear Dad's number, like me."

Yeah. Like that would happen. "I like this jersey."

Sam sat back against the couch and folded his arms across his thin beige sweater. "Penguins don't wear skates."

She pointed to Conner's jersey. "Fish don't swat pucks with their tails, either."

Sam opened a box of Dots and popped a few into his mouth. He watched her as he chewed, then said, "Crosby's a whiny little bit—girl."

She shrugged. "He's cute."

"Are you serious?"

She actually didn't really know what Crosby looked like, but Sam *looked* annoyed. Which, she admitted, amused her. "Yes. I don't want my guy to be ugly."

"*Your guy?* You pick a guy's number because you think he's cute?"

No. "Yeah." Just like women picked Sam's number because he was hot, but she'd never tell him that. Not that he didn't know it already. "Why else?"

"Why else?" He stood and dropped the empty box on the coffee table. "How about points? How about number of years in the NHL? How about taking a hit like a man. How about not crying like a girl? How about the mother of my child showing a little support and *not* wearing a Pittsburgh sweater?"

He looked serious, and she started to laugh.

He put his hands on his hips. "What's so funny?"

She slid a palm over her stomach. "You." She continued to laugh. She couldn't help it. "You're ridiculous." Conner gasped as if she'd committed blasphemy.

He motioned with his hand. "Take it off."

"Right." Like he could come into *her* house and order *her* around. Not going to happen.

Sam moved around the coffee table toward her. "Are you going to take it off?"

She shook her head and took a step back. "No."

"Then you leave me no choice here." He stalked her into the dining room, towering over her. "I'm going to have to take it off you." The corners of his lips twitched like he was joking, but his eyes were all about getting his way.

"You can't."

"Yeah, I can. I take off women's shirts all the time."

"That's not something to brag about."

"Not bragging. I'm just gifted." He held up three fingers, then lowered them one at a time.

"You're gifted all right." She didn't wait for the final finger before she turned on her heels and ran. His hand on the back of her jersey stopped her and slammed her back against the hard wall of his chest. "Sam!"

"Come help me, Conner," he called out, and wrapped one big arm around her ribs just beneath her breasts.

"No, Conner!"

The little traitor ran into the kitchen and

looked up at his dad. "What do you want me to do?"

"Hold her undershirt down so it doesn't come off with the jersey."

"Stop," she protested through a laugh. "Conner, go to bed! I mean it."

"No way." He reached his little hands beneath the jersey and grabbed the bottom of the long-sleeved thermal shirt creeping up her stomach.

"I'm your mom. You're supposed to be on my side."

"We can do this easy," Sam said into the top of her head. "Or we can go hard. You choose."

She tried to squirm out of his arms, but it was useless. "I'm keeping my Pittsburgh jersey. It cost me over two hundred bucks." Outmuscled and outmanned, the jersey was whipped over her head. For a brief second, it caught on her pony-tail, then she found herself in a tug-of-war with her son. "Let go."

"Hold—her—Dad," Conner managed be-tween peals of wild laughter and grunts of raw effort.

With both arms around her, Sam held her even tighter. "Take it and hide it somewhere," he told Conner.

"You're in big trouble," she warned her son. "No more cartoons for you."

In response, he tugged so hard his face turned red. She rose onto the balls of her feet and used her foot in his little tummy for leverage, but he ripped the jersey from her fingers. He tumbled across the kitchen floor, then took off. "Don't let her go till I hide it, Dad."

"She's not going anywhere." His arms tightened even more, and she suddenly became very aware of him pressed against her back and behind. Suddenly became aware of being surrounded by a heavy man blanket, throwing off waves of heat. She stilled as the heat of him seeped through her pores. Two of his fingers brushed her bare waist where her shirt had risen.

Other than the males in her own family or the occasional handshake, the last man who had touched her was the man touching her now. Yes, she felt the heat and pure male grit of Sam. Just like all those years ago in Vegas. What she didn't feel this time was the jump in her pulse.

"Let go, Sam."

Chapter Nine

Any Man of Mine:
Respects Boundaries

Y ou about done, Conner?" Sam called out. He
glanced from the doorway to the top of Autumn's head. Her messed-up ponytail tickled his
cheek. It had been a long time since he'd been this
close to a woman and been fully dressed. Especially this woman. He half expected an elbow in
the gut and head butt to his chin.

"Not yet, Dad."

Instead, she dropped to her heels and slid down
his body. A slow friction that ignited a fire and
burned down his stomach to his groin. His fingers

pressed into her bare skin. He couldn't help it. It just happened, and a deep, heavy groan vibrated his chest. A sort of sound that only meant one thing, and he hoped like hell she didn't notice.

"I need some water." She turned her face and looked up at him. "Want some cold water?"

That close, her eyes were very green. Not like emeralds. Warmer. Like when the trees finally turned in Saskatchewan. "No." He dropped his hands and turned from the kitchen. *Trees in Saskatchewan? Where the hell had that come from?* Yeah. He needed some cold water. He needed to dump it in his crotch.

He moved into the living room and reached for his coat on the couch. "I gotta get going." Before he did something totally insane, like starting to have sexual thoughts about the mother of his child. About Autumn. The women who hated and confused him more than any woman on the planet. "Conner!" he called out as he slipped into his wool coat, which thankfully covered the beginning promise of a full-blown erection.

"Yeah, Dad?" He came down the hall empty-handed. "Are you leaving now?"

"I've had a long week." True, but not the reason he had to go. "I'll call you Monday after practice and maybe we'll go to one of those kiddy fun centers you like."

"Can we golf? I'm good at golfing."

Autumn walked out of the kitchen, hair still in a wild just-got-laid mess, blue thermal shirt hugging her like a second skin and a glass of water in one hand. "Sure," he said as he looked down at the buttons on his coat.

"I have to work until around two. So he'll be at his day care Monday after school."

"I'll send Natalie to pick him up."

He looked across the room at her as she shoved one shoulder against the entrance into the dining room. There was something different about her that night. She was softer. More approachable, but that wasn't it.

"You probably know my newest clients." He'd noticed *it* a few weeks ago when she'd stood at the bottom of her stairs looking at him. "The Ross twins," she continued. "One of them is marrying Mark Bressler. I think he's your coach."

"Yeah, I know Mini Pit and Short Boss." Just a few months ago, he'd flirted with Chelsea at the Stanley Cup party. He liked her, and she was cute, but mostly he'd just wanted to piss off Mark. That's what friends were for.

"The other twin, Bo, is marrying someone in the Chinooks' organization. Someone named Julian."

"Jules Garcia?" He motioned for Conner to come give him a hug good-bye. "Didn't see that one coming." Mostly because Mini Pit scared grown hockey players, and a lot of the guys thought Jules was gay. Sam had never thought so, but the guy did favor pastels, moisturizers, and hair products.

He gave Conner a big hug, and it wasn't until he was locked up in his truck on the way home that he realized what was different about Autumn.

Nothing.

He took the 405 through Bellevue, the lights of the city a blur sliding across his windshield as he thought about Autumn and her deep green eyes. There was nothing in her eyes when she looked at him. No resentment nor hate. No passion or anger.

Good. Nothing was much preferable to the anger he'd seen in her eyes for so many years. He'd caused that anger. Deserved his share of it, but no one had ever hated him like Autumn. Not even hockey players he'd sent flying into the boards. Living with Autumn's hatred had always been a regretful fact of his life. One that had made his relationship with Conner difficult.

But what now? He just couldn't ever see them as friends. First off, he didn't have women friends, and second, there was too much bitterness and baggage. They'd been two combatants doing battle in the face-off circle for far too long. Guarded. Ready to fight. Except for tonight.

She'd been relaxed, and he'd let his guard slip, and for a few brief moments, things had been easy. Maybe too easy. Hearing her laughter reminded him of the girl she'd been long ago. The one who'd joked and laughed and made love all day. There was a lot about that time in Vegas he didn't remember, but there was enough that he did. Enough that twisted his head around and turned him inside out with guilt and confusion.

She was the mother of his child. The woman who blew hot and cold. The very last woman on the planet he wanted twisting his head and turning him any which way.

Least of all on.

Autumn sat across her desk from Chelsea and Bo Ross. She was all business, in a black crepe dress from the forties with little cap sleeves and rhinestone buttons.

The moment the identical twins walked into her office, she knew the double wedding ceremony they wanted wouldn't work. Bo's dark little ponytail and black suit made her look like she resided on the wrong coast, while Chelsea was a riot of color in a purple-and-pink Pucci dress and red platform heels. They were short and cute, with big breasts and large personalities.

Chelsea leaned forward and put her hand on the desk. "We decided on the third Saturday in July."

"The hockey season will be over," Bo clarified.

"Mark and I will be moved into our house in Chapel Hill."

"And Jules and I will hopefully have found a house by then." Bo put her hand over her sister's. "For our wedding, we were thinking understated. Black and white with a touch of pewter."

"I doubt Jules was thinking black and white, and Mark doesn't care as long as he doesn't have to plan any of it." Chelsea smiled and slid her hand out from beneath her sister's. "I want a garden theme with lots of color. Purples and pinks with splashes of red and yellow."

"No."

"Black and white is boring. You need more color in your life."

"And you're like an abstract painting that no one gets but you."

"Ladies," Autumn interjected. "How set are you on having a dual ceremony?"

They both looked at Autumn like she was speaking a language they didn't understand. "We got engaged within days of each other."

"It seems right," they said at the same time.

"A double ceremony is tricky." Autumn leaned forward in her chair and folded her arms on the desk. "And every bride deserves to have her day made special just for her. Bo, you're very understated, and Chelsea, you're bold and love color. You both deserve your moment, but I fear your tastes are so different, they're incongruent to the wedding of your dreams."

"But our family will have to make two trips to Seattle."

Bo shook her head. "Not if we have one wedding on a Friday night and the other on a Saturday."

Autumn smiled. "Exactly."

"I get Saturday."

Bo shook her head. "Jules has more family. I get Saturday."

"We don't have to decide that today," Autumn interrupted, and changed the subject to one every bride loved. "Have you two gone dress shopping yet? I can help you with that or give you the names of some great shops."

"I'm not looking at dresses until after Christmas," Chelsea said. "I'm having breast reduction surgery on the twenty-ninth, so I really don't see the point in trying on a dress now."

Bo looked at her sister, a deep scowl between her eyes. "I read a statistic about the number of people who die from cosmetic surgery."

"It's not cosmetic."

"Yes it is."

"No it isn't."

"It's mutilation."

Chelsea closed her eyes and took a deep breath. "Do we have to do this now?" She turned and looked at her sister. "Today?"

"No." Bo shook her head. "I'm sorry. You can have Saturday."

"No. Jules has a big family. You take Saturday."

Autumn felt a great stabbing pain in the center of her forehead. She was almost afraid to ask.

"How involved will the grooms be in the planning process?"

"Mark, not at all. Except for the two weeks he's taking off for my surgery, he's on the road with the Chinooks until spring." Chelsea raised a hand and waved it around. "And he's not really a planner anyway."

"Jules will help. Although . . ." Bo conceded, "his love of pastels might be a problem."

Chelsea smiled at her sister. "Jules has great taste. You should let him work with the planner instead of you."

Once the twins got past the idea of a dual ceremony and stopped arguing about who had the worse taste, the meeting calmed. Autumn quickly discovered that both women were very organized and knew what they wanted. They knew how much they wanted to spend and how much each wanted to be involved in the actual nuts and bolts of planning. They were very much alike in that regard, and the three of them went over the contracts quickly and thoroughly.

Both women were marrying high-profile men. Especially Chelsea. Mark Bressler was a hockey legend in Seattle, and she wondered if the two would mind if she submitted their photos to trade magazines. Once she became a little more familiar with the two, she'd broach the subject.

Bo pulled out her ponytail holder, then gathered her hair at the back of her head once more. "I think we're about done here, and I need to get some work done." Her brows lowered as she looked over Autumn's right shoulder. "That boy looks familiar."

Autumn glanced behind her at the many photos of Conner on the shelves behind her.

"He looks like the kid whose been in the players' lounge the last few games. He comes with one of Sam's tall, dark-haired, big-lipped women."

Chelsea folded her arms beneath her breasts. "Your basic nightmare."

"That's my son, Conner." She looked from one twin's face to the other, then added, "LeClaire."

Light dawned in Bo's blue eyes. "Ah."

"I didn't know Sam had a son. How old is he?"

"Five," Autumn answered. "Sam and I weren't married for very long." Which was an understatement. "Being married to a hockey player just wasn't for me." From the beginning, she and Sam had agreed for Conner's sake to keep the particulars of their marriage short and sweet. It was about the only thing they'd ever really agreed on. There were only three other people who knew the whole truth. Vince and Sam's two buddies. And as far as she knew, the buddies hadn't spilled the truth.

"That kind of life is hard on a family," Bo agreed. "It takes a lot of commitment and a strong woman. Hockey players are great, but some can be real dogs."

Chelsea gasped. "Bo!"

"Oh, I don't mean Mark."

Chelsea cut her eyes toward Autumn. "Watch what you say."

"It's okay." Autumn laughed. "Sam is a huge dog."

Chelsea smiled. "But he's a charming dog." She shook her head. "I'm sorry it didn't work out with you. I've always liked Sam. He used to come over to Mark's and pick him up when he couldn't drive. He's been a really good friend to Mark."

"Yes." Autumn didn't know how good a friend Sam could be, but she did know that he could be a charming dog. He'd certainly charmed her six years ago. Charmed her right out of her bikini bottoms.

Bo stood and reached for her little black backpack. "Jules and I usually sit in the owner's box for most home games. If you ever want to come and bring Conner, let me know."

"Won't Faith mind?"

"She's been hanging out in the lounge, and the box is usually empty unless Jules and I sit up there."

Autumn stood also.

"I'll ask Faith first, of course, but I really don't think she'll mind. In fact she'll probably be happy it's getting used."

Autumn had no intention of going to a Chinooks' game. She wasn't a hockey fan, and there was no way she wanted to be confused for a Sam fan. Their relationship was fine for the moment, but they weren't friends. "Thanks."

She showed the twins out, then moved back to her desk and put the contracts in a file. Sam was picking up Conner from his day care for a few hours. She didn't know how she felt about Sam's sudden transition from occasional to involved dad. She didn't know what had inspired the change in Sam, but ultimately, it was good for Conner. She missed him when he was with Sam, but she had to admit that it did give her a needed break. Like today, she had a ton of laundry and a house to clean, and it was always easier if her son wasn't making a mess behind her.

Before she left for the day, she pulled a few vendor files and put them on the pile of work she needed to take home. The cell phone on her desk rang, and she picked it up. She recognized Sam's number, and answered, "What's up?"

"I have Conner. I thought I'd let you know."

How considerate. How so unlike Sam. "Thanks."

"There's a game tomorrow night."

She sat on the edge of her desk and looked out the window at the parking lot beyond. "Yeah. Conner told me."

"He wants to go."

It was a school night, but as long as Conner's schoolwork didn't suffer, she could relax that rule. Sam was leaving for several weeks, and Conner wouldn't see him. "As long as he doesn't get tired, that's fine. Just have Natalie bring him home when he starts to wear out."

"Yeah. Uh-huh. Are you going to watch it on TV?"

"The game?" Why was Sam so chatty? "No."

"Are you working?"

"Not tomorrow night. No." She'd just bought

one of those Bedazzlers and wanted to glue tacky jewels on something. "November is typically a slow month for me."

"Natalie has the flu."

"Sorry." Maybe a cheap ugly vase or better yet, glass votive candle holders. That could be cool, and she could use them at events. Maybe.

"So . . . can you bring Conner to the game?"

Or on pens and . . . "What? Whoa. No. I'm busy."

"Doing what? You just said you're not working."

What did it matter? She didn't owe him anything. "Stuff."

"What stuff?"

"I've got a list of stuff."

"Of course you do, but what's on your list that's more important than taking your son to a hockey game to watch me play?"

Just about everything, but to show him how low he was on her personal food chain, she said, "My Bedazzler."

"Your what?"

"I got a Bedazzler, and I'm going to glue glass stones on a vase or something."

"Jesus."

"I don't owe you any explanation, Sam." She

stood and put a hand on her hip. "But if you want to know the truth, I hate hockey."

"That's like saying you hate Canada."

"I'm not Canadian," she pointed out.

"Conner is. Listen"—it sounded like he switched ears before he continued—"I wouldn't ask, but I'm leaving Tuesday for a week."

From the other side of Sam's car she heard a little voice plead, "Please, Mommy."

"That's not fair, Sam."

"I know."

Of course he did, and he wasn't sorry.

"You don't have to stay the whole game," he continued. "If you or Conner gets tired, you can leave. It's just this one time, Autumn. I wouldn't ask, but Conner really wants to see me put the big hurt on Sedin."

"Conner doesn't like violence."

"It's not violence. It's hockey."

Right. She was going to give him what he wanted this time, but she really didn't want to, and she wasn't going to make it easy for him. "What do I get?"

There was a pause, then he asked, his voice a deep rasp in her ear, "What do you want, honey?"

She rolled her eyes. "I want you to stop pushing me. You're spoiled and used to everyone's doing things your way. I don't work for you, and I'm not one of your women. My life does not revolve around your wants, needs, and desires."

"Autumn," he said through a sigh, "of all the women on the planet, I certainly know that your life does not revolve around my desires."

"Welcome to the Jungle" pounded the air inside the Key Arena in downtown Seattle. Two minutes into the second period, the score was even with two goals apiece. Walker and Vancouver player, Henrik Sedin, faced off behind the Chinooks' blue line. The puck dropped, the music stopped, and the sound of Axl Rose was replaced by the slap of sticks on ice.

Sam sat on the bench and squirted water into his mouth. He spit between his feet and wiped the corner of his lips with the back of his hand.

"Henrik's creating space and crowding the crease," Mark Bressler said from behind Sam. "Tie him up and get him off Marty's long side."

Sam nodded, his eyes following the action on ice. The Canucks had speed in their front line, but their blue line wasn't as fast. If the Chinooks kept the pressure on the defense and Luongo, they should give them a pretty good shellacking.

Beside him, Andre chirped at Burrows as he skated past the bench, "You're next, nutless."

Sam laughed and slid his gaze to the left corner behind the goal and landed on Autumn's pink ball cap. It was like Autumn was incognito. Hat on, collar of her coat up, like she was a double agent and didn't want anyone to recognize her. He guessed he was a little surprised that she wasn't wearing that Pittsburgh jersey just to piss him off.

Sam felt a hand on his back, and he rose and shoved his mouth guard against his teeth. He and Vlad scissored over the wall, and he skated to the far side.

Vancouver's Kesler brought the puck down ice, dangling the vulcanized rubber within the blade of his stick. Sam kept his gaze on Kesler's face, reading him, and the second he looked down, Sam hip checked him against the boards. The Plexiglas rattled as he dug at the puck with the curved blade of his own stick. "You must love getting your ass handed to you," he said as he slashed and hacked.

"Blow me, LeClaire."

"You first, chicken shit." He shot the puck

along the alley to Daniel and took off toward the red line. The whistle blew, and the ref called off-side.

He glanced at Conner and Autumn. His son waved a foam finger at him, and his heart swelled. The shadow of Autumn's cap hid her eyes and touched the bow of her lips. He was grateful that, despite her obvious dislike of him and hockey, she'd brought Conner.

He circled back to the goal line and checked the tape on his stick. He really couldn't ask for a better mother for his son, and as he passed Kesler, he bumped him with his shoulder. "My balls dangle better than you," he said.

"Your balls dangle 'cause you're an old man."

Sam smiled. He remembered when he'd been twenty-five and cocky. Hell, he was still a little cocky sometimes. "Watch yourself, dipshit. The season is young, and the ice is slick."

He stood near the goal line, shutting down firing lanes and waited. The puck dropped, Hendrik fed it back to Kesler, and from his right, Sam took a hard hit from Shane O'Brien that knocked him on his ass. He slid across the ice. His right shoulder slammed into the boards, and he heard the snap a split second before pain shot across his shoulder and down his arm. "Fuck."

He tried to sit up and rolled onto his right side. Stars flashed in front of his eyes, and the whistles blew. He shook off his glove and gritted his teeth. "Son of a bitch!" The pain took his breath away, and he lay on his back and looked up at steel girders. *This isn't good,* he thought. The arena was filled with the yelling of thousands of Chinook fans, and through it all, the pain and shock and the noise, he heard Conner. He heard his son's fearful wail, but that was impossible. The roar of the crowd was too loud. Then Daniel's and Vlad's faces crowded his vision, followed shortly by Bressler and head trainer, Scott Silverman.

"Where are you hurt?" Scott asked.

"Shoulder. My clavicle. I heard the snap."

"Can you move your hands and feet?"

"Yeah." He'd broken enough bones that he recognized the signs, and he wondered how long this break would keep him on the injured list. How long before he would meet with O'Brien on the ice and kick his ass. "Help me up."

Mark knelt beside him on one knee. "Just keep still and let Scott do his job."

Sam shook his head and gritted his teeth against the pain of that simple act. "My kid's here. I don't want him to see me laid out on the ice." And there was no way he'd let the bastards see how bad he was hurt. "Scott can do his job in the trainer's room." With his right hand, he pushed himself into sitting position. It hurt more than he let on. The last thing he wanted was to be taken out on the stretcher.

Scott wedged his shoulder beneath Sam's right arm, and he was able to rise to his knees.

Fuck! Shit! Goddamn!

"You okay?"

"Yeah. Yeah." *Son of a bitch!* He rose to his feet, and the arena went crazy with applause. Slowly, he skated toward the bench, his left arm tight against his chest. He was in so much pain, it crowded the corners of his vision. But more than the pain, he was pissed. Pissed that a piss-headed pissant had blindsided him. Pissed that he was going to miss a month—if he was lucky. Pissed that it had happened in front of his son.

Chapter Ten

Any Man of Mine:
*Doesn't Have Other Girlfriends
(especially skinny girlfriends)*

C onner dropped Autumn's fingers and pushed
the elevator button. In his free hand, he held
a little box with a cupcake inside. A brown cupcake with gummy worms and chocolate sprinkles
that they'd made that morning and Conner had
decorated himself. The door slid shut, and the two
rode the elevator to the loft on the tenth floor. It
was a little after ten in the morning. Normally,
Conner would be in school, but after last night, he
needed to see his father.

It had been well after one in the morning before

he'd finally cried himself to sleep. He'd been so sure that Sam was dying. "They took him away in the amb-amb-lance," he'd sobbed.

"That's just because it's more comfortable," she'd lied in an effort to soothe him. Shortly after Sam had skated from the ice, someone from the Chinooks' organization had found Autumn and Conner and told them that Sam was being transported to Harborview for tests and X-rays.

"I don't thi-ink so, Mom."

Conner was getting older and harder to trick, and those moments as they'd watched Sam laid out on the ice had been horrific for Conner. He'd burst into panicky tears, and Autumn had to admit that, even though she'd wished Sam harm on many occasions, the reality had given her a knot in her stomach.

"I want to go see my da-ad."

"I'll take you to see him in the morning," she'd promised, even though hanging out at Sam's was about the last thing she wanted to do.

The elevator opened, and they walked down a short hall. "Remember that we're not staying long. Just long enough for you to see that your dad's okay." Conner rang the doorbell, and within a few short moments, Faith Savage answered, looking tall and gorgeous and pregnant. Autumn didn't know who was more surprised. Her or the owner of the Chinooks.

"Well, hello, Autumn. You know Sam?"

"Yes. We have a son together."

"I didn't know that." She lowered her gaze to Conner's blond hair.

"Not many people do." She put her hand on her son's head. "Say hello to Mrs. Savage."

"Hi." Conner leaned to the left for a better peek into the loft. "How are you?"

Faith smiled. "I'm well. Thank you." She stepped to one side, and Conner shot past her.

"Dad!"

Autumn moved into the entry and shut the door behind her. "How is Sam?"

"Cranky." Faith looked over her shoulder. "I'm glad you're here."

Obviously, she didn't know her and Sam's relationship. "How are *you* feeling?" she asked Faith, as they moved into a living room filled with overstuffed leather furniture, a huge entertainment center, and a wall of windows looking out onto the city. The whole space was open and filled with expensive furnishings and art. Just the sort of bachelor pad she would expect of Sam.

"Good now. The first three months were a little rough. I just can't imagine how horrible it must be for those poor women who are sick the entire nine months."

Autumn laughed and raised her hand. "I was one of those women, and it *was* horrible." She unzipped her black fleece jacket as the two moved to the open kitchen, where Sam and Conner stood at the counter. "Do you know if you're having a boy or a girl?"

"Not yet. We've only had the first ultrasound."

"Oh. I remember that one. Conner looked like a chicken nugget." She laughed. "That's why we call him Nugget."

Sam looked up from the cupcake on the marble countertop. On the outside of his white T-shirt, he wore a figure-of-eight splint over his shoulders, and his left arm was in a sling held tight against his chest. The right side of the shirt was tucked into a pair of nylon running pants, while the left side hung down his hips. His hair was messed, and dark blond stubble shadowed his cheeks and chin. "I thought you called him Nugget 'cause he was conceived in Las Vegas."

She glanced at Faith out of the corners of her eyes and shook her head. The night Conner was conceived in Vegas wasn't something she wanted even to think about, let alone discuss. She and Sam had never talked about that time, and she didn't want to start now. Especially in front of Faith Savage.

"I'll let you enjoy time with your son," Faith said as she moved toward a barstool and gathered her red wool coat and Hermès handbag. "Sam, you let me know if there is anything you need."

"Thanks for coming by. I'll see you out." He moved toward her, but she held up a hand. "I can find my way. You rest." She smiled at Autumn. "It was nice to see you again."

"You, too."

And then Faith was gone, leaving behind the scent of expensive perfume. The door closed behind her, and Autumn was alone with Sam. In his loft. On his turf.

"Can you move your arm?" Conner asked his dad.

"Yeah," Sam reassured Conner. "I broke my clavicle." He pointed to his collarbone. "I'm just wearing the sling to keep my arm still."

Conner looked up at his father and shook his head. "I saw that man hurt you."

"This is nothing compared to the time I busted up my ankle. At least I can walk around this time."

She put her Hèrmes knockoff from Target on the barstool with Conner's Old Navy hoodie. She left her own jacket on because she wouldn't be staying long enough to get comfy. "But should you be walking around?" Autumn much preferred being around Sam in her house. Where she felt some semblance of control. Although with Sam, control had always been an illusion.

"Yeah. But I'm about to sit down." He pointed to the cupcake. "I'll eat the red worm. You have the green one."

"Okay." Conner grabbed a worm and stuffed it into his mouth.

"Later though." He shut the top of the cupcake box as if the sight of worms coming out of a dirty-looking cupcake made him a bit queasy. "I'm not sure a worm will agree with all the medicine I just took." Slowly, he moved past her, and Conner trailed behind. Maybe she should leave. Come back in an hour. She didn't belong there. In Sam's bachelor pad.

"Autumn, could you grab a bag of peas out of the freezer?"

"Sure." She moved across the stone floor to a stainless-steel side-by-side and opened the door. The first breath of chilled air hit her face and the hollow of her throat as she looked inside at frozen juice, a box of Toaster Sticks, and about ten bags of frozen peas. She grabbed the one on top and walked from the kitchen. Sam sat on a leather sofa, Conner by his side. With his arm trussed up and the straps of his splint around his shoulder, he looked almost helpless. Well, as helpless as a six-two, two-hundred-plus wall of solid muscle could look.

She handed him the bag of peas. "Should I call Natalie for you?"

"Why?" He put the peas on his shoulder and sucked in a breath.

"Isn't she your 'assistant'? Maybe she should assist you."

"Mostly she's Conner's babysitter. I don't need a babysitter."

Seeing him in pain, he not only looked helpless, but he really didn't fit her image of him. The image she'd had over the years of a man with multiple girlfriends and even more sexual partners. He looked like a regular guy. Well, kind of. A regular guy with a scruffy five o'clock shadow on his movie-star jaw. "Do you need anything else?"

"No." He shook his head and looked up at her through sleepy blue eyes. She didn't know if he was tired or doped up. Probably both.

She glanced at the watch on the inside of her wrist. Five more minutes.

"Dad, what does *conceived* mean?"

Both Autumn and Sam looked at Conner, then at each other.

"What?"

"You said I was conceived. What does that mean?"

"Well ahh . . ." Sam stammered, and slid his gaze to his son. "It means that when two people . . . It means that . . ." He shifted the peas on his shoulder. For a guy who'd had a lot of practice at conceiving, he sure was having a hard time explaining it. Not that *she* wanted to give it a try. Especially not in front of Sam. When she had "the talk," she didn't want an audience. "Well, it's when . . ." He winced as if he was in sudden and excruciating pain and couldn't possibly think. "Ouch. My shoulder hurts. Ask your mother."

"Me?"

He pointed to his collarbone. "Cut me some slack. I'm in a lot of pain here."

Which wasn't an excuse. "Fine." She could probably answer the question better than Sam anyway. Her answer would be safer, at any rate. She sat on the sofa and turned to face Conner. "It means made." There, that was easy.

"Oh." He stared up at her though blue eyes so much like his father's it was crazy. "I was made in Las Vegas?"

"Yes."

"Oh." He swallowed, and she could practically see the wheels turning in his little brain. "How?"

She'd always known that someday she'd have to answer this question. She was prepared. She'd gone over it in her head several times, but never in her imaginings had Sam been sitting two feet away, a bag of peas on his shoulder, looking like he wanted to know the answer, too. "Well, when two people make love, they sometimes make a baby."

"Oh." Autumn held her breath, waiting for the next "how." The questions were only going to get harder. He turned and faced Sam. "Can I have your gummy worm?"

"Go for it."

Conner jumped up and ran into the kitchen as fast as his little sneakers could carry him.

A sigh of relief escaped her lungs as she scrubbed her face with her hands. "I feel like I just dodged a bullet."

"I was kind of interested in how you were going to answer the questions working their way through his brain."

She frowned and dropped her hands. "You were no help." She leaned forward to make sure Conner was still in the kitchen before she said, "He asked you, and *you* certainly know what *conceived* means. Good God, you're the biggest perv on the planet."

He laughed, not at all ashamed. Of course not. He was Sam. "Not the biggest."

"You're right up there."

"Which is why I probably shouldn't answer such delicate questions."

Conner returned, munching on a red gummy worm. The little wheels in his head were still turning. Just because he'd taken a worm break didn't mean he was ready to let the subject go.

"Okay." Autumn jumped to her feet before

Conner could get his questions out. "We better get going now."

"We just got here."

"We talked about this, Conner. You knew we weren't going to stay long. Your dad needs to rest."

"What I need is a shower."

She started toward the kitchen. "Let's get your hoodie."

"I need your help."

That stopped her, and she slowly turned to face Sam. He was looking at her. "Me? You need me to help you take a shower?"

He chuckled and used his good hand to push himself up. "No. Not unless you insist." He tossed the peas on the coffee table and pointed to his sling. "Somebody hooked this thing up in the back, and I can't get it off." He moved past her, just naturally assuming she'd help him out. "I'm not so sure I need it anyway."

"Can I have your cupcake, Dad?"

"Knock yourself out, but just make sure you eat at the bar. I can't break out the DustBuster after you leave today." He looked back at Autumn over his shoulder. "Come on." When she didn't

221

move, he stopped and turned to look at her. "I'm not trying to push you around. I just need a little help."

That wasn't the reason her feet were glued to his carpet. Helping him out of his sling felt a little too intimate. A little too close.

As if he read her mind, he asked, "Do you think I'm going to try something on you?"

He made it sound so ridiculous that there was only one thing left for her to do. She shook her head and shrugged out of her fleece jacket. She tossed it on top of her purse and followed Sam. "Of course I don't think that." They moved down a curved hall and passed a room that could only be Conner's.

"That's good, because I'm in no condition to start something that I can't finish," he said over his shoulder. "No matter how pretty you beg."

If he hadn't already been hurt and moving kind of slow, she might have been tempted to hit him. Instead, she kept her attention focused on the dark blue figure-eight splint across the back of his white T-shirt and the beige strap of his sling. He was right. The figure-of-eight and sling were Velcroed in back.

She followed him into the large master bedroom with a spectacular view of Elliott Bay. The bed itself was still unmade and rumpled from the night before, and a pair of hockey shorts, socks, and big pads had been kicked to one side. The walk-in closet was as big as her bathroom at home and the bathroom as big as her kitchen. Only fancier. A lot fancier.

He flipped on a switch with his good hand and a brushed-nickel chandelier and rows of canned lights shone down onto white-and-black marble. The shower stall could comfortably seat a family of six and was enclosed in glass and black granite with tiny silver flecks.

He stopped in the center of a zebra-skin rug. She was fairly sure it was a cowhide dyed to look like a zebra, but it was still mildly disconcerting.

He turned to face her. "What?"

She ran her gaze up his legs, past his waist, over the arm pinned to his chest, to his face. "That rug is a whole cowhide."

"Yeah?"

She shook her head. "Aren't you disturbed by it?"

"No more disturbed by it than by your leather sneakers."

To her, it wasn't really the same. Her shoes

served a worthy purpose, and she thought animal skins used for nothing more than decorations were creepy. Like skulls and heads and antlers. Yuck. Her feelings didn't have to make sense to anyone but her. She moved around behind him and reached for the buckle just above his right shoulder blade. "Has Conner seen it?"

"Yeah."

Her knuckles brushed the warm cotton of his T-shirt. "Did he cry?"

"No, but he doesn't like to walk on it."

That was her boy. "He has a kind heart. He doesn't like to hurt people or animals." Which brought her to a subject she'd wanted to talk to him about. "Last night, he totally lost it when he saw you." She rose onto the balls of her feet and tried to touch him as little as possible. She lightly put one palm in the center of his back for support as she pushed a strap over his shoulder. "It really upset him."

"I know, but getting hurt is a risk that I take every time I step on the ice." She moved around him as he slowly lowered his arm. "Last night was a freak accident."

She carefully pulled the beige sling from his

arm, sliding it past his elbow. She wanted Conner to take a break from hockey games, but she supposed the subject was moot for a while. At least until Sam returned to the ice. "From where I sat, it looked on purpose to me." She glanced up into the grimace bracketing the corners of his mouth. She was so close, she could pick out every whisker on his stubbly chin.

"Oh, the hit was on purpose." He sucked in a breath and looked down into her eyes. "The injury was a freak accident. I slammed into the wall at a bad angle."

She set the sling on the black granite vanity top, then moved behind him once more. She ripped the Velcro on the figure-eight bandage and lightly slid her fingers beneath it.

"Shit."

"You okay?"

"I've been worse."

She slipped the bandage from his shoulders and set it next to the sling.

"Conner will learn that getting hit is just a part of hockey. He'll be okay."

She doubted it and once again moved to stand in front of him. "He's a pacifist."

"He's a LeClaire."

He was also a Haven. Nonviolent. Well, except for Vince. "Conner's a lover, not a fighter."

Sam gathered the hem of his T-shirt with his good hand and pulled it free. "You say that like he has to be one or the other. He's a LeClaire." He glanced up, and a slow smile curved his lips. "We're gifted in both areas."

She shook her head. "Even after all these years, I'm still amazed by your gigantic conceit."

"It's not conceit." He motioned for her to help him out with the T-shirt. "Not if it's true. I just don't suffer from false modesty."

Or any sort of modesty at all. She took a step closer and grabbed the edge of the soft cotton. She undressed Conner all the time. This was no different. It was mechanical. No big deal. She lifted his shirt past his waist and up his chest. See. No big deal. No biggie. No—*Holy mother of God*! She'd forgotten what corrugated muscles and six-packs and happy trails looked like up close. Her mouth went dry, and she swallowed hard. "Can you pull your arm out?" She didn't like him. She didn't hate him. Emotionally, she felt nothing. No pitter-patter of her heart, but physically . . . Physically, she felt like she'd been hit in the stomach with a flaming ball of lust. Reminding her for the first time in a very long time that she was more than just Conner's mother. She was a thirty-year-old woman who hadn't had sex in over five years.

He grabbed her hand and pressed her palm against his chest. His warm, hard, *bare* chest. Once upon a time, she'd licked that chest. Run her mouth up and down that flat belly like he was an all-you-can-eat buffet. "Did I hurt you?" When he didn't answer, she looked up. Up past his hand over hers. Past his thick throat, and parted lips, and into his blue eyes.

"The first time I saw you," he said, "I thought you had the prettiest hair I'd ever seen."

What? While she'd been thinking about his hard belly, he'd been thinking about her hair. "Are you high?"

He grinned. "Very."

He was goofy from pain medication and helpless from his injury. She didn't have an excuse for her mental wanderings.

"I still think your hair is pretty."

That was obviously the drugs talking. "Now, don't say anything you'll be embarrassed about tomorrow."

227

He brushed his thumb across the backs of her knuckles. "Why would I be embarrassed?"

"Because you don't like me."

"I like you."

He lifted his good hand and slid his big warm palm across her shoulder to the side of her neck. Suddenly, he seemed neither goofy nor helpless. "Sam."

"You smell good. Like cupcakes." He lowered his face and pressed his forehead into hers. "I like cupcakes."

She gave a little laugh, and her fingers curled into his T-shirt. "You've never had my cupcakes."

"Honey, I've had your cupcakes." His fingers plowed through her hair, and he held the back of her head in his hand.

Her voice sounded kind of breathy and strained when she said, "I didn't mean that."

By contrast, he didn't sound breathy at all. "I did."

"Dad?"

At the sound of Conner's voice, Sam lifted his head, and Autumn jumped back. Her hand fell to her side.

"Yeah, buddy?" Sam ran his gaze over

Autumn's face and hair before his own hand dropped to his side.

"The doorbell rang."

"It's probably Howie. Go ahead and let him in."

"What are you doing?" asked the little voice from the doorway.

"Chatting." Autumn moved from behind Sam. "And I'm just helping your dad out of his splint so he can take a shower."

"Oh." He looked from one parent to the other. "Okay." Then he turned on the heels of his little sneakers and disappeared.

"Who is Howie?" Autumn asked in an effort not to think. About abs and cupcakes and her son walking in and seeing . . . what? His mom and dad chatting? Yeah, chatting about cupcakes.

"One of the Chinooks' trainers. He's coming by today to check up on me and help with the sling."

She looked up and across her shoulder at him. His shirt had slid back down his chest, but the marks of her finger still wrinkled the cotton above his right pec. "So you didn't even need me?"

"Sure I did. I knew he was coming, just not when. And I stink."

He didn't. She wished he did, though. Wished he stank so badly that she'd thought of bars of soap instead of licking his abs. "Well, I'm sure he knows what he's doing and can help you with your shirt better than I can."

"Probably, but he doesn't have your pretty hair." He grinned. "And he doesn't smell like cupcakes."

"Sam?"

Autumn's gaze shot to the doorway, and the stunning woman standing there like she'd just stepped out of a fashion magazine. Autumn recognized her immediately.

Slowly, Sam turned. "Veronica? What are you doing here?"

"I came as soon as I heard that you were hurt."

"You should have called."

"I tried." Her dark brown gaze lowered from Sam's face to Autumn. Within the blink of an eye, the supermodel assessed and dismissed Autumn as any sort of threat. Autumn was more amused than insulted. Seriously, she didn't care until Veronica asked, "Are you one of the assistants?"

Autumn got hot and cold at the same time, and she forced a smile. "Time for me to go. You have lots of help now." She moved across the bathroom and slipped by the tall skinny woman in the doorway. She didn't know designers made women's jeans in little-girl-size 6X. "Excuse me."

"Autumn," Sam called out to her but she kept on going. She had an overwhelming urge to be anywhere but there, and she grabbed Conner's hand as she passed him in the hall. "Your dad has company, and we have to get going."

"Can we go to McDonald's on the way home. I'm hungry."

"Didn't you just eat your dad's cupcake?" She grabbed their jackets and her purse off the kitchen barstool.

"Yeah, but there's a dinosaur in the Happy Meal."

"You have dinosaurs." She could feel her cheeks flush. She wasn't angry. There was nothing to be angry about. She was *embarrassed*.

"Hold on." Sam caught up with them at the door and held out his good arm. "Give me a hug good-bye," he told Conner. He carefully gathered Conner to his side, then looked up at Autumn. "Why are you so mad?"

"I'm not."

"You're tearing out of here like you are."

She shoved her arms into her jacket. "I just

don't appreciate one of your many girlfriends mistaking me for another one of your many girl-friends."

"Natalie isn't my girlfriend." He lowered his voice. "Neither is Veronica. She's just—"

"Sam, I don't care," she interrupted, and held her hand up to stop him.

"You look like you care."

"I don't. This is your home. You can certainly entertain any woman you like here. Just as I can entertain whomever I like in my house." She hung her inexpensive purse on her shoulder. "I just don't like being confused for one of your women. I like to think I look smarter than that. That I *am* smarter than that." She *was* smarter, too.

Well, except for just a few moments ago when she'd stood in his bathroom touching his pecs, thinking about his abs, and talking about her cupcakes. Falling for his b.s. She knew better, too. She knew from painful experience that nothing good would ever come from falling under, over, or on top of Sam LeClaire's bullshit.

Chapter Eleven

Any Man of Mine:
Likes Muffins

What had just happened? Sam stood in the empty entrance of his loft, staring at the front door. Sure, he was fairly doped up and in pain, but that really didn't explain his confusion over what had just taken place.

It was Autumn. She blew hot and cold. One minute she had her hand on his chest, all warm and cozy, and the next she was shoving his son out the door, all pissed off because Veronica had mistaken her for Natalie.

I just don't like being confused for one of your women. I like to think I look smarter than that. That I am smarter than that. What had she meant? None of the women he dated were stupid-looking, and they really couldn't help it if they weren't the brightest crayons in the box. Some people accused him of only dating a certain type of woman, and that was true. He liked women as deep as puddles who moved on quickly to the next athlete or actor or rock star after the relationship ended. He didn't ever want to see the kind of pain in a woman's eyes that he'd once seen in Autumn's.

"Is there anything I can get you?"

Sam closed his eyes. He hated surprise drop-ins. Was a courtesy call, that he could then ignore, too much to ask? "No." He turned and headed into the living room to wait for Howie. His shoulder suddenly hurt like a son of a bitch. Taking off the figure-eight splint had been a mistake, but he'd thought he'd just take a quick shower and put it right back on.

He grabbed the bag of frozen peas from the coffee table and put it on his shoulder as he carefully sat on the couch. He gritted his teeth against the pain and leaned back. "I'm not going to be great company, V."

"That's okay. Do you want something to eat or drink?"

He looked up at Veronica, at her beautiful face and killer body. She had thick brown hair and puffy red lips, and he just wanted her gone. "No."

"Was that your little boy?"

"Yeah."

"He's handsome."

"Thank you."

She sat on the couch next to him. "So, was that his nanny?"

"His mother."

One perfect brow rose up her flawless forehead. "I never would have guessed that."

The pain throbbed along his shoulder and down his arm. He leaned his head back and shifted the bag of peas a little to the right. "Why?"

"She's . . ." She shrugged as she struggled for the right words. "Ordinary, I guess."

Ordinary? Autumn? With her red hair and deep green eyes and sassy pink mouth. Autumn wasn't ordinary, but he supposed he'd thought that, too, on more than one occasion. But there were those other occasions. Those times when he couldn't take his eyes off her. Didn't want to take his eyes off her. Like just a few minutes ago, standing in his bathroom beneath the chandelier shining in her hair. Those rare occasions when she didn't blow hot and cold. When she was hot and hotter.

"Where'd you meet her?"

He didn't want to talk about Autumn. He didn't even want to think about her. Thinking about her brought up memories of "conceiving" with her. For some reason, Conner's questions had triggered memories of sex with Autumn. Hot sex in a hotel room, against a wall, in a shower, and speeding through Vegas in a limo.

"Did you meet her when you moved to Seattle?"

"Not now, V." He was in pain, drugged up, and his thoughts about Autumn, about the past and present, about sex and her mercurial moods were as muddled and confusing as ever.

Veronica opened her mouth to argue, but the doorbell rang and saved him from the model's grilling. It was probably Howie. At least he hoped to God it was Howie and not some former girlfriend. He'd had enough drama for one day. "Would you get that for me, V?"

She gave him a look that said she wasn't through, but she did raise her skinny butt off the couch and answer the door. When she returned,

Howie trailed after her, and Sam could have kissed the assistant trainer on his bald head.

"Why aren't you wearing your figure-of-eight splint?"

Sam pressed the peas into his shoulder and stood. "I was going to take a shower."

Howie looked at Veronica and frowned. "What part of 'no physical activity' didn't you understand?"

Sam chuckled. Howie had the wrong idea and blamed the wrong female. "I thought I could handle it."

"All you hockey players think you're Superman."

Which was somewhat true. They spent their lives battling it out night after night, and it wasn't until they ended up on the injured list that they realized that they were, in reality, flesh and bone. That they weren't invincible. A fact that Sam was made aware of more frequently the older he got.

He spent the next four days at home alone, resting, recuperating, and going batshit crazy while the Chinooks hit the road for a six-game, two-week grind. That following Monday, he walked to the Key Arena and had Howie help him strap

237

on his skates. He participated in a light skate with some of the other guys left behind when the team hit the road. Since he shot right, he was able to dangle a few pucks one-handed. He didn't have to wear the arm sling, but still wore the figure-eight splint. He'd learned his lesson about taking it off for too long a period of time.

Sam hated staying behind. He'd stayed behind before, of course. There were eighty-two games in the regular season, and most players didn't play every game for various reasons, but he hated languishing on the injured list.

After a week, his shoulder didn't hurt as much, but he was still a month from returning to the game. He picked up Conner from kindergarten, and his son introduced him to his teacher and some of his little buddies. Parading him around as if to say, "See, I have a dad."

Sam took him to the rink, and they had the ice to themselves. His son didn't show a ton of aptitude on his skates. He couldn't seem to stay on his feet, but when he did manage, he wasn't a bad shot, for a five-year-old. Wednesday, Sam worked his legs and core muscles in the weight room at the arena, and Thursday, he asked Autumn to bring Conner to the Key. He told her

Natalie was in school and couldn't bring him. Which was kind of a lie. Natalie was in school, just not on Thursdays. He wasn't sure why he lied other than he was somewhat curious to see if she'd actually show. After that day he'd been all doped up and wanted to talk about her cupcakes, he wasn't sure if things were back to somewhat normal. Or what served as somewhat normal for him and Autumn.

He arranged for someone from the office to meet her and Conner and bring them to the lower level. He was half-shocked when she actually showed up around noon. Dressed in her peacoat over one of the Mrs. Cleaver dresses she wore sometimes. He wouldn't have put it past her to show up in Crosby's jersey.

Conner sat on the team bench, and she took off her coat before crouching in front of him to lace up his skates. Her red hair fell across her shoulder and cheek, and she brushed it behind one ear. The hem of her blue-and-white polka-dot dress slid up her bare thighs toward her waist. He liked it when women didn't wear nylons. Unless, of course, they were attached to a red garter belt.

"Knock knock, Dad."

Sam groaned inwardly and raised his gaze from Autumn's thighs. "Who's there?"

He grinned and answered, "Sam."

"Sam who?"

"Sam person who knocked last night."

Sam laughed. "That was a good one."

"I know."

Autumn chuckled and glanced up, her green eyes catching his for a brief moment before her gaze returned to Conner's skate. "How are you feeling?"

"Okay if I don't overdo." He sat on the bench and helped Conner strap on his elbow pads.

Autumn tied the last lace in a double knot and looked up at Sam, his blond head bent over Conner's as he worked with one hand. She'd picked up Conner and come straight from work. Earlier, she and Shiloh had met with Shiloh's friends, Lisa and Jen, to plan their commitment ceremony. It wasn't the first time they'd planned a same-sex commitment ceremony, but it was the first time they'd done it for friends, and they wanted their day to be perfect.

After she'd picked up Conner from school, she'd driven to the Key Arena and parked in the garage. The two had been met by someone within the Chinooks' organization and moved through the concrete maze within the belly of the arena. At the end, Sam had been standing on rubber mats near the entrance to the tunnel, waiting for them. He wore black sweats with a fish logo and looked huge in his skates. He wasn't wearing any pads or the sling on his arm. He looked hot and sweaty. His hair was finger-combed like he'd been working out. Alone or with one of his supermodels. Unfortunately, she knew about Sam's workouts. Knew that he had the stamina and determination of an elite athlete.

A frown creased her brow. Best not to think about Sam's thoroughness. "This isn't overdoing?"

"No. Not unless Conner hip checks me and slams my face into the Plexiglas. "

Conner laughed. "I won't put the big hurt on you, Dad."

Autumn reached for a fitted kneepad on the bench and strapped it on.

"I don't need those."

"You don't want them, but you *need* them."

"You'll get used to wearing your gear. Your helmet, too. It's part of the game," Sam said as he handed her the left kneepad. "My mom used to help me with my gear."

241

"And your dad, too?"

Sam shook his head. "He wasn't interested in my hockey."

Not interested in his own son? Autumn paused in the act of securing the Velcro behind Conner's knee. He had to be joking.

He looked at her without lifting his face, and said as if he'd read her mind, "He was a police officer. A very good police officer. He just wasn't a very good dad."

Like him. He lowered his gaze, but not before Autumn saw the thought clearly expressed in his eyes. She had to give Sam some credit. Lately, he'd been paying a lot more attention to Conner. He was trying hard and keeping his word to his son. If she were a betting woman, she would have bet against him. She'd have bet that he would have gone back to his old ways already. Then again, it had only been a month and a half since the arrival of the new and improved Sam.

She finished the last strap and rose. With his good hand, he put Conner's helmet on his head, then helped him to his feet.

"The ice is snowier today. You probably won't fall as much," Sam assured Conner.

"Good." Conner sounded relieved as the two

stepped onto the ice, and he moved in front of Sam and stood beneath Sam's much bigger feet. "I don't like to fall all the time. It hurts my bum-bum."

"Didn't we talk about *bum-bum*?"

"Yeah."

They moved their skates at the same time, inching forward. Looking a lot like—dare she even *think* it—penguins.

"What did we decide?"

"That just because Mom's a girl, she's not as smart as boys."

Autumn lifted her gaze as Sam whipped his head around to look at her.

"Uhhh . . . I don't remember saying that." Guilt worked its way across his face.

She lifted a brow and tried not to laugh. "You're a bad liar."

Sam chuckled, as the two slowly skated across the ice. He left Conner halfway between the center line and goal, then he lined up pucks in front of him. Even in his pads and helmet, Conner looked so small next to his dad.

"Could you bring me those sticks?" Sam asked, and pointed to the bench behind her. She shucked out of her bulky peacoat and set it on the bench. She pulled down the sleeves of her navy blue cardigan and adjusted the wide red belt around her waist before she picked up the two Reebok hockey sticks. One long and the other short. Both had cloth tape wrapped tightly down the handles and around the curve of the blades. Sam's number sixteen had been written in black Sharpie on the knobs of both handles.

As carefully as possible, she stepped from the matting and onto the ice. She stood still for a few short seconds, testing the surface to make sure she didn't fall on her behind. The bottoms of her red ballet flats didn't shoot out from beneath her, and she carefully moved toward Conner. Chilled air crept up her bare legs, and flakes of snowy ice slid inside her shoes. The rink looked bigger on this side of the Plexiglas. Longer from end to end.

She handed Sam and Conner their sticks, felt her shoes slide, and stuck her arms out to her sides for balance. "Whoa."

Sam dropped his stick and grabbed her arm with his good hand. "Now I know where Conner gets his balance."

"I can balance." She looked up. Way up into Sam's blue eyes. The skates gave him an extra three inches, which made him about six-foot-five or more. "Just not on ice." She turned to take a few steps, but his grasped tightened.

"Put your arm through mine."

"I don't want to pull you down if I fall."

He let go of her with his hand and stuck his right arm out from his side. "You're not big enough to pull me down."

Careful to touch him as little as possible, she threaded her hand under his arm and grabbed onto his hard biceps. Heat rolled off him and warmed up the tips of her fingers and palm. Hot, sweaty testosterone seeped into her skin, and an unbidden memory of his hot, sweaty skin pressed against hers doubled her pulse. The memory was purely physical and spread warmth up her arm and across her chest. "Jeez, you're really hot," she blurted.

He chuckled. "Thank you. You look hot in that dress, and I have no idea why. It's kind of frumpy."

She looked down at herself. "It's vintage."

"*Vintage* just means old."

"Some things get better with age. Like wine and cheese."

"And whiskey and sex."

She was not going to take that bait. "When I

said you were hot, I was talking about temperature."

"Yeah. I know."

She glanced up past the hard edge of his perfect jaw and into his blue eyes. "It's freezing out here."

"It's not that cold," said the contrary man who threw off heat like a bed of hot coals.

They stepped onto the rubber mats, and she dropped her arm, curling her hand against the warmth in her palm.

"Do you want to go into the lounge, where it's warmer?"

She looked past him to where Conner stood pushing pucks around. Then for no apparent reason at all, he fell on his behind. "I'll watch you and Conner." She sat on the bench and wrapped her coat around her bare legs.

"Sit tight." He headed down the tunnel, and she watched Conner rise to his knees. "Are you okay?" she called out.

He nodded, his helmet shifting about on his head as he got his skate beneath him and stood. In hindsight, she should have changed before she'd brought Conner to the rink. Changed into some ski pants and fuzzy boots, but her head was filled with all the last-minute things she had to do before the Kramer's fiftieth wedding anniversary the next day.

Fifty years. She folded her arms across her chest and hunched her shoulders against the cold. Her parents hadn't lasted fifteen years, let alone fifty. Her grandmother had died before their fifty-year wedding mark, and Autumn's own wedding . . . Well, that one didn't even count as a real wedding, and if she hadn't gotten pregnant, she never would have seen Sam again. The fact that there were people out there celebrating fifty years made her think that it was possible, despite her more cynical side.

"Stand up." Sam's black sweats and fish logo blocked her vision of Conner. Beneath his good arm, he held a deep blue and green blanket.

She stood, and he wrapped the blanket around her shoulders. Her coat fell and covered her feet as he pulled the blanket under her chin. "Are you sure you're going to be warm enough?"

She nodded, and the backs of his knuckles bumped her chin. "You're moving your arm."

"I can move my arm," he said as he looked into her eye. "Just not my shoulder."

"I'm ready, Dad," Conner called out to him.

"I'll be right there, buddy." His thumb brushed across her jaw. "Do you remember the other day when we were in my bathroom talking about your muffin?"

"You mean my cupcakes?"

He grinned. "I thought we talked about your muffin."

"You were doped up." She tried not to laugh. "It was cupcakes."

"I like muffins."

Yeah. Everyone on the planet pretty much knew that about Sam. "What's your point?"

"Just that I might have been out of line talking about your muffin, but since we were just talking about your cupcakes, then I'm—"

"Sam, what are you doing to that poor woman?" a male voice interrupted. Autumn turned to look at the man walking from the tunnel. Surprise stopped Ty Savage in his tracks. "Why are you harassing Autumn, the wedding planner?"

"Hello," she said. "How are you?"

"Okay." He looked from one to the other. "Evidently you know Sam."

Sam dropped his hands to his sides. "Autumn is my ex-wife."

Ex-wife? He usually introduced her as "Conner's mother."

Ty's dark brows shot up his forehead. "Oh."

Autumn was used to Ty's reaction. She clearly was not Sam's type of woman.

"What are you up to?" Sam asked his former teammate.

"Just viewing prospect tapes."

"Anyone look promising?" Sam asked, all nonchalant, as if he hadn't just been talking about muffins and cupcakes.

"A kid from Russia and a sophomore from Syracuse with a wicked wrist shot."

"You looking at rookies?"

"Yeah. We're loaded with prima donna vets like you."

"Dad!"

Sam turned to Conner. "I'm coming."

"It was nice to see you again, Autumn." Ty turned, and said over his shoulder, "If you see Jules around, tell him I'm looking for him." Then he was gone, the sound of his shoes silenced by the rubber matting.

"You think you're going to be warm enough now?"

Autumn nodded, and as Sam stepped onto the

ice, she leaned forward and picked up her coat. Sam skated next to Conner and picked up his stick. The two passed the puck back and forth, and she watched the way Sam paused to touch his son's head and back and patiently helped him when he fell. The two skated side by side. Sam made it look easy, smooth, while Conner struggled, teetering and almost falling every inch of the way. Sam said something, his low voice mixing with Conner's childish tones. The two laughed, and her heart lifted a little in her chest.

The blanket fell from Autumn's shoulders and pooled at her waist as she reached into her coat pocket. She pulled out her BlackBerry before her heart pinched, too. Before she got all weepy at the sight. She read her e-mails, sent text messages to Shiloh, and brought up the calendar on her phone. The Friday after Thanksgiving she and Conner were leaving on a minivacation. They needed to leave early Friday morning, but Thanksgiving was Sam's holiday this year, which was annoying since Sam was Canadian and didn't celebrate Thanksgiving on the third Thursday in November. Usually, if it was Sam's holiday, and *if* he was going to be in town, which was rare, he kept Conner overnight. She needed to talk to him about that and hoped like heck he'd let Conner come home that night so they could head out at daybreak. It was the first Thanksgiving in a long time that she wouldn't be making a big meal for her brother and Conner. Conner would be with Sam, Vince at work, and she'd have the whole day to herself.

"Are you waiting for someone?"

She looked up past black-and-brown plaid pants, black shirt, and paisley tie, beneath a peach-colored argyle sweater. Muscles bulged the arms of his shirt and the collar around his neck. He had dark skin, black spiky hair, and deep green eyes.

"I'm waiting for my son." She pointed to the ice where Conner once again stood between Sam's skates.

"You're Conner's mother?"

"Yep."

"I'm Julian." He sat next to her. "And I believe you're planning my wedding."

"Oh." She took in his pastel sweater, and said, "You're Bo Ross's fiancé." She stuck out her hand. "It's nice to meet you."

He took her hand in his. "I'm glad you talked Chelsea and Bo out of a double ceremony. Some-

251

times they finish each other's sentences, and I was afraid I might end up marrying the wrong sister."

Autumn smiled. She'd only met with the twins for a short time, but she thought Julian's concern was justified. She also thought, given Julian's fashion risks, it was probably a good thing Bo loved black and white.

"Nice day dress."

Her brows shot up her forehead, and she let go of his hand. He knew what a day dress was? "Thanks. I got it at Le Frock. A little vintage store on Pine."

"I know where it is. Last summer I got a shark-skin suit there."

"Blue?"

"Yeah."

"I remember it. I bet you look great."

"I'm the only one who likes it." He shrugged. "I met Conner a few weeks ago after the Stars game." His gaze skimmed her face. "You're different than I would have imagined an ex-wife of Sam's."

"Not a long-legged, big-lipped supermodel?"

"No. You're prettier than his supermodels."

Autumn laughed. "Right."

"Seriously. Until now, I thought Sam had horrible taste in women, but you're a surprise. A gorgeous redhead."

It was such an outrageous lie, she laughed even harder. She put her hand on his shoulder and gave him a little shove like he was Vince. He was built like Vince.

She glanced up as she heard the shh shh shh of skates on ice. Sam stopped a few feet away within a shower of glittering snow, his blue gaze icy as he looked at Julian.

"Savage is looking for you, jagbag."

Sam grabbed frozen peas from his freezer and shut the door. He shoved the bag beneath his sweatshirt and held it against his shoulder. He wandered into the living room toward the huge windows and looked out at the city and the bay beyond. When he'd seen Autumn laughing with Julian, touching him, relaxed and easy, something inside him had snapped. Snapped right in two, and he'd called Julian a jagbag. Not that he had any qualms about insulting another man. Not even men he liked. And he liked Julian, but he usually knew *why* he was insulting another guy.

253

You can certainly entertain any woman you like here, Autumn had told him the other day. *Just as I can entertain whomever I like in my house.* Until that day, he'd never really thought about her entertaining anyone. In her house or anywhere else. Probably because Conner had never mentioned any other man but Vince. So, Sam had always just assumed that there had never been anyone in her life. He'd never wondered if she had a boyfriend, a friend with benefits, or just the occasional hookup.

He wondered about it now, and he wondered why he was uncomfortable with the thought of her with anyone. He'd like to tell himself that it was because he didn't want his son exposed to random boyfriends. That Vince was already one too many men in his son's life.

There was more to it. Maybe he just didn't like the thought of someone sleeping in her bed, pressed tight against her smooth skin, in a house that he'd technically bought.

No, there was more to it than that. He didn't care about the money he gave her to support Conner. He couldn't say the same about someone pressed against her skin, though. But of all the men on the planet, he had the least right to have an issue with whomever she pressed against. He knew that, but that didn't stop him from thinking about her lately.

A lot. Autumn and that weekend in Vegas kept slipping into his memory like a dream that he couldn't shake. Like a hot, hazy dream filled with reckless desire and consuming need.

Maybe it was because he was spending more time with Conner and seeing her more often. Maybe because he was usually on the road, and these past few days he'd had too much time on his hands and had been thinking about putting his hands on her. Maybe because he hadn't put his hands on anyone for a while.

Maybe he was just bored.

Whatever it was, maybe it was time to figure it out.

Chapter Twelve

Any Man of Mine:
Does Dishes

Autumn sat at the head of her dining-room table, her head bowed. She held Vince's hand in her left and Sam's in her right. Conner sat beside Sam with his eyes closed. "Bless us Oh Lord for Thy gifts we are about to receive," she prayed as Vince and Sam glared at each other over the stuffed turkey in the middle of the table on her mother's lace cloth. "May our bodies be nourished and our hearts grateful." She squeezed her brother's hand, and added, "And can we all just get along. Amen."

Sam let go of her hand and smiled. "Amen. Great prayer."

257

"Especially that part where you channeled Rodney King," Vince added.

"Knock knock."

"Who's there?" all three asked at once

"Pass the mash potatoes."

"Pass the mash potatoes who?"

Conner shrugged. "Pass the mash potatoes to me. I'm starving."

Sam shook his head as he spooned potatoes onto Conner's plate. "You're going to seriously have to work on your jokes." He spooned some for himself, then handed the bowl to Autumn. The tips of her fingers touched his before she pulled back.

Usually on holidays, Autumn dressed for comfort, but today wasn't a usual holiday, and she'd dressed in a fitted white blouse and a black pencil skirt that hugged her body and made her look like a fifties pinup model. She'd had mixed feeling about dressing up because Sam was coming to dinner. On the one hand, she didn't want him to think she'd squeezed into her skirt because of him. On the other hand, she didn't want him to see her in old sweats. Once she opened the door and seen Sam, she was glad she'd made the effort. He looked cool and hot at the same time in black wool pants and gray V-neck sweater with a white T-shirt beneath. Not like the last time when she'd seen him, all sweaty and scruffy radiating body heat.

"Aren't you Canadian?" Vince forked sliced turkey on his plate.

"Yeah."

"So why are you here?"

Autumn kicked him under the table. "Be nice, Vin," she warned.

Vince turned and looked at her. His eyes wide and innocent. "I'm just asking. I'm sure Sam doesn't mind answering a simple question."

"Not at all." He looked across the table and give Vince a big kiss-my-ass grin. "Autumn and Conner were gracious enough to invite me."

Which wasn't really true. She hadn't even planned to make Thanksgiving dinner. Conner was supposed to be at Sam's and Vince at work.

"I thought you were going to spend a quiet day alone packing," Vince reminded her as he took the potatoes from her.

Which she had, until a few days ago, when she suddenly learned that Conner was bringing Sam to Thanksgiving at *her* house and *she* was cooking. She still wasn't quite sure how that had all transpired. Naturally, she'd had to invite Vince, who fortunately, or unfortunately—depending on how she chose to look at it—had an hour free for dinner. Just enough time to drive to her house, eat, stir things up, and go back to work. She supposed she should just be thankful that Vince would be there less than an hour. Not nearly long enough for Sam to get all comatose on L-tryptophan so that Vince could go commando on him.

"Where are you and Conner going tomorrow?" Sam asked, and forked turkey on and his and Conner's plates.

"I've rented a beach house in Moclips." Autumn added a little cranberry to her plate. "It's about a two-hour drive from Seattle."

"Never heard of it."

"That's probably because you spend your vacations in the upper rooms at Scores," Vince said.

Sam raised a brow. "What do you know about those upper rooms at Scores?"

"Just what I've read."

"Giving your fifth-grade education a workout with big words like *lap* and *dance*?"

"Yeah. And with letters like *f* and *u*."

"Little ears." Autumn lifted her finger off her fork and pointed to Conner. "We rented the same house last summer and really enjoyed it, but I've read that it's kind of stormy this time of year." She talked about clamming and sitting on the beach. She talked about Conner flying his kite and the little Moclips museum. She'd never talked so much in her life, but she kept it up until both men retreated back into their caves and shut the hell up.

"Are you about through talking?" Vince asked her before he took a bite of his croissant.

"Are you?"

"Not by half."

"Then I'm going to have Conner fill your ears with nonstop knock-knock jokes." She held up one hand. "I swear to God, Vince."

He took a deep breath and let it out slowly, defeated for the moment. Sam laughed, and Vince shot him a look that said he was retreating, but the war was far from over.

"Knock knock."

"Not now, Conner. Just eat your dinner please."

"Where's the green bean casserole?" Conner asked.

Of course the one thing she didn't make was the one thing he asked about. Since she was leaving in the morning, she hadn't gone all out.

She'd cooked just the basics, and not a ton, so she wouldn't have a lot of leftovers to rot in the refrigerator. "We'll have it at Christmas."

Vince poured gravy on his potatoes and turkey and looked across at Sam. "How's that shoulder?"

"About 60 percent." Sam lifted his elbow away from his body and grinned. "Thanks for asking, frog squat."

Conner laughed, Vince's gaze narrowed, and tension pulled at the back of Autumn's skull. She didn't know what a frog squat was. She was sure Conner didn't know either, but she was fairly sure it wasn't nice. She pointed to Sam. "Did you hear what I said to Vince?" She knocked on an invisible door. "Until your ears bleed."

He tilted his head back and laughed like everything was just hilarious. Then he settled in and ate as if he was on death row, and this was his last meal. He seemed happy and relaxed, like he ate dinner at her house every day. Like they were friends. Like they hadn't been going at each other's throat a few months ago, and like her brother wasn't staring holes through him. He didn't seem bothered by anything, and several times she caught him watching her as if he was looking for something.

"What's wrong?" she asked.

"Not a thing." He reached for more turkey and stuffing. "You're a very good cook. I didn't know that about you."

Why would he? "Thank you."

"Hey, Dad, you should move in here." Conner pushed his peas beneath his roll as if his mother wouldn't notice. "We have a bedroom downstairs."

Autumn's forehead got tight and achy.

Sam chewed and swallowed as if giving it some thought. "I don't know. I have a lot of stuff. And where would I put that water wall you like so much?"

Vince muttered something under his breath that sounded like an impossible suggestion for where Sam could put the "water wall." By the time dinner was over, Autumn was so tense her spine felt brittle.

Vince looked at his watch and placed his napkin beside his plate. "Gotta get back to the grind."

Vince was her brother, her friend and protector. Besides Conner, he was the only family she had, but she was relieved to see him go.

"I drew you a picture, Uncle Vince. It's in my

263

art center." Conner jumped down and ran from the room

Vince stood and tucked his Titan Security shirt into his Dickeys.

Sam leaned back and pointed to Vince's belt. "Where's your gun, cowboy?"

"I don't need a gun, asshole. There are more than a hundred ways to kill someone." He smiled. "And a hundred ways to dispose of a body in places it will never be found."

Autumn knew he was kidding. Kind of. "Well, I hope you come over while I'm gone and eat the leftover turkey. Or do you want to take some with you. Pie?"

Vince ignored her. "I wasn't around the last time you hurt Autumn. I'm here now, and it's not going to happen again."

Sam folded his arms across his chest and leaned the dining-room chair back on two legs. "I heard you the first time."

There'd been a first time? Where had she been? She stood and followed her brother into the living room. "What was that about?"

He gave her a big hug, the kind of deep squeeze that settled in her bones and let her know how much he loved her. The kind of love that would last forever. No matter how much he made her mad. "Call me when you get to your beach house tomorrow, so I know you've made it."

She didn't tell him not to worry about her. He would anyway. "I will."

"Here it is." Conner walked into the room and handed Vince the picture. "We're playing putt-putt like last year."

"Yep. There you are." Vince pointed to the little blond figure, then folded the paper and put it in his breast pocket. "I'll study it at work." He gave Conner a quick hug, then moved down the stairs. "I'll come over while you're gone, check up on things, and eat the leftovers."

"Thanks." She raised her hand as he walked out the door and shut it behind him.

She felt like a half-ton brick had been lifted from one shoulder. The other half ton was still in the dining room. "Are you going to help me clean up?" she asked Conner.

He shook his head. "I gotta draw Dad a picture." He took off down the hall to his bedroom. Typical. "Tell me when it's dessert time," he called out over his shoulder.

Autumn walked into the dining room and stopped in her tracks. Sam stood at the kitchen sink, the spray nozzle in one hand. Autumn's gaze stuck on the stretch and pull of his thin sweater across his wide shoulders and big arms as he reached for a plate on the counter. He whistled as he rinsed in one side of the sink and bent over to put the cleaned plates in the dishwasher. No man had ever done her dishes. Sam towering over her sink, squirting water all over, then bending over, was about the sexiest thing she'd ever seen in her life.

He rose and looked across his shoulder. "That was fun."

"That was the dinner from hell," she said as she grabbed the basket of croissants and moved into the kitchen, the heels of her red pumps lightly thudding across the vinyl floor. "I wouldn't have guessed you knew how to load a dishwasher."

"Growing up, I spent a lot of time in the kitchen. After my dad died, my mom went to work full-time, so Ella and I had to split up the chores."

She'd never thought of Sam as a kid, losing his father or stepping into his dad's shoes. A lot like Vince. Only their father hadn't died. He'd run off.

"Most of the time I paid Ella to do mine." Sam chuckled. "Which used to make my mom livid because then I'd have to ask her for more lunch money."

She'd met his mom a few times when she'd come to Seattle to spend time with Sam and Conner. "How's your mother?" she asked, as she set the basket on the counter.

His blue eyes looked across at hers and slid to her mouth. "Good." His gaze slowly moved down her body, over her breasts and the curve her waist and hips in the tight skirt, all the way to her red shoes. "She'll probably be here for Christmas."

"That will be nice for Conner." She ignored the tingle in her pulse and opened a drawer by his right hip, pulling out a roll of tinfoil. "You don't have to clean up."

"It's the least I can do for inviting myself." He raised his gaze to hers and dried his hands on a dish towel.

She'd cleaned as she'd cooked, so there wasn't much more to do. "I thought Conner invited you."

"Conner's five." One corner of his mouth lifted, and fine lines appeared in the corners of his eyes. "I might have planted the suggestion in his head."

She paused in the act of tearing some tinfoil.

"Why?" Why was he there? Rinsing her dishes, filling up her kitchen with his big shoulders and bigger presence. Running his gaze up and down her body and making her stomach take a tumble.

He flipped the dish towel onto her shoulder, then moved into the dining room. Her gaze took a journey of its own, moving down the back of his gray sweater to the back pockets of his black wool pants. There were just some men on the planet who filled out a pair of pants to perfection. Sam was one of those guys.

"Curious," he said as he returned with the turkey.

"No." She wasn't curious. She'd seen his butt, and even though it had been a while, she imagined that it was as tight as ever. The kind of tight that came from serious exercise.

"What?"

"What?" She looked up into his eyes and tore off a big chunk of tinfoil.

"You asked why I'd invited myself."

Oh yeah. She tossed the roll into the drawer and shut it with her hip.

He set the turkey on the counter. "And I said I was curious."

"About?"

"About what you and Conner do on Thanksgiving."

That's right. She'd allowed herself to get distracted, but in her own defense, she was a bit unnerved. "Probably the same thing you do. Only on a different day." She covered the platter with the tinfoil, scrunching it around the edges.

"I haven't done the whole Thanksgiving thing in years." He closed the dishwasher with his foot. "Here or in Canada."

"That's sad."

"Not really. I'm never sure where I'm going to be on that Monday or Thursday."

That explained his presence. He had nothing better to do. "You really don't have to stay and clean up."

"The quicker the dishes get done, the sooner I get pie."

"Seriously?" She'd been so tense, still was, that she hadn't eaten much, but Sam hadn't suffered from nerves. He'd eaten more than anyone. "You want pie?"

"Honey, I always want pie." He looked into her eyes and reached for the dish towel. Slowly, he pulled it from her shoulder. "It's been a while since I've had good pie."

Somehow, she doubted that. "No pie jokes." She lifted a hand and rubbed the back of her neck.

"I never joke about pie." He tossed the towel and moved behind her. He pushed her hand aside. "Pie is serious business."

"What are you doing?"

"You're all knotted up." He pressed his thumbs into the base of her neck and pushed inward. "You were so tense during dinner, I thought you were going to shatter."

She'd thought she might shatter, too, and his hands felt good. So good, she almost moaned out loud. Totally inappropriate, though, and she'd stop him in a minute. "That might have had something to do with you and my brother acting like idiots." Then he pressed his thumbs into the base of her skull, rubbed in tight circles, and she put her hands on the counter to keep from melting into a puddle by his size-fourteen loafers.

"It could have been worse."

She dropped her head forward and her hair fell across her cheeks. "Yeah. You two could have jumped across the table and stabbed each other with butter knives."

He laughed and slid his thumbs beneath the collar of her blouse. "Unbutton your shirt."

"Are you high?"

"Not today." He squeezed her shoulders in his big hot hands. "Don't you trust me?"

"Of course not."

"That's probably wise." He laughed, a soft little chuckle that slid up her skull with his thumbs. "Your collar is in the way."

"I'm not taking my shirt off."

"Not off. Just maybe two buttons to loosen up your collar." He pressed his fingers into her knotted shoulder muscles, and her eyes about rolled back into her head. "I get my kinks worked all the time. I'm pretty much a professional."

Two buttons. She raised her hands and unbuttoned her shirt to the white bow in the middle of her white bra.

His voice got a little deeper, and he said, "Slide your hair to one side."

With her right hand, she reached behind her and pulled her hair over her right shoulder.

He pushed the back of her collar. "One more. I promise I won't look."

She unbuttoned one more, and somehow the

271

top of her blouse was halfway down her shoulders.

"Better?" His hands squeezed her bare shoulders.

"Yes." Definitely not safer, though. But God, his hands were magic, sliding over her skin and pressing into her taut muscles. The tips of his fingers slid across her collarbone, and his thumbs worked the knots where her neck met her shoulders. Her tension eased, and she relaxed. With each magic squeeze of his warm hands, her guard lowered, and her body heated.

His palms worked outward, pausing to squeeze the balls of her shoulders and slipping down her arms. His hands spanned her ribs on the outside of her blouse, and he pressed his thumbs into her spine. "Are you sure you don't want to take off your shirt?"

No, she wasn't sure at all. She wasn't sure she didn't want to lean back into him, into his solid chest, and stay there a while. "I'm sure."

He slid his hands down her sides to her waist then to her hips. She felt his warm breath by her ear. "I like your skirt."

Her tongue stuck to the roof of her mouth, and she swallowed hard. "It's vintage."

"It's tight," he whispered against the sensitive side of her neck. "It makes your ass look good." His palms slid to her belly and pulled her back against his chest. The curve of her bottom pressed into his groin. "It gives me bad thoughts." Through the fabric of his pants and her skirt, his erection brushed against her bottom. "Wanna hear a few?"

Yes, she did, but she knew it was a really bad idea. Her voice was weak and not at all convincing when she answered, "No."

He kissed the side of her throat. "Is this still one of your sweet spots?" The wet press of his hot mouth forced a shudder to work through her relaxed body from the inside out. "Mmm," he hummed against her skin, adding delicious little shivers and sending her into a sensory overload.

She turned and put her hands on his chest to stop him. Through the thin wool of his sweater, and the hard muscles of his chest, she could feel the beating of his heart, much faster than the slow smooth touch of his hands. "We can't do this."

One of his hands moved across her bare shoulder to the side of her face. "I've been thinking about you a lot." His lips touched hers, and her

273

breath caught in her throat. "Thinking about you and wondering."

"What?" Her fingers curled into his sweater.

"Wondering what it is about you that made me lose my mind six years ago." His lips brushed hers, and hot little shivers tingled her spine. She couldn't help it. It was involuntary, just like her palms sliding up his chest, over his shoulder. His face was so close, his nose touched hers. She didn't want him to lose his mind. She didn't want to lose her mind, either.

"Wondering if being with you would make me lose my mind now." He slid his palms to her behind and cupped her bottom in his hands. "I wonder if it would be like the first time we had sex."

She wondered if he even remembered.

He pressed her against him, against the long length of his erection just left of his zipper. "When we were going at it so hard we fell off the bed. So hard we both got rug burns."

Okay. So he did remember.

He rocked against her pelvis. "Would it be like that again?"

Her breath caught in the top of her lungs, and

she moaned a soft, "Yes." She didn't know if she meant yes she remembered or wondered or wanted more. Maybe all three. She couldn't think straight, then he kissed her, and she couldn't think at all. It started with a gentle press of his lips that she felt in the backs of her knees and the soles of her feet. Her heart pounded, and she opened her mouth beneath his. His tongue touched hers, warm and wet, and he tasted like suppressed aggression, reminding her of something she hadn't had for a long time. Something she'd forgotten she liked so much.

Hot sex with a hot-blooded man.

Her pounding heart sped up, flooding every part of her body with liquid fire. Her emotions remained detached from the long, slow kiss, but her body was fully engaged. Aching with need. Itching for him to soothe the desire tightening her nipples.

His pectoral muscles bunched as she slid her hands up his chest to his shoulders and rose to the balls of her feet. She pressed the length of her body into his. Against her bare cleavage, she felt every fiber of his wool sweater. Against her pelvis, she felt his rock-hard erection, and she opened her mouth a little wider and devoured him with passionate, feeding, kisses. Undiluted lust twisted her stomach into knots. It had been so long since she'd felt so alive. So burned up inside. So long since the overwhelming urge to touch and be touched. To eat him up, run her mouth all over him. She moved her hands over his shoulders and back, ran her fingers through his cool hair. She wanted him badly. Wanted the hot push and aggressive tug of sex with Sam. The tumble and grind until she exploded and imploded all at the same time.

Just like before.

She pushed back from the insanity and gasped for breath. She couldn't do this. Not with Sam of all people, and not while her son was in his bedroom coloring pictures.

His hands on her waist tightened, and he pulled her toward him once more.

"No, Sam."

His hands on her waist tightened, his breathing hard as if he'd just finished an hour of sprint training. "Yes, Autumn."

"No." Saying no to Sam wasn't easy, but being with Sam was impossible. The last time had cost her a huge chunk of her heart and changed her life completely. She swallowed hard and shook her head. "No."

He looked at her through blue eyes smoldering with lust and determination. She'd seen it before. Years ago. She'd fallen for it then. She was older now. Wiser, too.

"What are you doing, Sam?"

"The same thing you're doing. Getting really turned on."

"Conner could walk in here at any second." But that was only a part of why she'd stopped him.

"I'm sure you have a lock on a door in one of the rooms in this house."

"That's tacky."

"That's what adults do."

She took a step back, and her shoulders hit the closed refrigerator door. "Is that what you do in your house? Lock yourself inside a bedroom with one of your girlfriends?"

His jaw tightened, and his gaze turned hard. "I've never had a girlfriend anywhere near Conner."

She pulled up the shoulders of her blouse. It didn't matter. "Why are you here? Why did you want Conner to invite you to Thanksgiving? Like we're a family?"

He ran his hands through the sides of his short blond hair, then dropped them to his sides. "I don't know. Just bored, I guess."

That's what she'd thought. "Go find someone else to play with you." She looked down and buttoned her shirt. "The last time you were bored, I ended up alone and pregnant in a Vegas hotel room."

Chapter Thirteen

Any Man of Mine:
Pushes My Buttons

Rain pelted the windows of Autumn's rented beach house as the storm pushed the black surging tide up the beach to crash within the long grasses whipping about in the extreme winds. A kitchen light illuminated her from behind as she stood in front of an entire wall of windows in the A-frame house.

Lightning flashed within the black clouds, and white cracks splintered the night sky a second before thunder boomed. She felt it through the hardwood beneath her bare feet.

Upstairs, in one of the two bedrooms, Conner

slept, blissfully unaware of Nature's chaos. He'd passed out about an hour before, after a full day of beachcombing in his rubber boots and rain-coat. The weather had been fairly tame until the storm had rolled in three hours ago. Autumn loved a good storm, and this one was proving to be spectacular.

She folded her arms across the thin top of her wiener-dog pajamas. If she hadn't been alone with only an exhausted five-year-old, it might have been nice to crack open the bottle of Cab-ernet Sauvignon she'd bought to take back to Shiloh. It might be nice to turn up the fire and listen to the thunder as she laid her cheek on a big shoulder and enjoyed a glass of wine with a man.

Yesterday had been tense, from the moment Sam had arrived until the moment he'd left. Beyond the general tension she usually felt near Sam, he and Vince had been at each other's throats, and both took it to a whole new level.

She hunched her shoulders against the air that chilled her skin and tightened her breasts be-neath the T-shirt material. There had been a few brief moments yesterday when her tension had eased. When Sam had smoothed it away with his hands. Then he'd kissed her neck and filled the void with a whole different kind of tension. And in those few moments, when he'd kissed her and she'd kissed him back like she was starving, he'd woken every cell in her body. He'd reminded her that she was thirty. That she wanted to be touched and held. She wanted to be wanted. He'd reminded her that she wanted more at night than the battery-operated boyfriend she had to hide in a box on her closet shelf, away from a snoopy five-year-old. He'd reminded her that dragging a chair to her closet and uncovering her special toy boy, was an empty substitute for a real flesh-and-blood boy toy.

And she wanted a boy toy. A hot, pretty one. Like Sam.

Thunder rolled across the sky and boomed beneath her feet. Lightning flashed like a strobe within the clouds. No. Not Sam. The fact that his name had even entered her head was horrifying. Proof that she needed some skin-on-skin time. That it had been *waaay* too long since she'd rolled around naked in a man's sheets.

The thunder boomed again, and she waited for the lightning. It didn't happen. Just a steady boom boom boom until she realized it was the front door. A frown creased her forehead as she moved across the carpeted living room, past the stairs to the entry. The storm wasn't bad enough for evacuation, and she made sure the chain was latched before she opened the door. She flipped on the lights, and through the crack, Sam stood in the downpour, his hair plastered to his head.

"What are you doing here?" she yelled to him above the sound of the rain.

"I don't know."

She closed the door just long enough to unlatch the chain before she opened it again. "There's a travel advisory."

Water dripped down his forehead and stuck his eyelashes together, but he didn't move. He just stood there staring at her like he was lost.

She flipped her watch over and looked at the face. "It's ten o'clock, Sam."

Droplets ran down his cheeks as his gaze lowered from her eyes to her mouth. "Is it?"

"Why are you here?"

"I don't know."

"You don't?"

He shook his head. "I don't know why one minute I was sitting at Benihana with Ty and Darby and some of the scouts, and I just got

282

up and left." The shoulders of his thick hooded sweatshirt were soaked, and his gaze continued lower, down her throat to her cold, hard breasts. "I don't know why I got in my truck and drove two hours through this god-awful storm." He looked back up into her eyes. "I don't know why I've been standing outside this house for ten minutes before knocking on the fucking door."

She wasn't going to ask why again. He clearly wasn't making sense. Maybe not playing hockey made him crazy. "Sam, I'm confused."

"That only seems fair." He reached for her and grabbed a big handful of her shirt just below her breasts. "You confuse the hell out of me." He pulled her across the threshold. Outside into the rain.

Cold droplets hit her face and neck. She lifted her face to tell him he was crazy, but his mouth silenced hers. Hot, slick, and demanding. She stood perfectly still while he kissed her, waiting for him to stop. Waiting for her hands to creep up his chest so she could shove him away and slam the door in his face. But the kiss was too hot, too delicious, and he must have slipped her some of his craziness because she rose onto the balls of her feet and kissed him back. Her tongue touched his, swirled and tangled. Heat radiated from his hand and mouth and warmed up places deep in her belly and between her thighs. Cold rain soaked her hair and arms. Thunder boomed, and rain slid past their sealed lips. She slid her fingers into his wet hair and sucked the air from his lungs.

He pulled back first, and the black night cast a shadow across his eyes and nose. Her heart pounded like the chaotic sky, and she fought for breath, sucking in cold air and water and him. She couldn't see him clearly, but she didn't need to see him to know that his eyes burned with his desire. It surrounded them both in hot waves. Pressing in and demanding satisfaction. The kind that could only be sated with hot skin against hot skin.

"Come inside, Sam." She'd felt it once before. Years ago. Big. Forceful. Dominating. Like the man himself.

"Where's Conner?"

"Asleep." This was dangerous. A dangerous game she'd lost in the past, but she was older. Wise enough to feed her lust while her heart remained detached.

"You know what I want."

Yes. She knew. She knew she was probably going to regret it in the morning. But that was hours away, and she wanted to spend those hours satisfying the ache pounding her like the thunder overhead.

She took his hand and pulled him across the threshold. She closed the door behind him and leaned back against it as he reached down his back, grabbed a fistful of his sweatshirt, and pulled it over his head. The bottom of the thick shirt lifted from the waistband of a pair of worn Levi's resting low on his hips. It rose from the five buttons and up the narrow blond line of hair on his flat belly. His happy trail circled his navel, then climbed up the ridges of his abdomen. He wiped his face and dropped the sweatshirt on the floor. Then stood before her in wet jeans and damp skin and his figure-eight splint. He shook his head like a dog, sending droplets everywhere.

Droplets landed on her cheek and top lip. She took a deep breath in an effort to slow her racing pulse. "How's your shoulder?"

"My shoulder's fine. Your shirt's wet."

She dragged her gaze from the short blond hair on his big defined chest and pecs that looked like they'd been chiseled by a Nordic god. She glanced down at the wiener dog on the shirt clinging to her chilled skin. In the middle of his long dog body, her nipples made two very hard points.

"You should probably go ahead and take it off before you catch a cold."

She tilted her head to one side and glanced back up, past his square chin and slightly crooked nose and into his blue eyes, all sleepy with lust. "You worried about me?"

"I'm worried you won't take off that shirt."

"You do it." She raised her arms above her head, and when he stepped toward her, the place between her thighs got all tight and needy. His fingers curled into the bottom of her shirt and racked her sensitive skin up her sides. He pulled the damp shirt over her head and dropped it next to his sweatshirt.

There was no turning back. She leaned forward and pressed her open mouth to the hollow of his throat. He tasted warm and musky, his skin damp from the rain. Her hard nipples raked his hot naked chest, and he moaned. Before she lost all reason, she said close to his ear, "Bored?"

"I wasn't bored, yesterday. I was turned on." He slid his other hand up and filled his palm with her soft breast. "And I wanted you. I couldn't think past all the parts I wanted and in what order I wanted them."

She slid her hands up his sides and chest. "Which parts do you want first?"

His voice a low gravel across her skin. "These parts." His thumbs brushed her nipples, forcing a soft moan from her lips. "I want these parts in my mouth before I go south to my favorite part."

She wanted that, too. Wanted it so bad she had to fight the urge to toss him down and take what she wanted. She chuckled, kind of breezy, like she wasn't burning up and feeling greedy. "My toes?" She had all night.

He shoved one hand down her pajama bottoms and beneath her panties. "This." He cupped her crotch in his hot hand, and she almost fell to the floor. "Right here where you're wet, and not from the rain." His fingers brushed upward, into her moist flesh, and everything got hotter, more intense. A blur. A rush. "I want deep inside you, where you're tight. I want to rub your little button with the head of my cock until you scream my name like you used to."

She didn't think she'd ever screamed his name, but she didn't care. It didn't matter as she tore at his clothes, and he pushed her pants and panties down her legs. She stepped out of them and reached for his erection. She wanted him, and she wasn't going to wait. She didn't want to take it slow.

Beneath the entrance light, he was naked and beautiful, and she took his penis in her hand. Huge and hot. Bigger than she remembered. The pulse of the thick bulging veins pounded in her palm. Beyond Sam, lightning streaked across the sky and flashed within the darkened room. Thunder shook the air and the foundation of the beach house. "I want that, too, Sam."

Sam looked at Autumn standing before him, her red hair slicked back, her green eyes bright and alive with lust. Pulsing urgency thumped through his veins. His lungs squeezed, and the pit of his belly got tight. His dick was so hard, he hurt. Her lips parted as she moved her hand up and down the shaft. He locked his knees to keep from falling and lowered his head. He wanted to take it slow. She deserved slow, sweet sex, but the instant his lips touched hers, the raw, naked edge of desire cut straight to the primal place in his core that demanded he go for it. No finesse. No thought beyond throwing her down and going completely caveman on her.

She inhaled, sucking his breath from him, and he was gone. Gone to the hot lust whipping through his body and grasping his testicles in a fiery squeeze. Her mouth opened, and she kissed him. A sweet liquid warmth. Like the sweet liquid warmth that waited for him inside her body. Their slick tongues touched, and he slid his palms over her breasts, her belly, her thighs. Once more, he slipped his hand between her legs. She'd shaved her red pubic hair into a landing strip. A little bare. A little hair. His favorite, and he felt her where she was warm and wet and waiting for him to thrust inside of her. He pushed his erection into her hand, in and out, simulating the ultimate act. Her thumb spread a bead of moisture in the cleft of his head, and he groaned long and loud, in pain as he sank to the floor, taking her with him. He kissed her mouth and her breasts and reached for the wallet in his back pocket. Somehow he ended up on his back with her on top, rolling the condom down his shaft to the base.

"I don't want to hurt you," she said, her voice husky with need.

"The only way you're going to hurt me, honey, is if you stop now."

Her chuckle was husky, like her voice, as she rose above him, then slowly lowered, and he slid into her hot, extremely tight body. He thrust up, and her head fell back with a long, drawn-out moan. The light in the entrance bounced off her round white breasts and tight pink nipples, down her belly to her red strip. Lost in waves of mindless pleasure, he growled, "That feels good, Autumn." She rose, and he lifted his hips and shoved into her hard. "Yes." He pushed deeper, the head of his penis pressed against her cervix, stretching and filling her up. He grabbed her thighs as she rode him like the queen of the Calgary Stampede. Within a few short thrusts, the first pulse of her orgasm squeezed him hard, milking him, and he set his teeth to keep from coming.

"Oh, God." A husky moan slipped past her lips, and she planted her hands on his chest. Her hair fell over her face. "Don't stop. Please, don't stop. I'll kill you if you stop."

No way was he going to stop, and when the last wave of her orgasm racked her body, he reached for her shoulders and turned her until he was on top. His penis deep within her body, he looked down into her green eyes, pulled out, and plunged even deeper. "Put your legs around my back." When he felt her tight thighs around his hips, he started slow, pumping his hips in a smooth rhythm. "More?"

"Yes."

He rested most of his weight on his right forearms, and he held her face in his palm as he gave her more, hitting just the right place deep inside her.

"Harder," she moaned.

"You sure?"

Her pink lips parted, and she sucked in a breath. "Yes."

He drove into her faster, harder, deeper. Stroking her walls, and sweet spot, with the thick head of his penis and hard shaft. Over and over, and he felt the familiar hard tug of her second orgasm. It started deep inside and radiated down his erection, squeezing him tighter than before. So tight he set his teeth against his own release. Against the sharp pleasure of holding back.

Then she cried out again. The sound of his name was drowned out by the boom of thunder, and he finally let the intense pleasure curl his gut and sweep across his flesh. It grabbed him hard and harder as her vaginal walls convulsed around him. He heard his own deep groan as he felt his own orgasm ripped from his groin. Ripped from his soul, almost as violent as the storm outside. Over and over until he was so spent he could hardly breathe, like he'd just finished a three-minute shift that ended with a fight in the corner. He lowered his forehead to the floor next to her ear. He'd had a lot of sex in his life, but this felt different. Bigger, better, more primal.

"Jesus Christ," he said, still panting hard. "I'm wrung from the inside out. If you came like that in Vegas, no wonder I married you."

Autumn stood in the kitchen and raised a glass of red wine to her lips. Several emotions churned and collided in her stomach. Shock and shame battled for the top spot, but more than anything, she was embarrassed by her total lack of control. She expected that sort of shameful behavior from Sam. Sam was . . . Sam. She didn't roll around on the floor having sex. Not these days.

And not with Sam, for God's sake!

In the back of the house, the toilet flushed, and the bathroom door opened. She looked down to make sure her terry-cloth robe was securely tied around her waist. After Sam had scooped up his clothes and retreated to the bathroom, she'd picked up her pjs and run upstairs. She'd thrown on a robe and fought hard against the urge to lock the door and hide under the heavy covers until she figured out what to do. Or until Sam left. Whichever came first.

Unfortunately, neither was an option. She was an adult and had to face the music.

Sam walked into the kitchen, shirtless, a ladder of hard muscles rising from the waistband of his jeans. He picked up the bottle of wine and looked at the label. "I'm usually a beer guy." He reached into a cupboard and pulled out a glass. "But I'm going to save you the shame of drinking alone."

She wished he'd saved her the shame of shoving her hand down his pants. She drained her glass and held it toward him for a refill.

He dipped his head, and his blue eyes looked into hers. "Are you mad about what I said?"

She shook her head. She hadn't heard anything beyond the rush of blood leaving her brain and her own voice yelling his name. Thank God Conner hadn't woken up. "What did you say?"

"If you don't remember, forget it." He looked a little relieved and filled her glass. "If you're not mad, why is your face all red?"

She put a hand on her hot cheek. "The wine."

"Does wine make you frown?" He poured the Cabernet into his own glass. "Do you want me to apologize?"

If he had to ask that, he wouldn't mean it anyway. And besides, an apology from Sam would be so unexpected, she just might pass out. "No. I'm not mad."

"Then what are you?" He set the bottle on the counter and took a drink.

"Mostly, I'm embarrassed by my spectacular loss of control."

He lowered the glass and smiled. "It was spectacular."

She shook her head and fought the urge to smack him. "Do you know how many times I've told myself that you were the last person on the face the earth that I would ever have sex with?"

One corner of his mouth turned downward. "I'm guessing a few."

"More than a few. Do you know how many times I told myself that I would never have sex with you again, even if it meant saving my own life?" She took a drink. "Just a month ago, if given the choice between having sex with you and getting hit by a truck, I would have taken the truck."

"Yeah, I think you mentioned something like that a few times in the past five years." He spread his arms wide. "And yet you chose me and spectacular sex."

"I meant my loss of control was spectacular."

"The sex was spectacular." He raised a finger off his glass and pointed at her. "You came twice."

She shrugged and turned her face away before her cheeks caught fire. "It had been a while."

"How long?"

"Never mind."

His finger on her hot cheek turned her face toward him. "A few months?"

"Drop it." She took a drink. Maybe if she got drunk enough, she'd think the whole thing was funny. There probably wasn't enough booze in the world for that, though.

"A year?" At her silence his brows shot up his forehead. "A year and a half?"

"I'm a mother. I work and take care of Conner. When I have time without him, I get a pedicure."

"A foot rub is no substitute for good sex."

"Depends on the quality of the foot rub. Some

people are good at it. Others just can't get the good spots."

"I wouldn't know." He chuckled. "How long since someone rubbed your good spots?"

"Really long." She moved into the living room, and said over her shoulder, "I have a son. Your son. Remember?"

He followed and stood next to her in front of the windows. Waves crashed just beyond the sea grass, and she felt rather than saw him raise his glass to his lips.

"Looks like the storm might be letting up," she pointed out.

"Two years?"

"Are we back to that?"

"We never left it because you didn't answer."

Lightning struck farther in the distance, but the rain still poured down in sheets. "More than five years. Less than six."

It took him a few moments to do the math. The second he figured it out, he choked on his wine. "That has to be bullshit. No one can go that long."

"Why? Why is it so hard for you to believe?" She held up her fingers and counted down the reasons. "I was pregnant for nine months, covered in baby vomit for an entire year after that, and trying to start a business on almost no sleep. I was tired for the first three years of Conner's life, and the last thing I wanted was another person in my life demanding my time. Being a working mother is very difficult."

"You haven't had sex in almost six years?" Out of everything she'd just said, he was stuck on the actual years. "Jesus. No wonder you're so mean."

"I'm not mean." She took a drink, and the sleeve of her robe brushed his bare arm. "It's just hard for you to believe a person can go that long because you've probably never gone without sex for six days."

"It's been longer than six days. Sometimes I'm on the road for two weeks."

"Big whoop."

"But I can tell you one thing," he continued, "if I went without sex for six years, I'd have gone blind by now. Then where would I be? I'm a hockey player. Can't play hockey if I'm blind. Now can I?"

She wondered if he believed his own warped logic. Sadly, he probably did. "On the rare nights I don't work and you have Conner, what am I supposed to do? Go to some bar and pick up a guy?" Hadn't she recently had this same conversation with Shiloh and Vince?

His voice was a low murmur in the darkness when he said, "Some women do."

"Well, I'm not some women. And despite what you might think of me, given the way we met and how I behaved in Vegas, I was never that woman."

"I never thought you were."

Sure. "You made me take a paternity test." He opened his mouth to defend himself, and she held up one hand to stop him. "I understand why you did it. At the time, it made me mad, but I understood."

"If I'd seen Conner first, I never would have asked."

"It doesn't matter. My point is, that the last time I hooked up with a guy I'd met in a bar, it didn't exactly work out for me."

"Yeah." He was quite for a long moment, then said, "But we have Conner. I haven't always been a great dad, but I've always loved him. I've never regretted that he's in my life."

Which brought the conversation around to,

"On the two-hour drive here tonight, did you think to call?"

"Of course, but you would have told me not to come."

"You're right. You can't just invite yourself on our vacation because you want to see Conner." Like Halloween and Thanksgiving.

"This isn't about Conner."

She looked across her shoulder at him. Into the shadows of his profile. "Then what's it about?"

"I'm still trying to figure that one out." He turned to face her and shoved a bare shoulder into the glass. "I think it might have something to do with unfinished business between the two of us."

"Whatever 'business' we had was finished a long time ago." When he'd divorced her.

He brushed his hand across her cheek and pushed her hair behind her ear. "That first night I saw you at Pure, you reminded me of the time when I was ten or eleven and mom took me and Ella to Washington, D.C." His gaze moved over her face and hair. "It was night, and we were standing at the Vietnam Memorial, and I looked out and saw bright blinking lights in the darkness. My mom said they were fireflies. I was so intrigued, I ran after them. Trying to catch one."

She tried to ignore the brush of his fingers on her neck. "Did you just compare me to a fly?"

"To a flash of fire. A bright intriguing light that I wanted to catch and hold in my hands."

When he said things like that, it reminded her of exactly how and why she'd fallen in love with him so easily. If she didn't know him, she might be in danger of falling all over again. "I'm not going to have sex with you again, Sam."

He smiled and dropped his hand to his side. "Okay."

Clearly, he didn't believe her, and the wisest thing to do would be for her to send him home. Or make him go get a hotel room. She pointed to the sofa. "That folds out."

She expected him to argue. To charm her. To kiss her until she gave in and shared her bed. Instead, he grinned as if he'd just gotten his way.

"See you in the morning."

Chapter Fourteen

Any Man of Mine:
Recognizes the Need for Speed

S am stood at the kitchen counter and lowered a couple of whole-grain waffles into the toaster. The previous night's storm had blown over, and the bright morning sun poured in through the windows.

"Mom makes pancakes that look like hearts." Conner knelt in a chair by his side, waiting for the waffles to pop up.

"You told me, but you shouldn't tell anyone else."

"Why?"

" 'Cause some guys at school might not understand heart pancakes and think you're a sissy. You don't want to get your butt kicked." He put his hand on Conner's head and ruffled his fine hair. Sam had risen with the sun pouring in through the windows and had already jogged five miles on the beach. He'd needed to clear his head. To think about the last two days. About Thanksgiving and last night. Had he been bored?

Yes. The Chinooks were on the road, and he was dying to get back in the game, but that wasn't the real reason. He could tell himself that it was about Conner. That he wanted to spend more time with his son before he was cleared to play. And that was true. He did want to spend as much time as possible with Conner before he left again, sometimes for weeks at a time, but Conner wasn't the only reason. And if Sam was honest with himself, he'd admit that his son wasn't the reason he'd jumped in his truck last night and driven through a storm. It was Autumn and the hot compulsion he felt whenever he was around her. The percolating memory of a few days in Vegas and not getting enough.

He'd arrived on her porch last night, rain beating on his shoulders and running down his face, staring at the door. Hot compulsion and percolating memory churning in his gut. He'd stared at the door, a tangle of confusion and desire. For the first time in a very long time, uncertain about a woman. Uncertain whether she'd let him in or slam the door in his face. Uncertain whether she'd let him touch her all over with his hands and mouth. Uncertain if she'd get naked and let him do something about the hard-on she'd given him the night before.

Sam had had a lot of sex in his life. A lot of sex with a lot of different women, but he'd never had sex like that. Autumn had been so hot and turned on. So wild in a way that had nothing to do with whips and handcuffs and naughty outfits but everything to do with how much she wanted him. She hadn't been faking it. Hadn't been trying to impress him or play games. She'd wanted him. Maybe it was just because she hadn't had sex in over five years. Maybe not. Either way, he wanted more.

A lot more.

Earlier, when he'd returned from his jog, he'd found Conner watching cartoons in the middle of the fold-out.

"Dad?" Some sort of long blue fruit snack had been hanging from one side of Conner's mouth. "You're on vacation, too?"

Sam had brushed the forearm of his sweatshirt over his sweaty forehead. "Yep. Is your mom up?"

Conner chewed, and the blue snack slipped up his chin. "Not yet."

"What are you eating?" he'd asked.

"Fruit By The Foot. Want some?"

"No." He'd checked the cupboard and was surprised that there wasn't any real food. Just coffee, some milk, and kid snacks. "Get dressed, and we'll go get some real food." It took them about twenty minutes of driving to find a strange little market that smelled like a weird combo of fish and kettle corn.

"Get a few plates down," Sam said as he slid his hand down Conner's back.

Conner climbed up on the counter and opened a cupboard. "I saw a slug yesterday. Yuck. I hate slugs."

"I smell waffles," Autumn said from the bottom of the stairs. "This is a 'no cooking' vacation. Where did you guys get breakfast stuff?"

Sam looked over his shoulder at Autumn, moving toward the end of the counter in her dried wiener-dog pajamas, and his throat got a little tight. He'd seen a lot of naughty lingerie in his life, for some reason, the wiener dog was hot as hell. Maybe it had something to do with the memory of her cold wet breasts the night before.

Conner peeked around the cupboard door. "Mom, Dad's here," he announced. Like she hadn't known that. Like she hadn't jumped on top of him last night.

"I can see that."

"We found a little store while you slept." Sam pointed to the toaster. "Up for some waffles?"

She raked her fingers through her hair and pushed it behind her ears. "Coffee first." Her bare feet moved across the kitchen floor, and she grabbed a mug above the coffeemaker. Morning light poured in through the windows and caught in strands of her red hair.

"What do we have planned for today?"

She looked at him as she poured. "Well, *we were* going to the Fireman's Breakfast Feed this morning."

"Oh." The waffles popped up, and he quickly

305

put them on the plates Conner had set on the counter. "Lucky you. Now you don't have to go." He put a little butter and syrup on both. "What else?" He handed the plate to Autumn, but she shook her head. Her hair fell across her shoulder.

"Kites." She blew into the mug. "At some point, clam chowder at Paddie's Perch."

He carried his and Conner's plates to a small kitchen table. He wasn't at all surprised she had everything planned out. In Vegas, she'd had a long list. Most of which she never got the chance to cross off. Thanks to him. He smiled at the memory. "What about building sand castles?"

"We don't have the stuff."

He cut into his waffle. "You do now." Her gaze narrowed and he held up one hand. "I know the world does not revolve around me, but it was Conner's idea to build a sand castle."

"Like it was Conner's idea to invite you to Thanksgiving dinner?"

He shoveled a waffle into his mouth and chewed. Yeah, kind of like that, but sand castles were so much better than kites.

She raised the mug to her lips, then lowered it slowly. "Where did you get those clothes?"

He glanced down at his Chinooks T-shirt and jeans. "I brought a duffel." He'd set out last night, spur-of-the-moment, sure, but he'd come prepared to stay. Prepared to figure out what it was about her. Now and five years ago that made him act like a kid again. Like he was thirteen, fantasizing about the girl down the street and riding by her house on his Haro Freestyler, just on the off chance he'd catch a glimpse of her. These days, he had a truck instead of a bike. He was a man not a kid. He liked to think he'd developed some skill with women. A little finesse. Maybe a little charm. That he didn't have to hunt a woman down. Stalk her through the night.

Yeah, that was what he liked to think, but there he was, with Autumn in Moclips, feeling like he was a kid again. Uncertain and freestyling.

"I thought you just jumped up from Benihana and drove here," she said.

She pursed her lips and blew into her mug, and his head got all twisted around with thoughts of what he'd like her to do with that mouth. Things he shouldn't even think about so early in the morning but couldn't help. "I may not have been an official Boy Scout, but I'm always prepared."

He looked at her and smiled around a bite of waffle, remembering her grabbing the condom from his hands and tearing it open with her teeth. "I always keep a duffel of stuff in the truck. Mostly to change at the Key."

"Well, Mr. Unofficial Boy Scout, I didn't particularly want to dig around in the cold wet sand today." She took a drink. "So I'll watch from the deck."

"Can I have some juice, Mom?"

She moved to the refrigerator and opened the door. Sam's gaze moved down her back and hips to her nice butt. "Do you want some, Sam?"

Oh yeah. "Yes, please."

She poured the juice, and he purposely kept his gaze off her wiener dog as she moved toward them. She set the juice on the table, and his hand slid up the back of her thigh.

Her eyes widened. "What are you doing?"

"Eating my waffle," Conner answered.

Sam didn't know and dropped his hand. He hadn't meant to touch her at all. It had just happened, like it was just a natural thing for him to do. Like they were a couple. A family, but of course, they weren't either of those things.

Autumn was his son's mother, but they weren't

family. She was hot and sexy and made him want more, but they weren't lovers. She was the girl he thought about, but she wasn't his girlfriend.

So what was she? To him.

It was fifty degrees, and a breeze blew Autumn's hair across her face. She wore a heavy sweater, jeans, and Ugg boots as she lounged on a chaise above the beach. She was glad she wasn't kneeling in the wet sand digging with little plastic shovels. Flying a kite had made much more sense, but she had to admit that there was a little piece of her that was glad she wasn't down on the beach, holding a kite and getting chapped lips. Up close to the house, the wind was a bit calmer.

She lowered the *Bride* magazine she held in her hands and peered over the top at Conner and Sam. They'd been at it for a couple of hours. Longer than she would have thought they'd last. From where she sat, the castle looked like a pile of sand with a moat. Mixed with the sound of the ocean and seabirds, snatches of their voices came to her on the breeze. Conner's childish giggles blended with Sam's much deeper laughter. More than his charm or the lust in his blue eyes or the touch of his hands on her aching body, or just the pure beauty of Sam, seeing those two blond heads bent together over a pile of wet sand, pinched one corner of her heart. She was in no danger of falling in love with Sam. She'd been there, done that, learned the lesson the hard way. But she might be in danger of liking him, and liking him was scary.

It had been two months since the Savage wedding and the afternoon Sam had brought Conner home late. Two months since Sam had become more involved in Conner's life. Somehow that had translated into Sam's being in her life more. So much so that she'd ended her more-than-five-year sexual drought with him on the entry-room floor last night.

She wasn't proud of herself, but not as appalled as she should be either. Like she'd told him last night, she was mostly embarrassed. And confused that she'd given it up with the one man on the planet that she'd sworn she'd never let touch her again. She was still confused about why he'd shown up at her door last night. Why she'd let him in and why he was still there.

"Hey, Mom," Conner called as he ran up the path toward her. "Come see the castle."

She set her magazine aside; she had known it was only a matter of time before Conner made her look at his castle. She stood and moved down the steps toward him. He met her in the middle of the tall grassy path and she cupped her hands over his red ears. "You're cold. Don't you want to go in now?"

He shook his head. "Dad made a dragon. Come see."

She took his cold little hand in hers and moved down the short trail. Sam stood in front of the "castle" with his hands on his hips. The knees of his jeans were as wet and sandy as Conner's, and his ears were just as red.

A cold breeze ruffled his hair, and dirt smudged his cheek. "What do you think?"

She cocked her head to one side and studied the castle. Up close, it looked less like a pile of sand. It was square, with four turrets and a moat, but the most impressive thing about it was the size. Like everything Sam did, it was big and over-the-top. "It's always been a dream of mine to go on a tour of European castles. Who knew I'd see one in Moclips."

"You dream about touring old, stone buildings?"

"Oh yeah. I hear Germany has some of the best and most haunted."

"See the dragon?" Conner pointed to what looked like a snake with a big head slithering through the sand toward the castle. "He protects the boy in the castle."

"From what?"

He looked up at his dad and squinted against the sun. "From what, Dad?"

"Girls."

She laughed and lightly socked him in the stomach. He grabbed her hand before she could pull away. "You're cold," she said.

"The other day at the Key, you said I was hot."

With her free hand, she pushed at the strands of red hair blowing across her face. "And today you're filthy."

Sam wrapped his arms around her and lifted her off her heels. He pressed his dirty sweatshirt against her and laughed. "You're too clean. I like you better when you're dirty, too."

"Sam!" She pushed at his shoulders and tried to squirm out of his hold. But Sam was bigger and taller, and she didn't stand a chance.

He tightened his grasp and lifted her until her toes dangled above the sand. His heated breath whispered across her chilled cheek, "Wanna get real dirty with me?"

She grabbed onto his shoulders, afraid if he didn't stop she'd get warm all over. That she'd *like* the way it felt to be held so tight by a strong man. By Sam. "Not in front of Conner!"

His lips brushed the corner of her lips. "Just a little dirty, then?"

"Stop, Sam. You'll confuse him." Like the confusing, hot riot tumbling in her stomach.

He raised his head and said as he stared into her eyes, "Are you confused, Conner?"

"Yes."

Sam looked over her shoulder, but he didn't let her go. "What about?"

"If the castle doesn't have a door, how will the boy get out to ride the dragon?"

Sam smiled and lowered Autumn, slowly sliding her down his body until her feet touched the sand. "There's a hidden door that the people who live inside know about."

"Oh." Conner nodded as if that made perfect sense. "I'm cold now."

Autumn looked over her shoulder at Conner. "You wanna take a bath?"

"Yeah."

She stepped out of Sam's warm arm, and together the three of them walked up the trail to the beach house. Like they were a family. The family she'd longed for when she'd carried Conner in her womb. The family she'd desperately wanted for her child, but that hadn't happened. They weren't a family, and they never would be. Sam was Sam. A spoiled athlete, so used to getting everything he wanted, when and how he wanted it, that he had no clear boundaries.

Autumn was a working mom with very clear boundaries. Or at least she did when Sam wasn't around touching her and whispering in her ear. Maneuvering her before she realized she'd been maneuvered.

Like before.

"Are we going to Paddie's?" Conner asked, as they entered the house.

Autumn closed the sliding glass door behind her. "I think your dad probably has better things to do."

Sam glanced up at Autumn through his clear blue eyes.

"At home."

His brows lowered a fraction, and he looked at

Autumn for several long moments. "Yeah. I gotta get back."

"No, Dad." Conner hugged his wet leg. "You can sleep in my bed."

"Thanks." He placed his hand on Conner's hair. "But I have some stuff to do."

"Tell your dad good-bye, and I'll go run your bathwater."

She moved toward the back of the house and walked into the bathroom. She was doing the right thing. Setting boundaries for Sam. Putting a protective distance between him and her. It was best for her. For Conner, too. Best not to confuse him because even though he said he wasn't confused at the moment, he would be. She ran four inches of warm water, then shut off the faucets.

"Get in there and get the sand out of your ears," she told Conner as she moved into the living room.

"Okay. Bye, Dad."

"Bye, buddy." Sam had changed into dry pants and a black polo and stood in front of the sofa, stuffing his duffel. He glanced up as Conner ran from the room. "You blow hot and cold faster than any woman I've ever known."

"And you come on stronger and more intensely than any man I've ever known. But we both know that it doesn't last with you, Sam."

"I have no idea what you're talking about."

"We're talking about my fear that Conner will wake up one morning, and you won't be around."

"Are you back to that?"

They were always back to that. And maybe it was a little bit about her, too.

"Conner is my son. I'm not going anywhere. I know I haven't always been the best father, but I haven't been as horrible as you paint me either." He shoved the sweatshirt into the duffel. "But this isn't about Conner. It's about last night."

Partly that was true. "It can't happen again."

He looked up, his brows lowered over his blue eyes. "Why not? I had a good time, and I know you did, too."

She couldn't deny that but . . . "There are consequences to that kind of fun."

"You can't keep using Vegas like a shield."

"I'm not."

He returned his gaze to the bag. "You are, and it's getting old."

"It's not something a person just gets over."

"It's not something *you* can get over because you don't want to. You want to hang onto the past. You want me to always be the bad guy." He zipped the duffel and looked across at her. "And I admit, I've done some bad things, but I thought maybe we were getting past all that."

How could she get past it? She'd patched around it. Sewn her life back together, but it was still there. It didn't hurt, but it couldn't be forgotten like it had never happened. The little boy in the bathtub was a constant reminder.

"But now I see that you want me to pay for Vegas for the rest of my life." He picked up his duffel. "Tell Conner I'll call him in a few days." He walked out of the house, and Autumn stared at the closed door. Was he right? Did she want him to pay for the past? Forever?

No. She wasn't that sort of woman, but she also wasn't the sort to whom forgiveness came easily. Not that he'd ever asked for it.

The Tuesday after Moclips, Natalie picked Conner up from kindergarten and took him to the Key Arena to practice with Sam. Around five, the assistant returned him home. Several days later, Natalie picked up Conner and his little backpack to spend the weekend with his dad.

That same Friday night, Autumn met with the Ross twins at a bridal store downtown so that Bo could try on dresses. Chelsea was still waiting until after her breast reduction surgery to try hers on, but she had plenty of advice for her sister. One gown was too poofy, and yet another too plain. They bickered about everything, and Bo tried on at least ten dresses before she walked from the fitting room in a sleeveless gown with an Empire waist and beautiful draping.

"Oh, Bo," Chelsea sighed. "That looks beautiful on you."

And it did. Perfect for a woman of her build. There was enough built-in boning that the top kept her heavy breasts lifted and covered while the draping elongated her body.

That night, Autumn checked the home phone to see if Conner had called. He hadn't, and she went to bed missing him. The next day she called vendors, checking in and touching base regarding an intimate Christmas charity event she'd been hired to manage at an estate in Medina. The hostess requested trays of hot and cold hors d'oeuvres be served an hour before the sit-down dinner for thirty. They'd planned on the standard four servers, but Autumn hired six. There had been times in the past when she'd had a last-minute no-show, and it was always better to err on the side of caution.

Always.

By the time Natalie dropped Conner off Sunday afternoon, it became very obvious that Sam was avoiding her. Things between them had gone back to the way they were before the Savage wedding. Back to neither her nor Sam speaking. She didn't like it. She'd hoped they could be friends. Friends was easier, but maybe no contact with Sam was for the best. Being friends with Sam had led to getting naked. And that was bad. Or rather good. Too good, and she couldn't be trusted. Although she was in no danger of another Hound Dog wedding and a wrist tattoo, she just might, *might* lose her mind and like him more than was wise. And as in business, the same was true in life. It was always better to err on the side of caution.

Always.

It wasn't until the fourteenth of December that she finally heard from Sam himself. It was Monday, a little before noon, and he called to tell her that he'd been cleared from the injured list and would be leaving for a week. Hearing his voice made her miss him. More than was wise.

"When?"

"Tomorrow morning."

She'd always known he would head out on the road again. He played hockey. It was his job. Still, she was a little disappointed. For Conner's sake, of course. "Oh."

"So tell Conner that Nat will pick him up on the," he paused as if he was looking at a schedule, "the twenty-second after school."

He was going to hang up. "Sam?"

"Yeah."

She picked up a pen and clicked it with her thumb. "Why are we back to this place?"

"What place?"

"The place where you have your assistant drop Conner off. I thought we'd become friends."

"You wanna be friends?"

Click click. Was that so impossible? Was he so mad, suddenly disliked her so much again, that he didn't want to be in the same building? "Yes."

"Friends like before or after we had sex on the floor?"

Her thumb stopped. "Before."

"Not interested."

"Why?"

"Because I don't want to be your friend."

"Oh." She swallowed her disappointment. It might be for the best, but she suddenly didn't want what was for the best. She didn't want to hate Sam and have Sam hate her. What choice did she have? "Okay."

"I want to be your lover. I can't pretend I don't want more. I want to be with you, Autumn. I want to get you naked and throw your legs over my shoulders."

She dropped the pen.

"I want to leave a mark on the inside of your thigh."

She rose and must have had some sort of out-of-body experience. It was the only way she could explain what she heard herself say, "I have two hours before my next client, and I'm not wearing panties."

She could practically hear him swallow just before he asked in a low, raw voice, "Are you at home?"

"My office." She gave him the address, and he was at the door in twenty minutes. While she waited, she reached beneath her polka-dot dress and took off her underwear. She put them in a desk drawer next to her thumbtacks and paper clips.

"Lock the door behind you," she told him, when he walked into her office. She picked up the phone and buzzed Shiloh. "I'm with a client," she said. "Take messages."

"Did I just see your baby daddy walk in?"

"I don't know what you're talking about." She hung up as Sam flipped the lock and leaned back against the door, waiting. Waiting for her to make the first move.

And she did. She rose and unbuckled the belt around her waist. "You got here in record time."

He might have waited for her to make the first move, but he didn't wait for the second. He pulled his shirt over his head as he moved toward her. "I may have run a light or two."

The dress slid down her arms and hips into a puddle of blue and white at her feet. She stepped out of it, wearing nothing but her white bra and silky slip. She reached for the buttons on the front of his jeans. He grabbed her hand and stopped her.

"Tell me what you want, Autumn. I'm never quite sure with you."

"I want you." She looked up into his hot gaze. The hot gaze that sent warm shivers across her skin. "Just like last time."

"Two orgasms?"

"Yes."

"Then what?"

"I want to be lovers."

"For how long?" He dropped her hand. "Until you get mad and kick me out the door again?"

"I don't want to be mad and kick you any-where." Not anymore.

She popped one button at a time then slid her hand into the pouch of his boxer shorts. And in case he worried that they might repeat the past, she added, "You don't have to worry that I'll fall in love with you again, either." She wrapped her hand around his erection, and he sucked in a breath.

His lids lowered and he brushed her cheek with the tips of his fingers. "What if I fall in love with you?"

She turned her face into his palm. "You won't."

Chapter Fifteen

Any Man of Mine:
Thinks I'm Hot in the Morning

H ow was your day at work?"
Autumn took a bite of a Take 'n' Bake
pizza and carefully laid it on the plate. She looked
across the table at Sam and Conner by his side.
When she'd come home around five thirty, Sam
and Conner had been downstairs, playing with
Conner's plastic golf set and watching *SpongeBob
Square Pants*. Sam had offered to "make dinner,"
and had found an organic pizza with fresh toma-
toes, goat cheese, and spinach.

"Interesting." She dabbed at the corner of her

325

mouth with a paper napkin. True to his word, he'd thrown her legs over his shoulders and given her two orgasms. "How was your lunch today?

"So good I'm having the same thing for dessert?"

Conner smiled around his bite. "Ice cream?"

"Yep."

After dinner, Sam helped Conner with his spelling at the coffee table while a Chinooks-Bruins game played across the television screen. The two sat on the floor and Autumn lay on the couch behind them. There was work she could be doing, but she much preferred watching Sam deal with the sometimes agonizing task of helping Conner spell.

At one point Sam jumped to his feet and yelled at the TV, "You've got to be f-ing kidding me."

"Little ears," she reminded him.

"What?" He glanced across his shoulder at her. "I said f-ing."

"What's f-ing mean, Dad?"

Autumn lifted a brow.

He returned his gaze to Conner and sat back down. "Freaking, but you probably shouldn't say it."

Several times he touched the back of her leg through her jeans or rubbed her bare ankle.

"When are you leaving, Dad?" Conner asked as he flexed his writing hand.

"In the morning."

"Oh." Conner's brows lowered, and he cracked his knuckles. "When are you coming back?"

"Saturday, but then I'm gone again Tuesday."

"Please don't crack your knuckles," she reminded him.

He stopped and picked up his pencil. "You'll miss my school holiday program"

"I'll be home for Christmas though. And your mom can tape your program for me."

On the surface, it looked like a nice family scene. Like Moclips. Mother, father, and child, and Autumn got that uncomfortably anxious feeling in her stomach again. Like the nice picture wouldn't last. That at some point it would crumble at her feet.

She was no longer afraid that Sam would backslide and put his son on hold while he lived the hard-partying life of a popular athlete. Some switch had flipped in Sam, and he truly wanted to be the father Conner needed. But that didn't make them a family. It never would, and she worried that Conner might get the wrong idea. That he might start to hope for things that just weren't going to happen.

So far, he seemed okay. He hadn't mentioned Sam moving in for a while.

"Your *h* is backward," Sam pointed out to Conner, then he glanced at the screen and jumped up again. "Control the damn puck, Logan. Settle down and control the damn puck. Pass it!"

"Language, Dad."

He glanced down at Conner. "What did I say now?"

"Damn."

"Oh. I don't think damn really counts."

At nine o'clock, Sam put Conner to bed, and Autumn moved into the kitchen to answer the telephone hooked to the wall next to the refrigerator.

"Hey, sis."

She walked to the sliding glass door, stretching the long cord. "Hi, Vince."

"Are you busy?"

It was definitely not a good time for a visit. "Yeah. I'm putting Conner to bed," she lied. "And then I think I'll hit the sheets myself." With Sam.

"At nine?"

"Yeah. It's been a busy day." She looked out onto the dark deck and the yard beyond. "What's up?"

"I'm on a break and just wanted to ask you what to get Conner for Christmas."

She smiled. "Well, he told me he wants Santa to bring him a Harley like yours."

Vince laughed, something she didn't hear often enough.

"I told him he wasn't big enough, and he said I could ride on the back and put my legs down to hold us up."

"Maybe someday, but in the meantime, anything else he wants?"

Even though he'd never admit it to himself, Vince was lonely. Why else would a thirty-five-year-old man call his sister at 9:00 P.M. to ask what his nephew wanted for Christmas? "He has his eyes on some Lego race cars."

"That'll be fun. Do you have to share him this year with the idiot?"

"The idiot" chose that moment to walk into the kitchen. Autumn spun around and put a finger to her lips. "Yeah. I think Sam has him in the morning this year."

"I wonder how much it would cost me to have him killed."

"Vince, don't even talk like that." She looked at Sam, standing there with his arms across his long-sleeved T-shirt, all belligerent. "I gotta go and make sure Conner didn't put his jammies on backward."

"Tell him I love him."

"I will." She walked back across the kitchen. "Bye," she said, and hung up the phone

"Was that your brother?"

"Yep."

"You didn't mention I was here."

"Nope." She shook her head and looked over at him. "Vince hates you, and I just didn't want to deal with the stress of that right now."

"I had a sister once, too, and she had a man in her life that I absolutely hated." He moved toward her and took her hand. "I understand your brother. I don't like him, but I understand him."

She didn't even understand her brother sometimes.

"I understand why he doesn't want me in your life. I believe him when he says he isn't going to let it happen."

Her lips parted. "What? Vince said that? When?"

"It doesn't matter." He shook his head, determination crowding his brow. "All that matters is that you believe I'm not going to let your brother stand between me and my family."

She took a step back. "You and Conner."

"What?"

"Stand between you and Conner."

"Yeah. That's what I said."

No. That hadn't been what he'd said. This wasn't about family. It was about him spending time with Conner and having sex with her. It wasn't about her falling in love and hoping for things that weren't going to happen. It wasn't about being a part of a beautiful wedding and a white-picket-fences and happily-ever-afters.

She moved into the living room, her thoughts a speeding mess. It wasn't about eating dinner and Conner doing homework with his dad. What was she doing? And what if Vince found out she was sleeping with Sam? He'd blow a gasket, and she wasn't so sure he had many more to blow. She was confused and raw and didn't want to think about it. Not then. The next day, when Sam was gone, and she could think. "Why did you hate the man in your sister's life?" she asked.

"Because he was a controlling son of a bitch."

She moved to the big picture window and looked down at Sam's red truck in the driveway. If they were really a family, it would be in the garage. Next to her Subaru. "What happened?"

He was silent for so long she didn't think he was going to answer. She glanced over at him, standing in the middle of the room. A tall powerful man, a deep furrow pulling his brows together over his blue eyes. "He killed her." He looked away. "When she finally got the nerve to leave him, he hunted her down and shot her."

Her heart dropped, and she turned to face him. In an instant, her own thoughts forgotten. "Sam."

"I was across the country enjoying my life. Living in Toronto, then—" He shrugged and glanced back at her. "Then my life stopped."

Without thinking about it, she moved toward him. "When did she die?"

"June 13."

The date was not lost on Autumn, and she recalled his mentioning something about his sister's death in Vegas years ago.

"She was young and smart and beautiful and had a wonderful life planned for herself. She wanted to teach little kids." He paused and shrugged a shoulder. "Instead, we had to plan a funeral and box up her stuff."

Without thinking, Autumn wrapped her arms around his waist and laid her cheek against his heart. "I know what it's like to put a person's whole life into boxes. I'm sorry."

He was so stiff, like stone covered in warm skin. "She was my little sister, and I was supposed to take care of her. Our dad died when she was ten, and she depended on me. I helped her with her homework and bought her first prom dress. I was supposed to keep her safe. I didn't."

She'd never known any of that. She'd known his sister had died, but not the details. "It wasn't your fault, Sam."

"I know that now, but I felt so guilty and pissed off for so long." He raised a hand to the top of her head and slid his fingers down the back of her hair. She felt his muscles relax a bit. "I still feel Ella's loss. I still get pissed about it, but I don't take it out on myself or anyone else so much these days."

She listened to the heavy thud of his heart and turned her face to press her lips into his chest. She'd always thought Sam was superficial. Interested in momentary pleasure, and he was, but

333

there was also something deeper behind his blue eyes. Something he liked to keep hidden. The boy who'd filled his father's shoes and the disciplined man who'd worked hard to reach his goals lay beneath that charming smile.

"For years after that," he continued, "I did some reckless, reckless things. You were part of that reckless fallout."

She looked up into his face, at his strong jaw so tight.

"There are things in my life I regret. That I'm ashamed of. Probably not as many as I should be." He gave her a lopsided smile. "But I regret Vegas."

So did she. Funny thing was, not as much as she had a few months ago.

"Not that I met you. I can't regret that, or I wouldn't have Conner, but I do regret that I married you in a ceremony that I largely don't remember. I regret that I hurt you. I regret that I didn't act like a man. That I left you in a hotel without a word. With nothing but a marriage certificate and a stuffed dog. I regret that a lot. I feel a lot of guilt and embarrassment about that." He pressed his forehead into hers. "I'm sorry, Autumn. I'm sorry I left you alone at Caesars."

For the first time since she'd met him, he uttered the s-word. For the first time since she'd pieced her heart back together, she felt a small tug at one of the strings. She dropped her hands to her sides and took a step back. The one word she'd waited to hear could destroy her carefully reconstructed life. "Don't." *Don't make me forget. Don't make it better. Don't make me love you again.* "I don't want to like you *that* much."

"You already like me *that* much." A smile worked one corner of his lips. "I think lunch in your office today showed how much you like me."

"That was sex. That's all." She shook her head and raised a hand as if to stop him. "No attachments."

He dipped his head to look into her eyes. His smile gone. "You don't think you can get past what happened in Vegas, do you?"

Could she? "I don't know. I'm not very good at the whole 'forgive and forget' thing." And if she did forgive and forget, what kind of fool would she be if it happened again? When it happened again? Sam was a hockey star. His life was huge. Hers wasn't. "That was a time in my life I try not to think about." Impossible as it was sometimes.

"Tell me about it."

"Why?"

"Because you can't help but think about it, and I need to hear about it as much as you need to tell me." He reached for her. "Because I've always wondered."

She stepped back, and his hands fell to his sides. He'd wondered? He'd wondered, but he'd never thought to pick up the phone and ask? "I was scared, Sam." She pushed her hair behind her ears. "I was scared and pregnant by a guy I didn't even know. It should have been the happiest time of my life, but it wasn't. Every child deserves parents who are ecstatic. Conner didn't have that.

"While other women were going to baby classes with their husbands, I was getting divorced. What's there to say beyond that?" Evidently a lot because the rest just poured out. "My mom had died a few months before, and Vince was off in Iraq or Afghanistan or South Korea or wherever. I hadn't seen my dad in about ten years, and I was all alone. Sick as a dog and all alone. I didn't have anyone. I didn't know how I was going to support myself or my baby. You're a man, so you'll never understand that kind of fear." She moved to the coffee table and straightened Conner's papers. "I didn't understand why any of it happened. I didn't understand how I'd gotten myself into such a foolish position." She fussed with his pencils. "And I didn't know why you'd married me and dumped me. It was a very bad time in my life and I was"—she bent down to pick up crayons and pencils—"scared."

Sam watched Autumn fuss over Conner's schoolwork. Emotion flushed her smooth white cheeks and wrinkled her forehead. He'd hurt her. He'd always known that, of course. He'd just never known what to do about it. Until now.

"I really didn't understand any of it either." But he was beginning to. His instant attraction. The intensity of it all. He was beginning to understand that maybe, just maybe he'd fallen for a girl in a crowded bar. A girl he didn't know, at a time in his life that was filled with crazy chaos. That maybe his heart had really shitty timing.

Every coach he'd ever played for, every captain he'd ever played with, had all told him the same thing: "You never learn the first time. You always have to get hit twice before you see it coming." He was seeing now what he'd seen that first night at Pure. A bright shiny light he wanted to catch in his hands and hold forever. If she let him.

"Well, if it's any consolation," he said, "you've always scared the shit out of me."

She looked up at him out of the corners of her green eyes. "Right."

"It's true. You're so sure of yourself, and you don't take crap from nobody. That's kind of intimidating." This time when he reached for her, she let him take her hands. "You're a good mother and you run your own business. You could sit back and live off the money you get for Conner. Other women might, but you don't. You work really hard." He'd always admired that about her. "You should be proud of yourself."

"You think I'm a good mom?"

"Of course. I couldn't ask for a better mother for my son." He smiled to lighten the mood. "And I'm not just saying that to get laid."

She bit her bottom lip. "Thanks."

"Thank you." Then he thanked her the only way he knew how. He took her to her room and undressed her. He pushed her down on the bed and covered her body in kisses. He made love to her, and as he slid into her body, it felt like coming home after weeks on the road. Like he wanted to stay there forever.

He placed his hands on the sides of her head,

338

and whispered into one ear, "Let me love you, Autumn."

"Yes," she said as she arched and met his thrusts. "Don't stop, Sam."

They were talking about different things, and for the first time in his life, he understood the difference between great sex and making love. For the first time in his life, Sam wanted more from a woman than she wanted from him.

Later, she lay in his arms, in the warmth of her bed and soft glow of good sex and two small lamps. With her back pressed into his chest, he ran his hand down her smooth arm to her wrist.

"You covered my name with wings." He raised her hand and kissed her pulse. "Does that mean you think I'm an angel?"

She laughed. "A dark angel from hell."

"When did you get my name tattooed over?"

"A few weeks after I delivered Conner."

"Ouch." He winced. "That soon? I at least waited."

She glanced over her shoulder at him. "How long?"

"A few months after."

She turned on her back and looked at him. Within the soft light, her beautiful green gaze met his. "Every person I've ever known who has had someone's name tattooed on them has lived to regret it."

"It wasn't one of my better drunken ideas." He smiled and rested his hand on her bare stomach. "It's right up there with the Hound Dog wedding and that Cher concert."

She laughed, a lush sound of pure pleasure. "Cher wasn't as painful."

"Says you."

"How would you even know? You slept through it, and we left early."

Maybe that's why he didn't recall the actual concert. He'd always blamed it on the booze and mental self-preservation. "Well, the good news is that Cher's had about five 'farewell' tours since. Barbra, too."

She grinned. "Are you volunteering to go to a Barbra Streisand concert?"

Hell no. He'd rather get a puck shot in his nuts. Wait . . . "What would you give me?"

"A ONE NIGHT WITH BABS T-shirt. You could keep it in a drawer next to that Cher BELIEVE T-shirt you got married in." She turned on her side to face him and a smile shone in her eyes. "Or you could wear it when you go out with your buddies."

He didn't do that so much anymore and really didn't miss it. He'd much rather be there, with his family, in Autumn's bed in her split-level house with bad wallpaper and old carpet.

His family. He wasn't sure when he'd started to see them as a family, maybe in Moclips, but it felt right to him.

"The guys would probably stage an intervention and kick my ass. Instead, maybe you and I and Conner can go tour some castles in Germany this summer."

Her brows lowered. " 'Old stone buildings?' "

"Sure." He'd much prefer white sandy beaches and Autumn in a bikini, but what the hell? "If that's what you and Conner really want to do."

"Don't you spend your summers in Cancún with the guys?"

"I'd rather spend time with you and Conner than on a boat with girls in bikinis." When had that happened? "Who needs girls in bikinis?"

"You."

He slid his hand down her hip. "I just need you in a bikini. All that white skin in need of sunscreen and someone to rub on it on you."

"That got us in trouble in Vegas."

"I remember. I remember how beautiful you

341

looked." He softly bit her shoulder and tasted her skin. "You're more beautiful now. Even in the morning."

"You don't know what I look like in the morning."

"Yes I do. You looked really hot in those wiener-dog jammies in Moclips."

She laughed as if he were joking. "There you go again, trying to charm me into falling in love with you."

"What if I fall in love with you?" His hand slid up and cupped her breast.

Her gaze met his. "You won't."

He didn't like the way she said it. As if it wasn't possible. As if he wasn't capable of falling in love with a woman. As if he wasn't capable of loving her.

Chapter Sixteen

Any Man of Mine:
Is Observant

E ven before Autumn opened her eyes, she knew he was gone. Of course he was. He had a game in New Jersey, and he wouldn't be home for five days. She touched the indent his head had left in her pillow.

What if I fall in love with you? Last night hadn't been the first time he'd mentioned love. He'd said the same thing earlier in her office. The first time, she'd just thought he was saying it because she'd had her hand down his pants. The second time because he'd had his hand on her breast. Men

343

couldn't be trusted during sex and were likely to say anything.

Autumn sat up and swung her legs over the side of the bed. She hurriedly pulled on a pair of sweatpants and a T-shirt so Conner wouldn't catch her stark naked in bed.

Five years ago, Sam had married her and never mentioned love. Never even hinted at it, and she'd just assumed he'd loved her. Look where that had gotten her.

She glanced at her bedside clock, then walked across the hall to Conner's room. He lay on his side, his arms stretched out, and his eyes were already open. "Get up, lazy." Conner would start Christmas vacation next week, but of course he wouldn't think of sleeping in. Which meant she wouldn't get to sleep in either.

He sat up in his new sailboat bedding and his Handy Manny pajamas. She wondered how much longer he'd like Manny. How much longer until Manny went the same way as Barney. "Can I have heart pancakes?" he asked.

"Yes." She smiled. He was still her boy. For a while yet anyway. "Yes, you can."

For the next five days, Autumn fell into her normal routine. Only it didn't feel so normal.

Not without Sam, and she felt uneasy about how quickly that had all changed. During the day, she tried not to think about him, and at night when he called, she tried to ignore the heated rush warming her skin and pulling at her heart. At the sound of his voice, she bit her lip to keep from smiling.

Friday night, he returned home. To her home, like they were a family. "How was your day, honey?" he asked as he slid into bed. She talked to him about the Ross twins and their latest wants and needs for their July wedding. She told him about Chelsea's breast reduction surgery scheduled for the next week.

"Ah. That's why Mark is taking a few weeks off." He lifted her hand and looked at her fingers. "Although I don't know why she'd want to do something like that."

"Probably because of backaches."

"I hadn't thought of that." He looked at her, his blue eyes serious. "You'd never do something like that. Right?"

She didn't have double D's, so she didn't have to worry about it. "No."

"Good. I like you just the way you are." When he said sweet things like that, she could almost

345

forget that he was a self-indulgent jock who spent most of his time in a locker room.

"I have a weird little toe," she felt compelled to point out.

"That's okay, honey. Your rack makes up for it. You have a great rack, and I don't think that makes me a perv. Just observant."

She laughed because he was totally serious.

Two nights later, she and Conner went to his game against the Carolina Hurricanes. They wore Chinook T-shirts and bought hot dogs and Cokes and tried not to cringe when Sam got knocked around or put the "big hurt" on someone. He skated up and down the ice, passing the puck or firing so fast Autumn lost track of it altogether. She noticed that he talked a lot out on the ice, and she was sure she was better off not knowing what he said. Especially when he had to sit out four minutes in the penalty box.

"That player there"—Conner pointed to a Carolina player—"is crashing Dad's zone. He's not going to like that."

Autumn really didn't have a clue what her son was talking about until Sam slammed the player into the boards and the Plexiglas shook. Autumn gasped as he dug at the puck with his stick and shot it down ice. He looked up, sweat dripping down his nose. For one brief second, his gaze met hers, and he smiled.

Suddenly she knew how that Carolina player felt. Like she was getting slammed around. Like he was putting the "big hurt" on her, only she liked it and wanted more.

Her chest got kind of tight and panicky. She had to pull back. She didn't trust Sam. She didn't trust herself. Like before, everything was moving too fast. And this time, if and when it ended, she wasn't the only one who would suffer.

And yet, that night he came to her house like he belonged there. He said good night to Conner, then moved into the kitchen. "Do you have any frozen peas in here?" he asked as he opened the freezer.

He wore black sweatpants, a blue Chinooks T-shirt, and a big red mark on his cheek. "Mixed veggie medley."

"That'll do." He took it out and shoved the bag beneath the elastic of his sweats. "The organization just hired a new forward from Russia."

She smiled. She liked how he told her things about his day and asked about hers.

"He's young, though," Sam continued. "Seems kind of irresponsible, selfish, and reckless."

He sounded like a hockey player to her, and she lifted a brow and looked at him.

He chuckled. "I'm not that reckless these days."

"Well, I guess one out of three is . . ." She paused, as if searching for the right word. " . . . progress."

He grinned like a proud, reformed sinner. "I'm working on the other two."

She leaned her behind against the counter and folded her arms across the fish on her shirt. "You might want to work a bit harder."

"I have been working harder. I thought maybe you noticed."

"Maybe a little."

"Maybe you should show me some appreciation." He grasped her forearms and slid them around his waist. "Show some encouragement."

And she did. She encouraged the hell out of him all night long, but the next morning, he was gone. They'd both agreed that he should not be there in the morning when Conner got up. Or rather, she'd set down the rule, and Sam had *reluctantly* agreed. He didn't see anything wrong with Conner seeing so much of his parents together, but he clearly wasn't thinking about the future. About the day when he wouldn't be around as much. Autumn thought about it, though. A lot. Thought about it and felt like she was sitting around, waiting for the axe to fall on her throat.

"I made a picture," Conner told her at the breakfast table the next morning. While she poured his Cheerios, he ran to his art station. Conner was officially on Christmas break from school, and she had an event planned for a local charity that afternoon at the Four Seasons. Normally, she'd take Conner to his day care, but Sam wanted to spend time with him before hitting the road for Chicago later that night. She expected him at eleven after his morning practice.

Conner ran back into the dining room and set a piece of white notebook paper on the table. "Come look, Mom."

Autumn poured herself a cup of coffee and sat next to Conner. On the paper beside his cereal bowl, he'd drawn a picture of her and Sam with himself in the middle. The figures were all holding hands and had big lopsided smiles. For the first time, he'd drawn them all as a family. "This is you and me and Dad."

Her stomach fell as she drank her coffee.

"That's a good picture. I like my pink skirt." She swallowed hard. "But you know your daddy just comes over sometimes to see you. Right? He doesn't live here."

Conner shrugged. "He can if he wants."

"He has his apartment downtown."

"But he can move here. Josh F's dad lives at his house with him."

"Conner, not all dads live in the same house with their children. Not all families are like Josh F's. Some families have two dads," she said to take his mind of things that weren't going to happen. "Or two moms."

Conner shoveled Cheerios into his mouth. "Dad can move in if he wants to, Mom. He has a big truck." Like it was just a matter of Sam packing up his truck and moving in. "And then you can make me a little brother."

She gasped. "What? You want a brother?"

Conner nodded. "Josh F. has a little brother. So Dad has to move here so I can have a brother."

"Don't get your heart set on it, Conner." He suddenly wanted his parents under the same roof *and* a brother?

"Please, Mom?"

"Don't talk with your mouth full," she said by

rote, her mind tumbling as fast as her stomach. A brother for Conner wasn't going to happen.

She pushed her coffee aside, the acid burning a hole in her chest. There had been a time when she'd wanted the same thing as Conner. She'd wanted it in Vegas, and the day she'd signed the divorce papers. She wanted it the night she'd discovered she was pregnant and the morning she'd given birth to their son. She'd loved Sam. It had taken her a long time to get over him, and somehow, she'd fallen in love with him again. Only this time it was worse. This time it felt deeper, comfortable. Like they were friends and lovers. She actually knew him now, and it was so much worse than the first time. The first time, she'd fallen in love with a charming, intense stranger. This time she'd fallen for a charming, intense man. He was real.

She rose from the table and moved to her bedroom. She took a shower as if her nerves weren't a wreck. As if her mind wasn't racing and her heart not pounding. She got ready for her day and dressed in a pair of black wool pants and cashmere sweater with pearls on the collar. Her hands shook as she pulled her hair back into a ponytail.

She loved him, and there was a tiny piece of her silly heart that held out hope that maybe he loved her this time, too. He'd joked about it twice, but that's all it had been. A joke. Like before.

This time she wasn't a scared twenty-five-year-old. This time she knew the outcome.

The sound of Conner's current favorite movie blared from the television as Sam walked downstairs to Autumn's basement office. He wanted to talk about Christmas and spending it together that year.

He paused in the doorway to watch her profile for a few moments. Her red ponytail slid over one shoulder and brushed her white throat as she slid a planner into her tote. He swallowed past the sudden constriction in his throat. He remembered a time when he'd looked at her and hadn't even thought she was beautiful. Hadn't *wanted* to think it. Had purposely dated women the exact opposite of Autumn, so he wouldn't be reminded of her and the reasons he'd fallen for her in Vegas. He outweighed her by about a hundred pounds at least, but she had the power to wipe the floor with him.

"When will you be home?" he asked.

She looked up and quickly glanced back down. "Late. You should probably stay at your own place."

Something was wrong. Different. It was there in the ridged stillness that suddenly surrounded her. "I'll be gone for eight days," he reminded her.

She turned and grabbed a pen off her desk. "Conner will look forward to your nightly calls."

He cleared the constriction in his throat. "Will you look forward to my calls?"

She pulled open a drawer but didn't answer.

He moved into the room and took her arm. "What's going on, Autumn?"

She looked up at him, and he saw it. In her green eyes. The look he'd never hoped to see again. Pain and uncertainty and withdrawal. Like the first time she'd laid Conner in his arms. "Conner is confused," she said, and she took a step back, separating herself from him with more than just space. "I think it's best if we don't spend as much time together."

This had little to do with Conner. Frustration tightened his skull, and he wanted to shake her. He purposely loosened his grip and dropped his hand. "You can't keep blowing hot and cold. You can't pull me in even as you push me away." He took a step back, too. To protect himself from the pain rushing at him. "You can't keep looking at me like you expect me to break your heart at any moment."

"And you can't expect me not to."

Something happened between the time he left last night and now. What it was didn't matter. "I'm not going to hurt you, Autumn. I promise."

"You can't make that promise."

He held out a hand. "Honey, just trust me."

She shook her head. "I don't know if I can."

"This is about Vegas." He dropped his hand. "Still."

"It happened, Sam."

"You're right. It did, but we were different people then." He pointed to himself. "I was different. I'm not asking you to forget what happened. I don't believe that's even possible for either of us. But if you can't get past it, then how can we move forward with our lives?" How could they make a life together? Something he wanted as badly as he'd ever wanted anything in his life. More than winning the Stanley Cup, he wanted to win his family.

She shook her head, and the pain in her eyes tore at his heart even as it pissed him off. "I don't know." She picked up her tote and headed toward the door. "I have to go."

Sam watched Autumn leave, and it was one of the hardest things he'd ever forced himself to do. Over the sound of Conner's movie, he heard the garage door shut down the hall. He loved her. He wanted a life with her. But he didn't know if it was going to happen, and he didn't know what to do.

He moved up the stairs, past Conner lying on the couch with a remote in one hand. "Can you turn down that TV?" he asked as he moved into the kitchen

The sound faded, and he opened the refrigerator. "Thank you." All of his life, he'd fought hard for everything. He'd fought and, most of the time, he'd eventually won. He was dogged that way, but he wasn't so sure he could win Autumn. She was an immovable force. Stubborn as hell, and he didn't know if he had enough fight left in him to change her mind.

He took out a bottle of water and twisted off the top. The telephone hooked to the wall rang until it went to voice mail. Maybe he should just walk away. He wanted a future with her, but maybe there was too much damage for her to ever get over it. Maybe he should just get out now before he sank himself even further. Until he choked and went under completely.

The telephone immediately rang again. He was angry. If he was a violent man, he'd go kick the living shit out of someone. If he hadn't just returned from the injured list, he might ram his head through the wall. The telephone kept ringing, a nagging annoyance snapping his control. He walked across the floor and glanced at the caller identification. Normally, he would have just picked up the receiver and slammed it back down.

Instead he picked up. "Hello?"

"You have a collect call," the automated voice said, "from . . . *Vince* . . . an inmate at Clark County Jail. Will you accept the charges?"

Chapter Seventeen

Any Man of Mine:
Shocks Me with Random Kindness

D o you think bailing me out is going to win
points with my sister?"

Sam looked across his truck at Vince and the
shiner closing one eye and the knot on his forehead. He didn't think there was anything that
was going to win points with Autumn. She was
a hardheaded woman with an immovable heart.
"I'm not going to tell Autumn. She doesn't need to
worry about you."

"I'll pay you back."

Sam slowed and stopped at a red light. "I know
you will."

Vince had been charged with assault. Apparently, he'd kicked some ass in a biker bar. Sam didn't hold kicking a little ass against a guy, but he didn't like Vince any more than Vince liked him. "It probably wasn't wise to take on a whole bar."

Vince grunted. "Says the guy who takes on a bunch of hockey players almost every night."

"That's different. That's my job. I don't fight for free." Not anymore. The light changed, and he stepped on the gas. "I have a really good lawyer. I'll give you his card."

"I don't want your help."

"I know, but you're going to take it." He was tired. Tired of fighting the past. There was no way to win with Autumn. He was probably better off knowing that before rather than later. Before he bought a big ring and made a fool out of himself. "I don't want you upsetting her with your bullshit."

"Me? Oh that's rich. You're the one who knocked her up and left her in a hotel."

He looked across at the former Navy SEAL. At the man people thought was a hero. "We all know what happened six years ago. Autumn and I are working past it," he lied.

Vince laughed. "You sure Autumn is working

to get past it? I know my sister. She's a Haven. Forgive and forget is not in our vocabulary."

Yeah. He'd figured that out on his own. Received the message pretty clear. "Tell me something, frogman. Have you ever done something you regret so much that the guilt stays with you for years? Maybe the rest of your life?"

Vince was silent for several long moments, then said, "Once or twice."

As much as he really hated to admit it, in that moment he saw a bit of himself in Vince. "I regret what I did to Autumn, and I've been trying like hell to make it up to her." He slowed and took an exit to Kent.

"Huh." Vince took a pair of aviator sunglasses out of his breast pocket and slid them onto his swollen face. "How's that working out so far?"

Not so well. After that morning, he wasn't so sure it would. He'd told her he'd never hurt her again, and she'd hadn't believed him. Hadn't trusted him and the more he thought about it, the more it pissed him off.

"I guess I should thank you for bailing me out," Vince said, as if the mere words caused him added pain.

It was Sam's turn to grunt. "Don't hurt yourself."

Vince crossed his arms over his chest. "And don't go thinking this makes us square. I'm still going to kick your ass someday."

Sam smiled. "You're gonna *try* and kick my ass someday. You might know a hundred ways to kill a man, but I know a hundred ways to make a man wish he were dead."

Vince chuckled. "If it weren't for you being a colossal dickweed, I might actually like you."

Sam didn't call. He didn't call the night before he left town, nor for the next two days. Finally, on the third day, he called and asked for Conner. Just the sound of his voice lifted Autumn's heart even as it plunged to her stomach. She could hardly breathe past the pleasurable ache. When he was through talking with his son, he hung up. Clearly, he didn't want to talk to her that day. Nor the day after, when he called and only spoke with his son.

It was for the best, she told herself. Best for Conner and her. The backs of her eyes stung, and she could not hold back the tears that splashed down her cheeks. She'd never thought the heart she'd carefully pieced back together could break even more, but it did. She was miserable and didn't know what to do.

Just after noon, Vince pulled his big black truck into the parking space outside her office window. She wasn't in the mood to see her brother, but maybe he'd take her to lunch and help take her mind off her troubles. Maybe he had a really great Christmas present for her that would cheer her up.

"Wow. You look like shit," he said as he walked into her office.

Autumn blew her nose. "Thanks." She pointed to his black eye. "So do you. What happened?"

Of course he didn't answer. "Why are you crying?"

She shook her head. If he could keep a secret, so could she. "I don't want to talk about it."

Normally, he would have pressed and worn her down until she told him. Instead, he asked, "Is Sam in town?"

Sam? Autumn couldn't remember a time when Vince hadn't referred to Sam as "the idiot" or worse. Something was very wrong. Like maybe

361

Vince had fallen and hit his head really hard and not only given himself a black eye, but brain damage as well. "He's in L.A. Why?"

"I wanted to talk to him. When will he be back?"

"Tomorrow night sometime."

"That's too late. I won't be here."

"Why?" She rose from behind her desk. "Where are you going?"

"I'm leaving town."

"No!" Her jaw dropped. "Why?" Why was her life turning to crap all at the same time?

"I have to do something."

"What?" She moved around the desk toward her brother.

"Nothing I can talk about."

"Are you running from the law?"

"No."

"An angry girlfriend?"

"No."

"Boyfriend?"

"NO!"

She placed her hand on her chest, and concern for her brother pushed her own troubles aside. "I'm your sister. You can tell me anything, and I'll always love you. No matter what."

"I love you, too, but there are just some things it's best you don't know." He put up one palm. "I'm not going to talk about it. So don't ask."

Sometimes he was so secretive, it drove her crazy. "When will you be back?"

"Soon." He pulled out a thick envelope. "Give this to Sam."

The envelope was filled with money, and she gasped. "When did Sam loan you this much money?"

"Just tell him thanks."

"What did you do?" She looked at the envelope in her hand and wondered why her brother would need so much money. Had he gotten kicked out of his apartment or gambled or hired a soldier of fortune from the back of one of his magazines? No, Vince wouldn't hire someone to do his dirty work.

"Sam bailed me out of jail Monday."

"What?" The possibility of jail hadn't entered her head. Sam hated Vince. Why would he bail him out? "What happened? Are you okay?" she asked through a haze of stunned disbelief. Then she listened as Vince told her about getting into a fight with a bunch of bikers and getting arrested.

"Why didn't you run away?"

He frowned. "I don't run."

"But that was three days ago. Why didn't either of you tell me?" Okay, so Sam wasn't speaking to her but, "Why didn't you tell me?"

"Sam doesn't want you to know. I think he loves you and doesn't want you to worry about me."

She wasn't so sure Sam loved her. Not after their last conversation. She wasn't sure like her brother seemed to be.

"I don't want you to worry about me either."

She looked at him standing there, her big hard-nosed brother. The back of her throat hurt, and her eyes watered. Again. She didn't want to make his life hard for him. Harder than it already was. "What will I do without my big brother?"

"Don't cry." He enfolded her in his big arms. "I'm not leaving forever." He leaned back and looked into her face. "Maybe Sam isn't as big an idiot these days." He wiped her cheeks with his thumbs. "He'll look out for you and Conner."

She was confused and scared for Vince. "You like Sam now?"

"Hell no, but the bigger question is, do you like him?"

Of course she liked Sam. She loved him. She couldn't help it. She loved the sound of his voice and the smell of him on her pillow. She loved that under all that muscle and enormous ego, there was a kind man with a giving heart. She nodded.

"Then you have to think about forgiving him, because sometimes a person needs to hear you forgive them so they can start to forgive themselves."

She looked into her brother's troubled green eyes and wondered if he was talking about Sam or himself.

Sam walked into his loft and knew something was different before he turned on the lights. It was 3:00 A.M., and Conner's jacket was tossed across a barstool, and his door was ajar. He looked inside at his son curled up in his bed, asleep.

Sam was exhausted, and sore as hell. He'd played the shittiest games of his career consecutively because he hadn't been able to clear his head of Autumn. He was living in a gray fog, but he was fairly certain it wasn't his night to have Conner. Not unless Autumn needed someone to watch their son. Natalie's door was shut, and he moved into his room and flipped on the light. In the middle of his dark blue quilt, Autumn lay curled up in his bed. Her red hair fanned out across his pillow. If he hadn't been standing up, with his duffel in his hand, he might think he was dreaming the whole thing.

"Autumn?"

She stirred, and her green eyes fluttered open. A smile tilted up the corners of her mouth.

The duffel hit the floor. "What are you doing here?"

"Waiting for you."

"Why? What's wrong? What happened?"

"Nothing's wrong. I just wanted to see you, and you're obviously avoiding me."

He looked around. "How did you get in here?"

"You have your ways. I have mine." She stretched her arms, and it looked like she was wearing a white hockey jersey. "And aren't you glad you didn't come home with some other woman?"

"There is no other woman."

"I know." She sat up, and the quilt fell to her lap. She was wearing that damn Pittsburgh jersey. "Vince left town."

He shrugged out of his blazer. "Why?"

"He said he had something to do. I'm very worried about him."

"He's a big boy." Were they really talking about Vince? "He'll be okay."

"Why did you bail him out?" She swung her bare legs over the side of the bed. "You hate Vince."

"But I love you."

"I love you, too."

His chest felt like he'd cracked a few ribs. Sore like someone caught him in the corner and punched the wind out of him. He pointed at her. "Then why are you wearing Crosby's jersey?"

" 'Cause the last time I wore it, you threatened to tear it off me if you ever saw it again."

He smiled. "Is that what you want?"

She nodded and wrapped her arms around his neck.

"What else do you want, Autumn?"

"Me and you and Conner. I want us to be a family." He sucked in a breath as she unbuttoned his shirt. "I want to always be here when you get home. I want to hear about your day. I want that for the rest of my life." She kissed the hollow of his throat.

"If you want that for the rest of your life, you have it." He grabbed her hand and kissed the inside of her wrist. "I want you to always be here when I get home. I want to hear about your day. I love you and I will love you for the rest of my life." He closed his eyes and took a deep breath. He didn't want to choke up. He didn't want the woman he loved to see him cry like a girl. "You and Conner, that's all I'll ever need."

"No, that isn't all." She brushed his hair from his forehead. "I love you, Sam. I fell in love with you five years ago, and you broke my heart. For a long time, I couldn't get past that, but I've fallen in love with you again. Only harder and deeper and more maturely this time. You don't need my forgiveness for the past. Like you said, we were different people then, but if that's what you want, if that's what you need, then I forgive you."

He lowered his face to her neck and breathed in the scent of her warm skin. He hadn't realized how long he'd waited to hear those words. Didn't know how much he wanted to hear them until she'd spoken them. He ran his hands down the back of her jersey and grabbed two bare cheeks. "You seem to have lost your panties again."

"Oops. I bet that happens around you a lot."

"Not anymore." He slid his hands up her smooth back. "You're the only woman I want around. The only woman I want to see drop her panties. The only woman I've ever really wanted."

She leaned back and looked up at him. Her green eyes smiling with laughter. "Up until a few months ago, I wasn't even the kind of woman you dated."

"No." He pressed his forehead into hers and brushed his mouth across her lips. "But you're the kind of woman I marry. If I'm really lucky, you're the kind of woman who will marry me twice."

Epilogue

Any Man of Mine:
Gives a Good Lei

T he setting sun hung just above the white sands of Lahaina Beach in Maui. Orange and red beams caught in the curls of Autumn's hair and touched the side of Sam's square jaw. Dressed in a simple oyster silk sheath, Autumn wore a lei of white orchids that Sam had given her that day. She'd pinned roses in her hair, and a slight breeze ruffled the veil attached to the back of her head. Sam and Conner wore matching black tuxedos with white orchids in their lapels and white bow ties.

When it came to planning her own wedding,

Autumn had opted for small and intimate. Sam's mother and Vince stood within the wedding party to the bride's right. The Ross twins and their husbands just back from their respective honeymoons and Ty and Faith Savage, their baby girl asleep on her daddy's big shoulder, watched Sam take Autumn's hand and raise it to his lips. He kissed the backs of her knuckles and smiled just before he said the vows he'd written.

"I'm a hockey player," he began. "I'm not romantic, so I asked Conner what I should say to you today. He suggested a few knock-knock jokes." He laughed. "Mostly, he wanted me to tell you that you're the best mommy in the world. And that's true, but that is only one reason why I love you so much. I love the way you make me feel when you walk into a room. You fill my life with light." He paused and looked into her face. "Autumn, I love you because I can't imagine my life without you. I don't want to even try."

Autumn gazed into Sam's eyes as the sinking sun streaked his cheeks with smears of orange and lavender. "I love you Sam. You healed my heart and taught me that forgiveness is about love. I used to think that any man of mine had to live up to a list of my expectations." She shook

ROGUE
By Danielle Steel

For Maxine Williams, being married to Blake was an amazing adventure. Brilliant, charismatic, and wholly unpredictable, as an entrepreneur he had made millions and grabbed headlines. His only shortcoming was as a husband, and now they have worked out an odd but amicable divorce, and share three children they both adore. Blake gets to keep his globe-trotting lifestyle – dating a succession of beautiful, famous and very young women – while Maxine raises their kids in Manhattan and pursues her passion, working as a child psychiatrist. Then, everything changes . . .

Maxine finds a new love just as a tragedy transforms Blake from carefree playboy to compassionate, responsible grown-up. He wants Maxine in his life again – as a partner in a humanitarian project that could affect countless lives. But Maxine is on the cusp of a new life and almost certain that Blake, a.k.a. the Rogue, is a man capable of doing anything – except change . . . Or is he?

A journey of choices, and the amazing opportunities that come together - just when life seems to be falling apart.

9780552154758

NEW YORK VALENTINE
By Carmen Reid

Love is in the air!

Personal shopper Annie Valentine has a dream job in the heart of fabulous Manhattan.

Daughter Lana is lost in the heat of first love, but has she fallen for a heart-breaker?

In London husband Ed faces a scandal at work and knows, in his heart, he needs Annie back.

What's a girl to do when her true love is in London but her new love is New York?

Does it have to be fashion *or* family, or can Annie Valentine have it all?

'Cleverer than the average slice of chick-lit and much more entertaining too'
Heat

A fabulous read. A sexy read. A Carmen Reid.

9780552163170

DIRTY TRICKS
By Jo Carnegie

SEX IN THE CITY OR SEX IN THE COUNTRY?

As long as it's hot, who cares?!

Fashion queen Saffron is leaving the London party scene for the country, to write her bonkbusting novel. It means six months without gorgeous boyfriend Tom . . . but at least his supermodel twin brother will be there to keep her company!

Good girl Harriet, meanwhile, has swapped country life for the bright lights of London, and finds herself working with quite possibly the sexiest man she has ever met. But what dangerous secrets lurk behind those twinkling blue eyes of his?

New lives, new temptations. Have both girls bitten off more than they can chew?

'A blush-inducingly naughty, funny and deliciously addictive read'
Heat

9780552163170

her head and her veil brushed her bare shoulders. "I was wrong. Love has no list." A tear splashed past her bottom lashes. "You are the pinch in my heart. The catch in my breath. The reason my stomach tumbles and why I lie awake at night just to look at you. And every time I look at you, I know that I want to look at you forever."

Sam brushed her tear with his thumb and lowered his face to hers.

"We're not to that part yet," the minister reminded him.

Sam grinned into Autumn's face. "Get there. I'm not a patient man, and Conner tells me he wants a baby brother."

LAYING THE GHOST
By Judy Astley

'Warm, funny and unnervingly true to life'
Katie Fforde

Have you ever wondered what your ex is up to?

When Nell was a student, she and Patrick were a serious item. Nell really thought Patrick was The One, despite their often tempestuous relationship. But then Alex came along. He seemed the safer, more restful option, and thanks to her over-controlling mother she opted for him instead.

Now nothing is going right. Alex has left her to live in New York with a younger, blonder woman. Escaping to the Caribbean for a recuperative holiday, she is mugged at Gatwick and her bag is stolen. It's crisis time – and she makes two decisions:

First – she will take lessons in self-defence.
Second – she will try and find Patrick again.

Is she trying to put the past behind her – or setting out to ruin her future?

9780552773218

YOU DON'T HAVE TO SAY YOU LOVE ME
By Sarra Manning

Sweet, bookish Neve Slater always plays by the rules.

And the number one rule is that good-natured fat girls like her don't get guys like gorgeous William, heir to Neve's heart since university. But William's been in LA for three years, and Neve's been slimming down and reinventing herself so that when he returns, he'll fall head over heels in love with the new, improved her.

So she's not that interested in other men. Until her sister points out that if Neve wants William to think she's an experienced love-goddess and not the fumbling, awkward girl he left behind, then she'd better get some, well, experience.

What Neve needs is someone to show her the ropes, someone like Max. Wicked, shallow, *sexy* Max. And since he's such a man-slut, and so not Neve's type, she certainly won't fall for him. Because William is the man for her . . . right?

Praise for Sarra Manning's *Unsticky*:

'We were superglued to the pages of this book, and you'll be hooked too . . . this sexy, gritty tale is Sarra Manning's first novel and she's nailed it*****'
Heat

9780552163293